PRAISE FOR *OUR SISTER, AGAIN*

"A beautiful exploration of grief, hope, and what it means
to be human, Cameron weaves themes of ethics, AI, friendship
and first love with a compelling mystery and bewitchingly-described
Scottish location. This is an outstanding middle-grade debut
from one of my favourite authors."
Simon James Green, author of *Life of Riley*

✳

"I loved this book, it was perfect soft sci-fi with very real themes
of love and loss"
L. D. Lapinski, author of *The Strangeworlds Travel Agency*

✳

"*Our Sister, Again* expertly weaves family drama with high concept sci-fi.
It's a captivating tale about AI written with real, human heart."
Annabelle Sami, author of *Llama Out Loud*

✳

"A book about family, friendship, and what it means to be you.
One of those books you read in one day and think about forever."
Wibke Brueggemann, author of *Love is for Losers*

✳

"A powerful exploration of grief, technology and what makes us human,
Our Sister, Again skilfully combines warm-hearted contemporary with
a sci-fi twist to create a thought-provoking, thrilling read"
Lucy Powrie, author of *The Paper and Hearts Society*

✳

"A truly remarkable story. Sad and life-affirming all at the same time.
These characters are going to stay with me for a long time."
Lee Newbery, author of *The Last Firefox*

✳

"*Our Sister, Again* is a rich, heartfelt story about family, grief, and what it
means to be human told with immense gentleness and skill"
Ciara Smyth, author of *The Falling In Love Montage*

To Fof, who is much missed

Our Sister, Again contains content that some readers
may find distressing, including the death of a teenage
relative through illness.

LITTLE TIGER
An imprint of Little Tiger Press Limited
1 Coda Studios, 189 Munster Road,
London SW6 6AW

Imported into the EEA by Penguin Random House Ireland, Morrison Chambers,
32 Nassau Street, Dublin D02 YH68

www.littletiger.co.uk

First published in Great Britain in 2022
This edition published in 2023
Text copyright © Sophie Cameron, 2022
Illustration copyright © Little Tiger Press Limited, 2022

ISBN: 978-1-78895-701-4

The Forest Stewardship Council® (FSC®) is a global, not-for-profit organization dedicated to
the promotion of responsible forest management worldwide. FSC defines standards based on
agreed principles for responsible forest stewardship that are supported by environmental, social,
and economic stakeholders. To learn more, visit www.fsc.org

10 9 8 7 6 5 4 3 2 1

Our Sister, Again

Sophie Cameron

LITTLE TIGER

LONDON

Prologue

I'm watching the videos again. I'm supposed to be doing my German homework, but twenty minutes ago I picked up my phone to find the word for watermelon, got distracted by a notification from the Sekkon app, and now I'm watching my sister serenade our cat.

On the screen, Flora sits cross-legged on her bed, singing into a hairbrush. When she gets to the chorus, she holds the pretend mic out to Sìth. The cat lets out a long meow that's so perfectly in tune with the song that Flora jumps back and falls off the bed. The video has over twenty thousand views, 132 comments. I can see a few of them at the bottom of the screen.

Too cute!

Omg your cat is channelling Ariana Grande

Rest in peace, Flora. We miss you.

The video ends and rolls on to the next one, then the next. There are 389 videos on Flora's Sekkon account. I've seen them all a million times before, but I keep watching anyway. I watch Flora unbox an American snack pack that a friend sent for her birthday and dance to a K-pop song with three girls from her swim team. I watch her try to copy a make-up tutorial, then crack up when it goes horribly wrong. (That one's my favourite. I snuck into her room to watch after I heard her giggling hysterically and had to press both hands to my mouth to stifle my own laughter.)

The playlist reaches the end and loops back to the most recent videos – the ones that Flora took when she was bored in hospital, and a tearful update after the doctors told us there was nothing more they could do. I skip those. I like seeing Flora laughing and joking around, being silly and carefree. That's the way I want to remember her: my loud, funny, bossy big sister.

Mum comes into the kitchen carrying a stack of mugs and plates. I put my phone face down on the table and turn back to my German grammar exercises. Bringing up Flora around my parents is always a risk. Some days we end up laughing about happy times or funny things she used to say, but on others it plunges them into darkness. I can tell from the cloudy look in her eyes as Mum walks to the sink that today is one of the bad days.

"Do you need a hand, Mum? I can wash those up, if you like."

"Hmm?" Mum looks round at me. Her voice sounds faraway, like she's talking from the bottom of a very deep pit. "Oh. No thanks, Isla, it's fine. You carry on with your homework."

She falls silent as she washes the dishes, lost in her memories. In the living room, Dad is watching an interior design show while my little sister Ùna lies on the carpet, reading. Everything looks quiet and calm but the atmosphere is heavy as a storm. Great big thunder clouds of grief rolled over our house when Flora died.

A year and a half later, they still haven't cleared.

Of course I knew I'd miss her. But I didn't know how much, or that I'd even miss the way she hogged the bathroom and snapped at me for borrowing her pens. I also hadn't expected how much I'd miss Mum and Dad. That sounds strange, since they're still here in the house with me, but they're not the same. Especially Mum. She doesn't sing along to the radio or quote old TV shows like she used to. It feels like forever since I saw her smile – her real smile, not a quick turn-up of the lips.

Dad is a little better. He has his down days but lately he's started cracking his terrible jokes and puns again. Hearing them is like a ray of sunlight slipping through the dark clouds, even if they still make me groan. He keeps suggesting that we sort out the things in Flora's bedroom for charity shops, or that we finally scatter her ashes, but Mum always finds an excuse not to. Those things are all we have left of Flora.

She's not ready to say goodbye yet.

And that means none of us can.

Mum leaves the plates and cups to dry and goes back to the living room. When I pick up my phone again, an advert has popped up on the screen.

HOMEWARD HEALING
A free online support group for those
struggling with bereavement.
Join us and take a brave step
towards a happier future.
Find out more

Sekkon is full of ads but I've never seen one like this before. They usually show me football boots or cat T-shirts, whatever I've searched for recently. My friend Murdo's dad is always going on about how big tech companies are tracking us and selling our personal information to advertisers. This feels different, though – it's almost like they've read my mind.

I click on the link. It takes me to a really basic website with a short description about how the group is open to anyone who has lost a loved one, and a form to enter your contact details. Maybe this is what Mum needs. We live on a tiny island in the Outer Hebrides, just 163 inhabitants. There are no support groups like this nearby. We all did online sessions with a grief counsellor last year but Mum and Dad gave up on theirs pretty quickly. They said it was too expensive, and that it wasn't helping much either. A group would be good for them. They could meet other people who have lost a child. People who really know what they're going through.

In the living room, my parents' faces are lit up blue in the glow of the TV screen. Without asking their permission, I type Mum's name and email address into the form and click send. The thought of scattering Flora's ashes, boxing up her things ... it makes me feel sick with sadness. But nothing is going to bring her back. We need to be brave and start taking steps forwards, like the ad says. Maybe this will be the first.

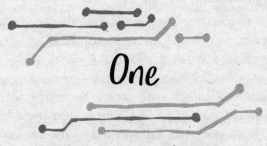

One

Eighteen months later

Almost everyone on the island comes out to see the boat arrive. They stand in two uneven lines along the harbour walls, whispering and nudging each other as they look towards the water.

Mum parks the car opposite the wee shop and sighs. "I told them not to come tonight. The guide says to act normal. Not to throw a welcome party."

Behind us, Ùna unclips her seat belt and checks her reflection in the rear-view mirror. "They're excited, Mum." She pats down a few flyaway strands of hair. "This is a big deal for the whole island, not just us."

"You're right." Some of the tension leaves Mum's shoulders. "I'd rather have kept things quiet, though. This is overwhelming enough as it is."

Outside, the crowd is still growing. My best friend Adhiti and her older brother Suresh step out of the tiny post office that their dad runs and cross the road towards the harbour. Adhiti stops to talk to Finley Graham, who's in the year above us at school. As usual, Finley has his phone out. He slowly moves his arm to film the scene, then scowls when Adhiti jumps in front of him

9

and pulls a face for the camera.

Mum touches my arm, and I remember with a jolt of nerves why we're here. "Are you ready, Isla?"

I want to say no. I thought I was helping Mum move on when I signed her up for that support group. Instead she's taken ten giant steps in the wrong direction. Dad's moved out, and our family is even more broken than it was a year and a half ago. But it's too late to say no now. The papers have been signed, the money is in our bank accounts. We are part of this project, whether I like it or not. And it's all because I saw that advert on Sekkon. It's all because of me.

I bite my tongue and force a smile. "Ready. Let's go."

The cool air nips at my skin as I climb out of the car. It's July and the sun won't set for another few hours but the overcast sky and dense sea fog have shed a murky twilight over the island. Heads turn towards us as we walk to the harbour. Reverend Jack is standing by the door to the church, his hands clasped behind his back as he looks out to sea. Next door, Georgie Campbell is sitting on the front step to her house, absent-mindedly stroking her dog Lola's ears. Her mum comes outside wearing a bright orange anorak and waves at us. "Good luck, Sarah!" she shouts to Mum.

Georgie looks up at her mum and cringes. Annie blushes too, as if worried she's said the wrong thing. What do you say in a situation like this? There are no ready-made phrases, no greetings cards.

Mum smiles and nods back at her. "Thanks, Annie. We're feeling very lucky indeed."

The tide is low this evening, so Mum walks down

the stone steps to the jetty where the boat will come in. Ùna and I follow, pulling our coats tight round us. Curious stares and whispers fall down from the high harbour walls. It reminds me of a funeral, when the family are ushered to the front of the church after everyone else has taken a seat. That uncomfortable, unwanted spotlight.

"I feel sick," Ùna whispers. "This is too weird."

Weird doesn't even cover it. I could read the English and Gaelic dictionaries back to back and I still wouldn't have enough words for how mind-bogglingly bizarre this all is. No wonder Dad wanted out.

"It's way too weird," I agree. "But at least we're in it together, right?"

I nudge my glasses up my nose with the knuckle of my index finger. Ùna gives a small smile and does the same to hers. It's a thing we started doing last year, when we were caught between our fighting parents or stuck in some strange, intense training session about the trial. It became our way of checking in – a subtle means of telling each other "I'm here, I get it" when we couldn't say anything at all.

"Right." Ùna lets out a long breath and flattens her dark brown hair again. "Besides, weird is OK. Weird can even be good."

She skips forwards and takes Mum's hand. I cast a glance up the harbour steps, towards the big house on the left of the church. That's where my other best friend Murdo lives. The lights are on in the rooms upstairs. Murdo might be watching from his bedroom window but his dad is dead set against the trial – there's no way he'd let him come out to see the boat arrive. I wish he was here. Murdo is like a lighthouse, big and bright and secure. Being around him always calms me down.

As I turn back round, Ùna lets out a gasp that makes me jump. "I think I see them!"

Slowly, a light emerges from the fog. An engine's whirring grows steadily louder and closer and then a boat comes into view. It's a flashy white yacht, small but at least twice as fast as the old ferries that chug between here and the bigger islands. Behind us, one of the wee kids lets out a gasp of delight. The sight of a fancy boat is enough to provide a few bars of staccato in the sleepy rhythm of life on Eilean Dearg.

"It's time." Mum presses a hand to her mouth. "Finally."

The low evening sun bounces off the boat's metal railings as it curves neatly into the harbour and comes to a stop at the long wooden jetty. Behind the cabin window is a man I don't recognize. He's white, probably early thirties, with a thick beard and red hair a shade lighter than my own. Sitting beside him is a striking Japanese-American woman with dark hair in a neat bob: Marisa Ishigura, our Family Liaison Officer at Second Chances. She waves at us through the glass before disappearing to the back of the boat.

"Oh my gosh." Mum's voice is thin, trembling. "I can't believe this is really happening." She reaches for our hands and takes a few steps forwards, right to the edge of the water. My stomach is turning cartwheels, Mum's entire body is shaking and I can hear Ùna's breathing coming fast and shallow. The red-haired man turns off the engine, and a moment later Marisa climbs down the small ladder at the back of the boat. The buckles on her shiny black ankle boots jingle as she steps on to the jetty.

"Hey, there!" she calls in her high-pitched American accent. She glances up at the overcast sky and shivers. "Bit colder than California, huh?"

The boat rocks slightly as the man follows her down the ladder. He smiles briefly at us, then turns back and holds out his hand towards the last passenger. My pulse pounds in my wrists, my ears, behind my ribs. This is it. After months of planning, the time has finally arrived. I stare at my trainers and take a deep breath, preparing myself for ... for what? Not disappointment. Like Dad, I never had any faith in the trial. Not even fear, though there's definitely a bit of that churning in my gut.

It's change. I'm steeling myself for yet another change.

But then I look up and everything disappears. Gasps and muffled cries in English and Gaelic ring out from the crowd above us. Mum takes a sharp breath and squeezes my hand so tightly the tendons crunch but I barely notice. The sun, the sky and the island itself could melt into nothing and I wouldn't even flinch. Right now, the only thing in the world that matters is the girl climbing down from the boat.

She's small – shorter than me now – and thin, dressed in skinny black jeans, white Adidas trainers and a denim jacket. Her dark blond hair is tousled from the sea breeze and her pale cheeks are flushed pink with cold. She looks up at the crowd, nervously twirling the pearl stud in her right earlobe with her thumb and index finger.

Marisa puts a hand on the small of the girl's back and gently steers her forwards. "Here we are," she says. Her voice sounds distorted in my ears, as if we've been

13

plunged underwater. "Home at last."

Turning her gaze towards Mum, Ùna and me, the girl's eyes widen. For a moment she stares at us, her lips open. Then she pushes them into a shaky smile and echoes Marisa's words. "Home at last."

If I hadn't known from looking at her, the voice would have confirmed it. This isn't the cheap fake that I've been dreading for months. She's not some imposter. Along with my parents and Ùna, this is the person I've known longest and best, someone so familiar I could recognize her in the dark. She has the same small grey-blue eyes that we all inherited from Mum, the same sharp jawline as Dad, the same wobbly smile she'd always put on when she was trying to hide her nerves. It's really her.

It's really Flora.

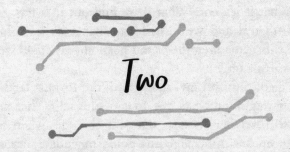

Two

It wasn't a real support group. Or maybe it was – Mum was so vague about it, and I'm still not clear about all the details. Either way, somehow the Homeward Healing group I signed her up for led her to Second Chances, a tech company based in Silicon Valley, California. They told Mum they were running a trial "recreating" people who had recently passed away. They said Flora was the perfect candidate.

They said they could really bring her back.

Mum didn't tell Ùna and me about it straight away, just like I never told her that I was the one who signed her up for the support group. I overheard her whispering something to Dad about a trial as they washed the dishes one evening, then a few days later I saw them watching a video on her laptop. Dad's face had gone chalky but Mum's eyes were bright with excitement. Brighter than they'd been in a long time.

A couple of days after that, I woke up in the middle of the night to hear them arguing downstairs.

"How could you be taken in by something like this? It's a scam!"

"What if it's not? What if we find out in a few years that it's real and we missed our chance to have Flora back? If there's even the tiniest possibility it could work, it's worth a try."

I crept out of my room and on to the landing. Mum was standing at the foot of the stairs, her arms crossed over her chest in that way she does when she's made up her mind and isn't going to budge. The way Dad was staring at her, it was like she'd announced she was moving to Narnia.

"Sarah, this is ridiculous. It's impossible." He was holding a glass of whisky in one hand and some slopped on to the floor as he gestured up the stairs. "Did you even think about Isla and Ùna? They've already been through so much. You can't do this to them too."

"I'm doing this *for* Isla and Ùna," Mum said, her voice cracking. "I can hardly even look at them without thinking about everything that's missing. I need our family to be whole again."

Mum broke down then. She cried harder than she had in the days after Flora died, much harder than she had at the funeral – as if months of grief had built up, up, up and now came overflowing out of her. As I gripped the bars of the banister, my own eyes started to sting. I wanted to run downstairs and hug Mum tight, but then they'd know I'd been eavesdropping.

"Please, Innes," Mum said, wiping her eyes. "Please let me try."

Dad's shoulders drooped, the anger seeping out of him like a punctured balloon. He went to Mum and put his arms round her. "OK, love. We'll give it a go."

They told us about their plan a few days later. At first, Dad kept warning us that the trial probably wouldn't go ahead. They needed everyone on the island to agree to it and he didn't think that would happen. But that was before we found out how much money Second Chances were offering everyone to take part. It was a lot, and I mean a *lot*. There's not much work on Eilean Dearg. Not many people around here could afford to turn down that kind of money.

So here we are. Eighteen months, hours of interviews, countless training modules and dozens of signed contracts later, Project Homecoming has begun.

For weeks now, I've been imagining some creepy remake of my sister coming back into our lives. Something almost-but-not-quite human, a monster from a bad sci-fi film. But the girl who steps off the boat… She's *actually* Flora. This is the same girl who pierced my ears when Mum and Dad wouldn't let me, who came to my football matches and shouted my name louder than anyone else. I know her the way I know that my heart is beating or how to breathe. This really is my sister.

Suddenly, Mum lets out a gasp so loud it makes us all jump. I look at her, at her flushed complexion and her stunned expression, and realize she's been holding her breath since the boat reached the shore. She lets go of our hands and moves forwards, her footsteps slow and uneasy on the wet sand.

"*Mo nighean. Mo chaileag.*" *My daughter. My girl.* Mum whispers the words over and over, though she never usually speaks to us in Gaelic – that was always Dad's thing. "It's you. It's actually you."

She puts her hands on either side of Flora's face and gently turns it from side to side, like a jeweller examining a diamond. Flora swallows. There's a silvery scar below her lip where she fell and hit her head on Gran's windowsill when we were little, and a few faint pockmarks that acne once left along her cheekbones.

"Of course it's me, Mum," she says. "Who else would I be?"

She gives a light, nervous laugh. The sound makes my heart clench tight in my chest. I've heard Flora's laugh recently, in her Sekkon videos and voice notes and in my memories, but it's different hearing it in person again. Like coming across a once favourite song that you'd forgotten quite how much you loved.

"*Mo chaileag*," Mum says again, her voice thick. "Look how perfect you are."

Silent tears start to pour down her cheeks. I'm too shocked to cry, too shocked to even move, but a strangled sob bursts out of Ùna. She bounds forwards and throws her arms tight round our sister. Flora is stiff for a moment, almost as if it were a stranger hugging her, but then her eyes soften and she hesitantly slides her arms round Ùna's back.

"Hey, you." Flora's voice trembles but she's smiling. "Oh my gosh, how did you get so grown-up?"

Watching them feels like seeing past and present collide. Ùna was seven when Flora died, a skinny wee kid in dungarees and Disney T-shirts. She's ten and a half now and really tall for her age, not much shorter than me. Her sobs are loud enough to rival the seabirds' cries: raw, choked sounds that fill the whole sky. Mum wraps her shaking arms round both Ùna and Flora and pulls them close. Flora smiles and holds out her free arm towards me, but I still can't move. I would think this was a dream but everything is far too vivid for that. The smell of salt and seaweed and the goosebumps rippling over my skin. Flora's twitching smile and the way her hair flutters in the breeze.

"Did you miss me, Lala?" she asks.

Lala. That was what I called myself when I was little, when I couldn't pronounce "eye-la" properly. It became Flora's nickname for me. Hearing it again makes my heart throb with happiness. My body finally remembers how to move and I tentatively step towards her as my own wave of tears rises up.

"I did," I say in a tight voice. "I missed you."

The words are far too small. They can't hold even a fraction of the past three years. Not her brightly coloured funeral on the beach. Not the aching gap at the kitchen table or the looming silence behind her bedroom door. Not every tiny moment of forgetting and the guilt that hit afterwards. But nothing ever could, so for the moment, that's all I say: that I missed her.

Flora smiles and beckons to me with her free hand. "Come and give me a hug then, silly."

The tears finally spill over as she pulls me towards her. Her hair and clothes smell different, the way they used to when she came back from trips away with the swim team or sleepovers at her friends' houses. Mum wraps one of her arms round my waist and holds us there, her three girls together again. I think about Dad and feel a pang of guilt and sadness that he's not here with us, but it doesn't last long. We are Flora and Isla and Ùna again.

The way we're supposed to be.

I'm not sure how long we stand there but it's long enough for the sky to dim and the one lonely street lamp at the harbour to flicker on. After a while, I start to notice voices around us. I look up and see the people watching us from the harbour walls, their hazy forms outlined in the soft golden glow of the street lamp.

"You'd never be able to tell, would you?"

"*Nach eil i brèagha…*"

"It's a miracle. It must be."

They must have been talking all this time but I was too stunned to notice. I'd forgotten about Marisa and the red-haired man from Second Chances too, but now I turn and see them watching us with gentle smiles on their faces.

"How about we head back to your house?" Marisa asks. "We can help get Flora settled in."

Mum lets us go, and Ùna and I both take off our glasses to wipe our eyes. As Flora turns towards the harbour steps, her hair falls to the side and shows the back of her pale neck. And everything inside me flips.

Carved into her skin, only just visible above the collar of her jacket, is a small square. It's a couple of centimetres high and wide, with rounded corners and a thin metal border. I know what that shape means and what it does. I've seen it on the Second Chances videos, in diagrams in their training modules. I thought I was ready but seeing it in the flesh is different. It's a reminder that things aren't the same at all.

Because while this Flora may be a miracle, she's also a machine.

PROJECT HOMECOMING:
A GUIDE FOR FAMILIES

Module 1: Introduction

Welcome to Project Homecoming,
an exclusive trial by Second Chances Ltd.

If you are reading this, congratulations!

You are part of one of the most ambitious and
pioneering projects ever carried out in the field
of Artificial Intelligence. One that, if successful,
will change how we think about and experience
life and death forever.

As you know, you will soon welcome a new version
of your loved one back into your home.

This "returnee" has been created using vast amounts
of data, in addition to photos, videos and extensive
interviews with your loved one's friends and family.

Despite being machines, our returnees look entirely
human – in a recent survey, 98.1 per cent of
respondents could not tell them apart from
human beings.

We are confident that this new arrival will be an
extremely close match to the person you remember.
However, please be aware that there are some
differences. Returnees do not need to sleep, they
cannot be fully submerged in water and they don't
fall sick with human illnesses.

Most notably, their bodies do not change and age as ours do, though we at Second Chances are working hard to find a solution to this.

While it may be difficult, please try not to fixate on these differences or bombard the returnee with questions about their new body. The best thing for them now is simply to adapt to their normal life as quickly as possible.

Your most important job is to make them feel safe and loved, and to give them a warm welcome home.

Three

Everything is a blur. The moment we finally leave the shore and walk back up the harbour steps, Finley rushing towards us with his camera until Adhiti pulls him back, Mum nervously babbling the whole way to the house on the drive home… All the while, I can't stop staring at Flora. Everything about her is just like I remember, from how she kicks off her shoes without undoing the laces to the way her eyebrows rise as she looks around our kitchen.

"This is so strange," she says, fiddling with her hair. "I can't believe it's been three years. It feels like I was here a few weeks ago."

"Your perception of time might be a little off," Marisa says. "We find that happens quite often during the transition period. We'll work on it, don't worry."

Reverend Jack lent Marisa his car to help her get around the island, so now she and Toby, the red-haired man, are both sitting at our kitchen table with mugs of tea in front of them. We don't often have visitors at home, especially not ones as glamorous as Marisa, but I barely notice them. All I can focus on is Flora. I have to stop myself from reaching out and touching her to check that she's real.

Mum takes Flora's hand and squeezes. "It doesn't matter how long it's been, love. All that matters is you're home now."

Flora smiles. It's a little unsteady, but warm. She takes a small sip of tea and turns to me and Ùna. "You two are so quiet." She sticks her arms out at right angles and moves in a robotic shuffle. "Were you expecting some C-3PO deal?"

Ùna laughs, snotty, bubbly laughter still thick from crying. I shake my head, trying to find the words. This girl is Flora, she has to be, but the sight of the charging port at the back of her neck still niggles at my mind like a splinter. "I… I didn't think you'd be so like you," I say eventually. "You look exactly the same."

Flora died when I was ten and she was fifteen. I'm thirteen now, but she still looks fifteen. Even if she's still my big sister, the gap between us has shrunk. Back then she seemed so grown-up, almost like an adult. Now I see she's just a kid, like me.

"And you both look so different. Marisa showed me photos but it's still weird." Flora pokes Ùna in the rib. "Are you part giraffe or something, beanpole?"

"You're just mad because you're going to be the shortest soon," Ùna says in a shy, hesitant voice that doesn't sound like her own.

Flora smiles. "You got me. If I'd known I'd have asked them to give me an extra couple of inches."

Marisa chuckles. "Sorry, Flora. Doesn't really work like that."

Toby joins in with her laughter. Marisa has been to the island twice before but this is the first time we've met Toby.

Apart from introducing himself as Marisa's assistant, he hasn't said much since he arrived. He sits with his hands cupped round the tea that Mum made him, his smile calm. Maybe he's jetlagged after the long journey from California.

"I know you're all excited to welcome Flora home, so we won't stay long," Marisa says, pulling her handbag on to her lap. "But we have a few things to go over first."

She places a thin black box on the table and takes off the lid. Inside are a small, rectangular tablet, two white cables and a user manual. Marisa presses a button on the tablet and the screen lights up. "This is what we call a Returnee Health Hub. You must have seen it in the online training modules you completed, right?"

We nod. It looks a lot like the panel on the wall in Finley's kitchen that his mum uses to control the central heating and turn the lights on and off. Marisa points to an orange bar on the left of the screen. "This part shows Flora's energy levels. She needs to recharge for seven to eight hours every day using this cable. Flora's already done this lots of times back at the Second Chances centre, so she can handle it herself."

Flora nods. "It's really easy. I plug it in and turn off for the night, as if I was going to sleep."

"If there are any serious problems, the Health Hub will start flashing red and you'll hear an alarm," Marisa says, looking up at Mum. "But we'll also have weekly check-ins to monitor Flora's progress, so our team will usually be able to pick up on any issues as they—"

Before Marisa can finish, Flora gives a gasp so loud that everyone except Toby jumps. Sìth, our Siamese cat, has walked into the kitchen. Flora pushes her chair back and rushes towards her. "Sìth! Hi, gorgeous!"

The cat lets out a strangled mewl and darts straight back out of the room. Flora's face falls. Before she died, she and Sìth were inseparable. Flora was forever taking selfies with her or trying to get her to cooperate for Sekkon videos, and Sìth always slept on the foot of Flora's bed. Nowadays the cat mostly splits her time between my room and the third step on the staircase.

"Don't take it personally, love," Mum says, squeezing Flora's arm. "Sìth's become a real scaredy-cat lately. She's getting old."

"Animals often have a hard time adapting to returnees," Marisa says with a sympathetic smile. "But we've found they get used to them with time."

"OK." Flora sits back down, her bottom lip turned out slightly. "I hope so."

Marisa turns back to the Health Hub and goes through the rest of its functions. I picture Flora inserting the cable into the port at the back of her neck or pressing buttons on the screen to control her body temperature. A shiver runs over me. This is all so, so strange. Flora looks completely human – I can even see the pores on her skin, the faint hairs on her arms. It's hard to believe there aren't bones and organs under there, but chips and bolts and wires.

"Are you all right, Isla?" Marisa asks. "I know this is a lot to take in."

My cheeks flush. "I'm fine. Just trying to get used to everything."

"The tech aspect can be hard to get your head round at first, but returnees really are just like us in most ways." Marisa nods to Toby. "I've been all around the world with this guy, and people never guess that he's anything other than human."

My mouth falls open. From the way Ùna's eyes bug behind her glasses, I can tell she's surprised too. Even now that I've seen how lifelike the returnees really are, I never would have guessed Toby was one of them.

"Seriously?" Ùna cranes her head to the right, trying to glimpse the port at the back of his neck. "How did you get through all the scanners at the airport?"

"We fly by private jet, and Second Chances make arrangements so we aren't required to pass through security," Toby says. He has an American accent and his voice is low and melodic. The sort of voice that could send you to sleep if you listened to it for too long.

"The jet was amazing. The seats were like this," Flora says, stretching her arms out wide. "And Toby flew it himself! I got to sit in the cockpit and everything. It was awesome."

"You're a pilot?" Mum asks him, blinking in surprise.

"Oh, Toby's extremely well qualified," Marisa says, putting a hand on his shoulder. "We still have one more thing to go over, though, and that's confidentiality."

Part of me wants to ask why Toby works as Marisa's assistant if he's trained as a pilot but that might sound a bit rude. The question fades when Marisa's gaze shifts to Ùna and me. She's still smiling, yet I feel like I'm about to get a telling-off.

"As you know, Project Homecoming is top secret for now," Marisa says. "We need to assess how well returnees integrate back into their families and communities under normal circumstances, or at least close to normal.

That won't be possible if word about the trial gets out and Flora suddenly has international press bothering her."

We all nod. Everyone on the island had to sign non-disclosure agreements promising that we wouldn't tell anyone about the trial. Even some people outside Eilean Dearg had to sign for it to be able to go ahead – people who are likely to come and visit, like our aunt Kirsty and Murdo's older brother Ranald, who lives in Berlin.

"That means Flora can't leave the island under any circumstances," Marisa continues. "She also can't use social media or get in touch with any of her friends who aren't part of the trial."

"We know this," Ùna says. "This was all in the online training we did."

"I know you do, Ùna, but it's really important you understand how crucial this is. If confidentiality is broken, we'll need to make adjustments to allow Project Homecoming to continue." Marisa glances at Flora, who's staring down at her cup of tea. "In the worst-case scenario, that could mean ending the trial altogether."

"But what about when we go to Eilean Gorm? What if I forget and mention Flora to someone?" Ùna asks, chewing on her fingernails. My little sister has a big mouth – I've lost count of how many birthday surprises she's spoiled for the rest of us.

Mum reaches for her hand and gives it a squeeze. "Don't worry, love. It'll be fine. We just need to be really, really careful."

"Even if you do let something slip, people will think you're making it up," I say. "No one's going to believe the truth without seeing Flora for themselves."

"Isla's right," Marisa says. "Our returnees have gone far beyond the general public's experience of AI. Most people could never imagine someone like Flora could exist. But even so, you'll have to be extremely careful. Promise?"

"Promise," Ùna and I echo.

After that, Marisa reminds us how we can get in touch if we have any issues, passes the box with the Health Hub and cables to Mum, and tells us they'll pop in before they leave tomorrow. I follow her and Toby to the door to say goodbye, nodding as Mum thanks them again and again, but my head is a messy knot of thoughts. Flora's charging port. The Health Hub. The fact that Flora is here with us at all.

And tangled through it all, the scary realization that if we make any mistakes, we could end up losing her twice.

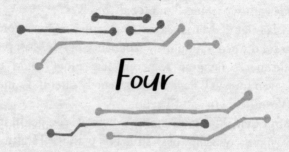

Four

I had lots of dreams about Flora after she died. Some were so vivid, it was almost like being with her again. She'd be filming a Sekkon video or getting ready for a swimming gala, normal things Flora used to do, and when I woke up I'd actually forget for a moment. I'd expect to hear her humming in the bathroom or her footsteps thundering downstairs to breakfast.

But then my sleepiness would clear and reality would come crashing back over me. The bedroom next door was still empty. Mum and Dad were still roaming the house like zombies. Flora was still gone.

When I wake up that Thursday morning, there's a horrible moment when I wonder if yesterday was all a dream. I throw back my duvet, leap out of bed and hurry downstairs to check. And there she is – Flora, sitting at the kitchen table, wearing her old polka-dot pyjamas and filling out the puzzles in the back of yesterday's newspaper. Ùna is beside her, talking through a mouthful of cereal. Mum leans against the fridge and sips her coffee, a look of pure wonder on her face.

The sight is so, so strange. But it's so normal too.

Flora looks up at me and smiles. "Morning, Lala. Sleep well?"

It takes me a moment to answer. "Yeah. Did you?"

As soon as the words are out, I realize what a silly question it was. My cheeks turn red, but Flora laughs.

"Something like that. Sweet dreams of electric sheep." She pats the seat beside her. "Are you planning on lingering in the doorway all day? Come and have some breakfast."

My stomach is full of jitters but I take a bowl from the cupboard and pour myself some cereal. Outside, Sìth is sitting on the boot of Mum's car, her sapphire-blue eyes fixed on the house. It's not like her to go out so early. Usually she lounges around the front room until lunch. I guess she's still a bit freaked out by Flora.

If I'm really honest, I am too. Having her here is amazing but it's a lot to take in. More than my brain can handle. Much more than I was expecting.

"What's another word for airy or celestial?" Flora asks, tapping her pen against the newspaper. "Eight letters, begins with E."

I think about it as I sit down at the table. "Ethereal?"

Flora counts the letters. Her eyebrows rise when she sees I'm right. "Whoa. You got smart as well as tall."

I smile and hope it doesn't look as awkward as I feel. Ùna slurps the last of the chocolately milk from her Coco Pops and wipes her hand on the back of her mouth. "So, what are we going to do today?" she asks Flora.

'Well, I've been gone for three years," Flora says, stretching her arms above her head. "I must have some TV to catch up on, right?"

There's not a lot to do on Eilean Dearg. Unsurprisingly, my sisters and I have watched a *lot* of series in our time. Ùna was too little to join us back then, but sometimes Flora and I would spend entire Sundays curled up on the sofa bingeing episode after episode of our favourite shows.

While I eat my cereal, she and Ùna go through Netflix on Mum's laptop and try to decide which series to catch up on first. "Ooh, let's watch this!" Flora points at the thumbnail of a comedy she used to love. "How many more seasons are there?"

That was the last show we watched together, squashed into her bed as Flora drifted in and out of sleep. A few more seasons have come out since then but I haven't watched any of them. It didn't feel right without Flora singing along to the theme tune and cracking up at her favourite characters' lines.

But this version of Flora doesn't know that. Her memories cut off right before she got sick.

"OK," I say, pushing the bad thoughts away. "Let's start from season four."

We get our duvets from upstairs and squash on to the sofa together, with Mum in the armchair beside us. I squirm around trying to get cosy but I can't settle. This is all such a big change, and I don't like change. According to Mum, I sobbed for an hour and a half when she bought a new microwave when I was three. It's not that I'm not happy Flora is back, of course I am. But it's all so overwhelming.

"I think I'll make pancakes," I say, pushing myself up from the sofa when the first episode ends. I need to do something to take my mind off all this. "Does anybody want some?"

Ùna's hand shoots up. "Ooh, I do!"

Mum starts to protest that we've just had breakfast, but she quickly gives up. She's in too good a mood to worry about things like our sugar intake. I go to the cupboard, take out the flour, then grab the milk and a couple of eggs from the fridge. I whisk up the batter while the others watch the show, and by the time the pancakes are ready, I feel myself start to relax. Cooking and baking always calm me down. As the second episode ends, I carry two plates of blueberry pancakes dripping in maple syrup and pass one to Ùna.

"Are you sure you don't want some?" I ask Flora.

"No, thanks. I already had toast." She pats her stomach, or rather the part of her body where a stomach would normally be. "Don't want to overload the food compartment."

Ùna pauses before biting into her pancakes. "Can I see it?"

Mum chokes on her coffee. "Ùna! Don't ask Flora things like that."

"It's OK, Mum," Flora laughs. "Look, it's here."

Flora lifts up her pyjama top a bit. On the right side of her waist there's a faint circle marked into her skin, about six or seven centimetres wide. She presses on the skin and it spins outward to reveal a long cylindrical container. She pulls it out and lifts it up. Inside it's filled with chewed-up bits of toast.

"Bit gross, right? Marisa says to clean it not long after I eat or it'll start to smell bad. I can't eat too much, either, or else it'll overflow."

We're all quiet for a moment. I cut into my pancakes and take a big mouthful, trying to fill the space left by the words I can't find. Even Ùna has gone silent and Mum doesn't know what to say, either.

Flora sighs. "I know it's weird but there's no point pretending these parts of me don't exist." She gets up and goes to the kitchen. There's a clatter as she empties the toast into the bin. She comes back tugging down her top. "I'm still me but some things are different now. I don't want to have to hide that."

"You don't have to hide anything, Flora," Mum says quickly. "We know things are different. It'll just take us time to get used to it."

"I think it's cool," Ùna says, swirling her pancakes in the maple syrup.

My appetite has totally vanished but I take another nervous bite. The online training that Second Chances made us do explained how returnees were built and how they worked, so I should be ready for stuff like this. But it's so hard to get my head round. Everything about this girl, from her laugh to the way she twirls her earrings, is Flora… Except Flora didn't have a big metal hole in her neck or a tube that slotted into her side. Flora wasn't a robot.

Then I remember something Marisa said the first time she came to meet us. She said it was lucky Flora was on Sekkon so much because it gave Second Chances enough data to create the returnee version of her. The app was also the reason Mum found out about the trial. For months now I've been so furious with myself, thinking that if I'd

34

done my homework instead of going on Sekkon, we never would have heard of Project Homecoming and Dad would still be at home. But if I hadn't, this new version of Flora wouldn't be here now. Somewhere in the world, a different family would be welcoming their son or sister or mother home, and for us this would be just another day, missing Flora.

And when I think about it like that, I realize that technology isn't a barrier stopping this Flora from really being her. It *is* her, the entire reason she's here. I've been so worried about the ways the trial would change our lives again, I never really imagined that it might give us back our normal. But it has. Flora is home, and it's the most amazing thing in the world. I'm not going to let the mechanical stuff get in the way of appreciating that. Instead, I'm going to confront it head-on.

"Maybe you should stick to eating chips." I poke Flora in the side. "Get it? Microchips."

Flora blinks at me. For a moment I worry I've crossed a line but then she throws her head back and laughs. "That's so rubbish! That's embarrassingly bad."

Ùna bounces up on to her knees. "I've got one, I've got one! Make sure you take one *byte* at a time."

"That's even worse!"

Flora chucks a pillow at her and Ùna knocks it away, bursting into giggles. Mum rolls her eyes and chuckles at us, just like she used to. Smiling, I sink back against the sofa cushions between my two sisters, take another bite of pancakes and settle in for the next episode.

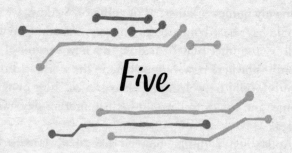

Five

Marisa and Toby come back to our house later that afternoon. Marisa is wearing a long green coat with a tartan scarf over a black dress, but Toby is in his Second Chances uniform again. Mum shows them through to the living room, where Flora, Ùna and I are still snuggled up in our duvets. We're now on episode eleven and halfway through a packet of biscuits.

"We wanted to say goodbye and good luck," Marisa says. Mum offers her the armchair but she waves her hand to say no. "We really can't stay long. We're flying out to our next assignment tomorrow, so we need to head back to the mainland soon."

"Where are you going next?" Ùna asks, licking crumbs from her fingertips. She offers the pack to Toby but he shakes his head with a smile.

"Oh, that's top secret." Marisa grins and holds a finger to her lips. "But I'll give you a clue – it's a lot warmer than here."

Ùna looks to the window, where heavy rain is lashing down from the slate-grey sky. "That could be pretty much anywhere except Antarctica."

"Good point." Marisa laughs and reaches for Flora's hand. "It's been an honour, Flora. We're really going to miss you at the base but we'll talk every week. I'll set up a time for our first check-in next Wednesday, OK?"

"OK." Flora pushes the duvet back and jumps to her feet. "Thank you so much for everything, Marisa. Thank you for bringing me home."

Instead of taking her hand, Flora gives Marisa a tight hug. When they pull apart, Marisa's eyes are shiny. Mum moves to give her a handshake, but then her eyes tear up and she pulls Marisa in for a hug too, babbling thank yous under her breath. Marisa gives high fives to me and Ùna, and Toby nods a polite goodbye to each of us in turn.

"It was nice to meet you all," he says. "I hope you'll be very happy, Flora."

Ùna leans over the sofa. "Are you going back to your family too, Toby?"

Marisa frowns but Toby's smile doesn't even flicker. "No, Ùna. Second Chances is my family now," he says in the same steady voice he always uses. "It's where I belong."

"Yes, Toby's situation is a little different to Flora's." Marisa puts a hand on Toby's shoulder and squeezes. "But don't worry. We take good care of each other, don't we?"

Toby nods, still smiling. So, he ended up working for Second Chances instead of going back to his family after he was recreated. I wonder why…

We all follow them out into the hallway to wave goodbye, but Marisa pauses near the front door. Her eyes linger on the family photos hanging on the wall – the five of us on the beach; squashed inside a tent on a camping trip;

smiling around a Christmas dinner with Gran and Kirsty a few months before Flora died.

"Did I ever tell you why I decided to work for Second Chances?" she asks.

Mum shakes her head. "No, I don't think so."

Marisa takes her phone from the pocket of her coat, taps on the screen a few times, then passes it to Flora. I lean over and see a photo of an adorable little girl with messy pigtails, dimples and a streak of chocolate ice cream on her cheek.

"My cousin, Hana," Marisa says. "She died of meningitis when she was six."

My heart gives a sudden pang. Mum sucks in her breath.

"I'm so sorry," she says. "That poor wee girl. Your poor family."

"I was a couple of years older than her but we lived two streets apart so we saw each other all the time." Marisa takes back the phone and touches a hand to the screen. "One minute she was running around in Batman pyjamas and a tutu singing the *Pokémon* theme song, and the next she was gone. Nothing was ever the same after that."

Mum squeezes Marisa's arm. We all know exactly what she's talking about. When Flora died, it was like someone had drawn a line straight through our lives. Everything was divided into Before and After; the time our family was whole and the time that it wasn't. Even the parts of my life that hadn't changed, like football and my friends, felt different afterwards. The whole world lost some of its colour without Flora.

"I always wanted to help families who suffer that sort of loss. I did my doctorate in Psychology, thinking I'd specialize in grief and bereavement counselling, but then

Second Chances found me." Marisa puts the phone back in her pocket and smiles slightly. "It almost felt like destiny. I really believe that what we're doing with Project Homecoming will change the world."

When she looks up at us, her dark brown eyes are shiny. I can see how much this trial means to her. "It's too late for my family," she says. "But I think it would make Hana proud, knowing I'm trying to help yours."

We spend the rest of the day lounging around doing not very much, until Mum makes veggie fajitas followed by raspberry and apple crumble (Flora's favourites) for tea. It's a cosy, easy, happy day – the best I've had in ages. But even so, Dad's absence throbs like a bruise.

Flora doesn't bring him up until later that evening, after we've tidied away the dishes and Mum's sent a reluctant Ùna to bed. I'm in Flora's room, helping her go through the clothes in her wardrobe. Everything looks almost exactly as it did the day she died – the purple duvet, the posters on the walls, the fairy lights strung above the bed and pots of nail polish lined up on the desk. And on her bedside table, the same framed Christmas photo that we have downstairs.

"So … time to talk about the elephant in the room." Flora taps the photo, where Dad is wearing a bright red Santa jumper and a wide smile. "A tall, Gaelic-speaking elephant who likes gardening and whisky."

My throat goes dry. "I thought Marisa already told you about Dad leaving?"

"She did, yeah, but she didn't really explain why." Flora reaches for a cream knitted jumper with a hole in the elbow. She smiles but her voice is wobbly. "Does he think I'm a crime against humanity, or something like that?"

I lean back against the wall and fiddle with my necklace. It's a gold pendant shaped like a leaf with the letter 'I' engraved in it. Ùna has one with a 'Ù' and Flora used to have an 'F'. Gran gave them to us for Christmas one year. Flora never took hers off until she lost it a few weeks before she died.

"Nothing that dramatic." I search for the kindest way to reword some of the harsh things Dad said. "He thinks it's impossible to recreate a human being, so you can't really be you."

It never felt like Dad was properly on board with the trial. He signed the contracts, did the training modules and came to all the community meetings. He even cleaned Flora's bike, which had been lying in the garage since she died. But I could tell from the way he sighed and shook his head when he thought no one was watching that he was only doing it for Mum's sake. Maybe he was hoping she'd realize how unrealistic what they were promising seemed and eventually back out.

That didn't happen, obviously. The closer Flora's homecoming grew and the more real it started to feel, the more fixated Mum became, and the more Dad withdrew. A few months ago, he packed up his stuff and told us he was going to live on Eilean Gorm with Kirsty and Gran.

"I'm sorry," he said again, as he hugged Ùna and me goodbye. "I can't be part of this. It's not right."

Watching him drive away made my heart hurt, but I couldn't blame him. I didn't think the trial was a good idea, either. For a while I even considered moving to Eilean

Gorm with him, but there's no room for me at Kirsty's, and I couldn't leave Ùna on her own. Especially not when I was the one who'd started all this.

"He'll change his mind once he sees you," I tell Flora now. "Definitely. We just need to convince him to come and visit, since you can't go there."

"I hope so. It feels weird not having him around."

She tosses the jumper on to the Throw Away pile. Her clothes have that musty smell from being trapped in the wardrobe for so long and moths have chewed through some of the fabrics. I haven't seen most of them in years, like the pale blue dress that Flora wore to our uncle Griogair's wedding, or the dungarees she loved when she was twelve. Each one gives me a little pang of grief, but then I look up and see Flora right beside me. It's so confusing.

"This place must look like a time capsule to you." Flora nods towards a poster of Pandora21, her favourite K-pop band. "Are they even still together?"

"Oh yeah, they're really popular now. One of their songs was number one for ages last year."

The chorus instantly pops into my head. It seemed like every time I went into the wee shop in the village or got the ferry to Eilean Gorm last summer, that song was playing. Hearing it always felt like a punch in the chest, knowing how excited Flora would have been by the once little-known band getting airtime on national radio.

"Oh my gosh, that's amazing!" she says, her tone brightening. "Maybe they'll finally tour over here now."

"They played Glasgow a while ago. Adhiti went with her cousins."

"No way!" Flora lets out a long sigh. "Damn it, I wouldn't

have gone and died if I'd known that was going to happen."

The dark joke trips me up but I try not to show it. "Adhiti said they were awesome. We should all go together if they come back."

Her face lights up. I wonder if I'd be having this conversation with eighteen-year-old Flora. If things had been different, she'd probably be getting ready to go to university now. Maybe she'd still love Pandora21, but maybe not.

"You'd come with me?" she asks. "You always thought they were so cheesy."

"Of course I'd come. I still think they're cheesy, mind," I say, grinning.

She bunches up an old yellow polo shirt into a ball and throws it at me. "Take that back, you absolute heathen."

I laugh and toss the T-shirt at her. The Flora I remember probably wouldn't have wanted to go to a concert with her little sister either, but that doesn't matter any more. This is the Flora who's here now.

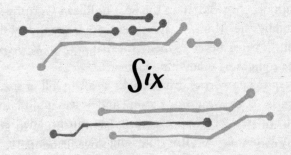

Six

The next day, the July rain finally gives way to blue skies and sunshine. Mum is keen for Flora to spend the day at home again but in Scotland you have to make the most of good weather while it lasts. She eventually agrees we can cycle to our favourite beach, the one on the north-west coast of the island.

"You keep saying we need to act normal," I remind Mum while Flora and Úna wheel the bikes out of the garage. "Going to the beach on a sunny day – that's normal."

"You're right." Mum runs a hand through her hair and sighs. "But you know what this place is like. Flora's going to be the centre of attention for a while and not all of it will be good. I wanted to keep her away from that for a few days."

Though everyone on the island signed up for the trial, not everyone is happy about it. There have been complaints at every community meeting about it. Some people think Second Chances will use Flora to spy on us, or that if we let one robot in, soon the island will be overrun with them. Most of that anger faded when the first payment arrived, but it hasn't fully disappeared. I can tell from the whispers when I walk into the shop or the post office, and the way certain people avoid us on the boat to Eilean Gorm.

"It'll be fine, Mum," I say, sounding more confident than I feel. "There's never anybody on that beach. We'll come home right away if anything happens."

Despite her worries, Mum packs us a bag full of snacks, reminds us to wear sun cream, and waves us off from the front step when we eventually set out for the beach. Sìth watches us leave from the long grass by the path, her tail bushing up when Flora wheels past.

There are days when living on Eilean Dearg makes me feel like the luckiest person on earth, and today is one of them. Above the hills, the sky is brilliant and endless. The clear air smells like sea salt and heather, and other than Ùna's squeaky brakes, the only sounds are the waves hushing and the occasional seagull cawing. Flora cycles ahead of Ùna and me, the fabric of her T-shirt rippling in the light breeze. She was always a fast cyclist and now she pedals even quicker than before. But I don't fixate on that, or how the sun glints off her port when her hair is blown to one side. Mostly I think about how healthy she looks. How alive.

Twenty minutes later, we arrive to find the beach deserted except for one lone dog walker in the distance. Nothing has changed here. The soft white sands and blue-green water look exactly like they did when we were little, and probably long before that too.

We dump our bikes and race to the big black rock, then help Ùna find shiny shells and bits of sea glass for her collection at home. I've brought my football, so we mark goalposts with pieces of driftwood and take turns shooting penalties. Ùna is so bad that she keeps kicking the ball straight into the sea. Each time she rolls up her jeans and splashes into the cold water to fetch it, her shrieks bouncing up to meet the seabirds gliding above us.

After an hour or so, Ùna gets hungry and insists we eat the picnic that Mum packed for us. I open my bag to pull out a big bag of cheese and onion crisps, some chocolate flapjacks that I made a few days ago and a few apples and tangerines. I do keepy-uppies with the ball while the others sit on the sand and nibble at the food.

When Flora reaches for a tangerine, Ùna stares at her. "You hate tangerines! You used to, anyway."

"I did?" Flora pulls off a segment and slowly chews it. "Huh. Really? Why? This is nice."

"Seriously? You used to run out of the room if someone was eating one." I catch the ball with my foot and balance it there. "You really don't remember?"

Flora looks down at the fruit in her hand. "No. I guess no one told them about that. It probably tastes different to me now, anyway. My tastebuds don't work the same way as yours." She peels off another piece, then shakes her head. "But OK, tangerines suck. Noted."

She turns and throws the fruit into the long grass that borders the sand. Ùna laughs, but an uncomfortable question is starting to itch at the back of my head. What else has Flora forgotten? What else did we forget to tell Second Chances? Her hatred of tangerines isn't a big thing to lose, but there could be other parts of her that have disappeared too.

"Can I ask you something?" I let the ball drop from my foot and sit down on the blanket beside Ùna. "What's the last thing you remember?"

"Getting on the ferry with Mum," Flora says. "I think we were going to Eilean Gorm to see the doctor. They told me what happened after that but I don't remember any of it."

Marisa warned us that Flora wouldn't remember anything from her illness. I thought it was strange, but Second Chances explained that it would let her carry on with life as if she'd never got sick. In Flora's mind, the tests and the chemotherapy and the endless bad news never happened. No sleepless nights writhing and vomiting, no mornings waking up with clumps of hair on her pillow. All that pain, erased.

It's a strange thought, but a comforting one. I'd delete it from my own memory if I could.

"The next thing I knew, I was waking up in the Second Chances centre." Flora picks up a handful of sand and lets it run through her fingers. "I wasn't scared or anything. I already knew what had happened, and I guess they programmed me to feel calm so I wouldn't panic."

She starts telling us about the Second Chances base, about her huge bedroom, the open-plan labs and the views over the valley. I try to listen but I'm still stuck on what she said earlier. *I guess they programmed me to feel calm.* There was something in the training guide about making returnees as comfortable as possible, but I hadn't clicked that meant adjusting her feelings.

A shiver runs over my bare arms. I grab the football and get to my feet. "Let's head back," I say. "The wind's getting cold."

This time, we go by the village so we don't have to cycle back up the steep hill. Nerves start to flutter around my stomach as we draw closer. It's a Saturday and the village is busy, or what passes for busy around here. There are a few elderly people chatting by the harbour steps who pause their conversation to gawp as we cycle past, and others walking their dogs along the beach.

Annie Campbell comes out of the shop carrying a loaf of bread. She does a double take when she sees us, then waves. "Welcome home, Flora!" she shouts. "Lovely to have you back!"

I grin. Annie's daughter Georgie is in the year above me at school. Georgie is really shy and quiet but her mum is the exact opposite – you can practically hear her laugh from the other side of the island. As Annie disappears into her house, Flora calls a "thank you" then comes to a halt on her bike. Ùna and I have to slam on our brakes to stop from bumping into her.

"What happened there?"

It takes me a second to realize that she's talking about the church next door. It was badly damaged in a fire and now its pretty stained-glass windows are gone and its walls are black with soot. For a moment I'm confused, wondering how Flora could have forgotten that – it was the biggest scandal to hit Eilean Dearg in decades. But then I realize it happened after she'd got sick, a month before she died. Flora can't remember any of that time.

"There was a fire," I say. "Three years ago now."

There's no fire station on Eilean Dearg. By the time the emergency services arrived, the fire had already spread to Annie and Georgie's house on the left, and Murdo's dad's woodwork studio on the right. Luckily everyone managed to get out in time, but Reverend Jack badly burned his right hand trying to put out the flames himself.

"They're still not sure how it happened," I tell Flora. "They said it looked like someone lit the fire on purpose but that doesn't seem possible. I mean, it's Eilean Dearg. Nothing that dramatic ever happens here."

"No way," Flora murmurs. "That's so sad."

We're quiet for a moment, all looking at the blackened building silhouetted against the Atlantic. Mum and Dad took us there sometimes, before Flora got sick. I remember playing under the pews when I was too small to listen; tea and biscuits at the end of the service. I wonder how many of those memories Flora still has, and how much got lost in the process of recreating her.

"Isla!" A voice from the end of the street shouts, breaking my thoughts. Adhiti is running towards us, wearing the yellow dungaree dress that she always wears on sunny days and waving her hands. Murdo jogs behind her.

"Is that Adhiti?" Flora asks. "Oh my gosh, look at you!"

Adhiti beams, her eyes sparkling. Apart from Mum, no one's been as excited about Project Homecoming as her. She taught herself how to code when she was six, started programming her own apps and games at eleven, and her aim is to study Artificial Intelligence and get a job creating smart prosthetics for amputees. For her, Project Homecoming is the world's best work experience.

"You look amazing," she tells Flora. "You look so like … so like you."

"You got so grown-up," Flora says. "And you got *tall*, Murdo."

Murdo gives a shy nod. "Welcome back, Flora."

Seeing them both smiling at my sister fills me with happiness. Murdo, Adhiti and I were all born within four months of each other and we've been best friends our whole lives. They're the ones who have kept me calm throughout the entire preparation process for Project Homecoming. Adhiti helped me get my head round the more complicated parts of the family guide and Murdo's a great listener – he was always there when I needed to vent all my doubts and worries.

We stand and chat for a while, pretending not to notice the curious stares of the people around us. Flora talks about her time in California and Adhiti fills her in on what Pandora21 have been up to in the past three years. Murdo casts a few nervous looks at the woodwork studio as we talk, but there's no sign of his dad. Soon, Ùna starts tugging on Flora's sleeve and complaining that she needs to pee.

"Why don't you come over to ours on Sunday?" Adhiti asks Flora. "That way you can see Suresh too. He won't be working then."

Flora's whole face lights up. She and Suresh were in the same class at school and were best friends. "Suresh is still on the island? I thought he'd have moved away by now."

"No, not yet." Adhiti pokes me in the arm. "You too, Isla. I want to show you the game I've been working on."

"OK." Flora actually bounces a little on the spot, making the tyres of her bike squeak. "We'll see you then!"

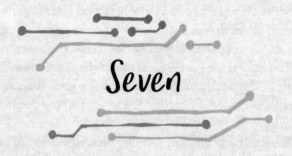

Seven

Ùna and I have to go to Eilean Gorm that Saturday. I don't want to leave Flora so soon, but we promised we'd visit Dad at least once a week during the summer holidays, and I always meet up with my friends to play football afterwards.

Flora sits on the bottom step and watches as we put our shoes and coats on, her arms wrapped round her knees. "Send Dad my best regards," she says, pouting her bottom lip in a way that's supposed to be a joke but clearly isn't. She looks like a little kid being left at home while everyone else gets ready to go out to a party.

"We're only going for lunch." I slip my feet into my trainers and tighten the laces. "You're not missing out on much. You know what Kirsty's cooking is like!"

"We'll talk to Dad about coming to see you," Ùna says as she flips her hair out from behind her coat collar. "We'll make him change his mind. Promise!"

I force a smile, but there's an uneasy feeling in my stomach. The trial was enough to make Dad pick up and leave us, his job, the whole island – it's going to take a lot of persuading to get him to come back. But I nod, and as Ùna and I wave goodbye and climb on to our bikes to go to

the harbour, I hope really hard that this is a promise we'll
be able to keep.

The crossing is choppy that day, the waves rising up
to brush the edges of the boat as it slices through the
water. After we arrive Ùna and I loop up by the high
street so we can take a look at the shops before going to
Kirsty's. Although Eilean Gorm is tiny by most people's
standards, it feels like a metropolis compared to our island
– there are four cafés and even a cinema. Flora had loads
of friends from the swim team here, so this place was like
a second home to her. I understand why she can't come
with us but it still feels so unfair that we have to leave her
behind.

When we get to the cottage, Kirsty opens the front door
to greet us and I instantly feel my mood lift. She's an artist,
and the youngest of Dad's siblings. There are a whole
sixteen years separating them and to me she's always felt
more like a big cousin than an aunt. Today she's wearing
paint-splattered dungarees with a striped top and giant
Pusheen slippers on her feet.

"Right on time!" she says cheerfully. "Lunch is almost
ready."

"Um, great." Ùna follows me into the house and slips off
her trainers. "Did, uh, did *you* make it?"

Ùna can't keep the nerves out of her voice. Kirsty is
probably the world's worst cook. She once made us a daal
that was as thick and bland as porridge, and another time,
she gave us all food poisoning after she left a bag of frozen
prawns out overnight.

Kirsty grins and rolls her eyes. "Don't worry, your dad's on the case. He's barely let me near the oven since he moved in!"

We follow her into a small, cosy kitchen filled with the colourful clay jugs and bowls that Kirsty makes in her studio. Dad is standing by the oven, dishing lasagne on to five plates. Out of the three of us, Flora looks the most like him by far. They have the same sharp jawline and sandy hair, and their noses are the same narrow shape.

"*Halò, a chaileagan*," he greets us, smiling. *Hi, girls.*

He holds out his free arm and I slide under it to give him a hug. His unshaven face is rough against my temple, and the feeling gives me a jolt of missing him. Not only present-day Dad, but the person he was before Flora died, before he and Mum began fighting all the time. The dad who knew an old folktale for every part of the islands and constantly made bad bilingual puns. Who tried so hard to be interested in K-pop and *The Great British Bake-Off* and anything else his daughters loved.

"How was the boat today?" It's what he always asks when we arrive, but today there's a quiver in his voice. He hasn't forgotten that the new Flora was due to arrive on the island a few days ago.

"Fine," Ùna says, shrugging off her jacket. "Nice and smooth."

To my surprise, she replies in Gaelic. Though we're all bilingual, Flora and Ùna almost always spoke to Dad in English – a sore point for him, given he's a language teacher. Making the effort is always a sure way to get him in a good mood. He smiles at Ùna, his eyes crinkling at the edges, and passes me a couple of plates of lasagne.

"Put these on the table, would you, Isla? And before you call PETA, yes, it's all veggie."

I roll my eyes. Dad is so old-fashioned about some things and vegetarianism is one of them. I set down the first plate in front of Gran. "Hi, Gran," I say. "It's me, Isla."

She turns round, peering up at me through her thick, round glasses. Gran's eyes are a little cloudy now, but they still sparkle when she smiles. "Oh, hello, there. Now let me see. Isla … you're one of Innes's girls, aren't you?" she asks with a hesitant glance towards Dad.

"That's right, Mam. The middle one," Dad says in a loud voice. "And that's Ùna, the youngest."

Ùna drapes her arms round Gran's neck in a hug and flops into the seat beside her. It still makes me sad when Gran gets confused about who we are. Today, though, she looks from Ùna to me and nods.

"Flora didn't come with you?" she asks.

There's a tense pause. Gran's dementia took a sudden dip about six months after Flora passed away. She went from sometimes forgetting that Flora was gone to having no memory of her illness or death at all. At first Dad would remind her about it but he quickly gave up on that. It was too upsetting, having to see Gran relive the shock over and over again, and it felt pointless when we knew it would fade from her mind in a few hours.

Kirsty takes the seat opposite Gran and begins filling our glasses with water from one of her sunflower jugs. "No Flora today, Mam," she says, the brightness in her voice as false as the painted clay flowers on the jug. "Just Isla and Ùna."

Ùna opens her mouth to say something but I shake my

head slightly. Dad can be really stubborn, and if we start pestering him about coming to see Flora too soon he'll never change his mind. We need to time this just right.

He comes to the table with the remaining three plates balanced on his arms like a waiter. "*Bon appétit*," he says in an overexaggerated French accent. "So, what's been happening this week?"

I cast around for something to say that doesn't involve Flora and end up rambling about a funny clip from last week's *Gogglebox*. Kirsty tells us about a commission she received to make a gravy jug shaped like a gannet holding a bag of chips in its beak, and Dad talks about the online Gaelic classes he's started teaching. All the while, Ùna picks at her nails and shifts in her seat. You can practically see the arguments bubbling inside her.

After ten minutes or so, the boiling pot blows its lid.

"Are we really going to pretend that everything's the same as usual?" she snaps. "You're really going to ignore the fact that Flora has come back?"

There's a long pause. Dad casts a worried glance towards Gran. Kirsty picks up their plates and leads Gran out to the garden, saying something about it being too nice a day to sit inside, though the sky is slate grey.

Once the door is closed, Dad turns back to Ùna with a sigh. "We've been through this, love." He's using his teacher voice, the one he saves for students who won't do as they're told. "That … person. It's not Flora. It's not possible."

"She *is*, though! You haven't seen her. Look."

Ùna takes out her phone and swipes at the screen. She holds out a picture taken at the beach yesterday – Flora with her jeans rolled up to her calves, laughing and jumping out of the way as a cold wave comes gliding towards her toes. Dad drops his knife and fork and jolts back as if he's been burned. I put my hand on Ùna's and turn the phone towards the table but she snatches her fingers away.

"No! He has to see this! You can't ignore her, Dad. She's your *daughter*."

Dad's face has gone ghostly pale. His gaze floats to the other end of the room, to the urn that holds Flora's ashes, now sitting on Kirsty's windowsill. He took it with him when he moved out and Mum didn't argue. No brand-new Flora was going to rise from those ashes. Only Second Chances could give her that.

"That girl isn't your sister, love," Dad tells Ùna now. His hands shake as he reaches for his glass of water. "She's not even a girl. It's a lookalike, a visual trick."

"I thought so too, Dad, but it's really not like that," I say. "She actually *is* Flora. You should at least come and meet her, see what she's like. Make up your mind after that."

Surprise flashes in Dad's eyes. Until Flora arrived, I was on his side about all this. He puts his head in his hands and stares at his food for a few long moments.

"This is exactly why I didn't want to do this. I knew you two would get too attached, and when this all goes wrong…" His Adam's apple bobs under his chin as he swallows. "We all need to try to move on, girls. That means accepting that Flora's gone. There's no bringing her back."

Ùna has tears in her eyes and her lower lip is quivering with anger. "When Flora got sick, you didn't accept it, did you? You needed science and technology to help her get better. Even if it didn't work, you had to try."

"Of course we tried. We couldn't sit around waiting for a miracle. But that's not the same thing at all, Ùna, and you know it." He picks up his knife and fork and pushes another bite of lasagne into his mouth, shaking his head as he chews. "I can't believe Sarah's actually going through with this. It's ludicrous."

The legs of Ùna's chair scrape against the wooden floor as she pushes it back. She grabs her jacket and pulls it on. "You're the one who's being ludicrous!" she shouts. "You don't get it. They've actually brought Flora back, and you're too stubborn to come and see for yourself."

Ponytail swinging, Ùna storms out of the kitchen and slams the door behind her. Dad mutters an exasperated "*an ainm an Àigh*" under his breath and gets up to go after her. I think of the moment Flora stepped off the boat, how dizzy with shock and happiness I'd been. I want him to feel that way too. He would if he gave her a chance.

"We did get a miracle, Dad," I call after him. "This is it. *This* is the miracle."

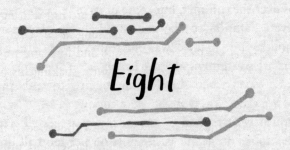

Eight

Ùna doesn't have strops very often these days but when she was little she was the queen of temper tantrums. Dad was always the best at coaxing her out of it. He'd distract her with his bad jokes and even worse impressions of animals or celebrities, and by the time Ùna was done laughing she'd have forgotten what she was angry about. He goes after her when she stomps out of Kirsty's and by the time they come back twenty minutes later, her stormy mood has been weathered by his jokes and the promise of apple strudel for pudding.

Even so, the atmosphere in the house is still tense when I leave to meet my friends later that afternoon. I hum under my breath as I walk over to the field by the high school, trying to clear the argument from my head. I didn't think Dad would refuse to even look at a photo of the new Flora. Talking him round is going to be harder than I thought.

My mood shifts when I see my friends kicking a ball around the pitch. Eilean Dearg is way too small to have its own girls' football team – or a boys' one – so I joined the Eilean Gorm team a few years ago. Our training stops over the summer, but some of us have been meeting up every Saturday to play. There are always players away on holiday but today Tiwa, our team captain, and a few others are warming up by the bench.

Tiwa waves when she sees me jogging towards them. "Isla! We didn't know if you were coming."

"You haven't replied to any of my messages all week." Rachel looks up at me as she puts on her football boots, squinting in the afternoon sun. "Did you see that video of those ice-skating goats that I sent you?"

"Uh, no, not yet," I say. "Sorry, I've been really busy."

Màiri tugs her hair into a high ponytail and frowns. "It's the summer holidays! What are you busy with?"

"Just … things," I say, waving my hand vaguely. "Helping my mum with some stuff at home."

I can feel my cheeks burning. It was hard enough keeping the trial secret from the rest of the team over the past year and a half, but now that Flora's actually here it's a whole different level of lying. It feels wrong to keep such a big thing from them, even if I don't have a choice: I can't risk putting the trial in danger and Flora being taken away again.

As I finish tying up my boots, Eilidh comes running across the field, her gym bag bouncing against her side. Behind her is a girl I don't recognize. She has a long black ponytail with purple tips and boots with rainbow laces. They both slow down to a walk and wave as they draw up to us.

"This is Holly," Eilidh says, panting slightly. "She just moved in down the road from me, into the yellow house."

"Oh, I love the yellow house! I wondered who'd moved

in there." Rachel tosses the ball from her left hand to her right. "Are you starting at our school after the holidays then?"

"Yeah. Third year, same as Eilidh," Holly says. Her voice is light and bouncy with an Inverness accent. "I hope you don't mind me crashing your game. I'll try out for the team properly after the holidays."

"Here's the best part." Eilidh does a drumroll on her thighs. "She's a goalie!"

"Oh, that's perfect!" Tiwa's eyes light up. "Our old one abandoned us. Clashes with drama group."

"And the one before left to focus on her violin lessons," Rachel says. "I call it the Eilean Gorm goalkeeper curse."

"Are you any good, though?" Màiri asks Holly.

Rachel and Tiwa pull faces at her. Màiri is always a bit frosty with new players. It's because she gets nervous around new people. I do too, but I go quiet instead. When I first joined the team, I barely said a word to the others for months. Now they're some of my best friends, after Murdo and Adhiti of course. It is a bit tough when new girls join, though. It changes the group dynamic, like adding different ingredients to an old recipe. Sometimes it turns out even better than before, but it always takes me a while to get used to it.

Holly tugs on her ponytail to tighten it. "I'm not bad. Plus, I'm terrible at acting, so I'm not going to abandon you for drama group. I do play the cello, though, so string instruments could be a threat!"

We do some warm-ups with Tiwa leading us through the drills since our coach Lily doesn't train us during the holidays. Soon, all thoughts of Flora and everything else that's going on at home float up into the sky. Football is a bit like baking for me. When I'm playing, I can completely shut out everything else. All that matters is getting the ball from my opponent or scoring a goal – like making sure the batter is exactly fluffy enough or the chocolate is the right temperature. It's stuff that isn't very important in the grand scheme of things, but in the moment it feels crucial.

With everything that's changed over the past four years, it's been good to have one part of my life that's more or less the same. Something that's just for me.

Before we finish, we take turns shooting penalties. It turns out Holly is much better than she let on. She only misses three goals, including one of mine. Plus she's funny – when Jess skids into her, Holly clutches her leg and starts wailing like those overdramatic professional players, to make us laugh. Even Màiri has stopped scowling by the end.

As I'm changing out of my football boots and back into my trainers, Holly sits down on the bench beside me. "You're good," she tells me. "Like, *really* good. You're like Megan Rapinoe but with red hair."

My cheeks flush at the compliment. "No way. Thanks, though. You're really good too."

She grins at me, then waves goodbye to everybody before following Eilidh off the pitch. I like this new addition to our team. She's going to be a good fit.

Flora's in her room when I get back home that afternoon. I knock on her door to the beat of that old song "Seven

Nation Army", something we started years ago. Sometimes I'd still tap like that after she'd died, a tiny part of me hoping she'd shout for me to come in, even though I knew it was impossible. When her voice actually does call through the door this time, my heart almost bursts with happiness.

"Hey." Flora's sitting cross-legged on her bed with her laptop in front of her. "How was football?'

"Good. Scored a few goals." I take a run-up and dive on to the bed beside her. "What are you looking at?"

On the screen is a photo of Flora and Suresh. They're around Una's age and dressed up as Smurfs, their hands and faces covered in bright blue paint.

"Some old photos of me and Suresh. I wanted to go through our memories before I see him tomorrow." Flora points at the screen. "What was this for? I remember dressing up, but not why we did it. Was it Halloween?"

I shuffle forwards on my elbows to look at the picture. Second Chances asked us to send them all of our photos of Flora to help them recreate her memories, and then they interviewed us and some of her friends about her. I did nine or ten sessions with them, and each one lasted a few hours. They dug around and teased out memories that had been buried for years: nine-year-old Flora singing a song from *High School Musical 3* in the car; an argument where she'd thrown my pencil case out of the window.

But even after hours and hours of talking about her, I still hung up the call feeling like I'd missed huge chunks of her past. It must be the same for Suresh. There will be parts of their time together that have been lost forever.

"I think it was World Book Day," I say. Something else comes back to me then. "Dad complained for years about how hard that blue paint was to get out of your clothes."

A light whirring noise from the doorway interrupts Flora's laughter. She whips her head round as Mum's robot vacuum cleaner trundles into the room.

I wave at him. "Hey, Stephen." Seeing Flora's confused look, I explain: "He was a present from Uncle Griogair a couple of years ago. Ùna named him."

"That's so like her to name the vacuum cleaner!" Flora chuckles but her smile quickly disappears. "Did Dad hate him too, or am I the only robot he's got a problem with?"

Though she says it like she's joking, the hurt in her words is neon obvious.

"Don't say that. Of course he doesn't hate you." I give her shoulder a playful bump with my forehead but the sad look in Flora's eyes doesn't fade. "We did talk to him but he still doesn't get it. He just needs some time."

"He's had loads of time." Flora flops back against her pillows with a sigh. Beneath the fairy lights strung above the bed, photos grin down at us. There's one of Dad on his fortieth birthday, blowing out candles on the lemon drizzle cake while eight-year-old Flora and three-year-old me clap our hands.

"It's hard for him," I say. "He doesn't want any of us to get hurt again."

We're quiet for a moment. The whirring of Stephen's wheels fills the silence as he chugs around the room gobbling up dust. Flora traces the swirls on her duvet cover with her finger. The colour makes me think of Holly – the purple tips of her hair swinging as she dived to block our goals.

"It must have been pretty horrible for him when I got

sick," Flora says. "For all of you. I can see why he doesn't want to be reminded of it."

I nod. Flora was diagnosed just after her fifteenth birthday. She'd been having pains and losing weight for ages, and eventually the doctors found she had a type of cancer called neuroblastoma – very rare for someone her age and already stage four. Mum and Dad tried to hide how serious it was from Ùna and me, even from Flora herself, but the odds were really, really bad. Even from the start, the doctors were clear that there wasn't much hope.

But we had to hope. Even when Flora went through rounds of chemotherapy and radiotherapy and none of it worked, we kept hoping. I never really believed she would die. That was something that happened to other people's families. Some clever doctor would come along and suggest a treatment that no one else had thought of and things would go back to normal.

It didn't happen like that. Eventually the doctors told us they had run out of options and there was nothing else they could do. Our parents brought Flora home and a couple of nurses from Eilean Gorm came to help them take care of her. We were told Flora would have around a month left with us, but it turned out to be even less – she slipped away in her sleep one night, without any warning. All the bad news, all the people telling us to make preparations, and in the end none of us had the chance to say goodbye. It felt like being hit by a car and only later realizing you'd been standing in the middle of the motorway for hours.

But I don't know how to say all of that to Flora now. I wouldn't know where to start.

"Yeah." My voice comes out strangled. "It was really horrible."

Flora presses her lips together. "I'm sorry."

"Don't apologize. None of it was your fault," I say quickly. "Anyway, we don't have to talk about it. It was a long time ago. It's over now."

But it's not. Not really. Those months changed who I am. I learned that normal can disappear with one doctor's appointment. That forever can drift away like a cloud. That sometimes life is unfair, unfair in a way that doesn't make sense, so unfair it hurts.

For Flora, those lessons were even sharper. I'm glad she can't remember it, but at the same time it's strange that she can't. Even though she's home now, losing her is a huge, important part of our family, something that reshaped us forever. I don't know who we are without that any more.

Nine

Adhiti's family live on the north coast of Eilean Dearg, in a cute white house with a red door and a thatched roof. Flora and I both spent loads of time there when we were younger, chasing their chickens around the garden or playing video games for hours on end. Before we can even ring the bell, Adhiti comes thundering downstairs and flings the door open.

"Hey! Suresh is upstairs," she tells Flora. "Come and say hi to Mum and Dad first. They're really excited to see you."

In the kitchen, Adhiti's dad Tamal is making tea while her mum Neerja sits by the window with a book in her hands and a blanket over her knees. They're both quite a lot like Adhiti – short, friendly and chatty, with Glaswegian accents that haven't faded even after living here for years. They turn to look at us as Adhiti pushes the door open, their eyes widening with matching expressions of shock and amazement.

"Flora!" Neerja says, spluttering slightly. "Look at you!"

Tamal is still gripping the kettle, pouring hot water into a mug. He doesn't notice it start to overflow until

Adhiti rushes over and takes it from him. Neerja starts to get out of her chair, but Flora shakes her head and hurries towards her.

"Don't get up!" She swings her backpack from her shoulder and takes out a small bunch of wild flowers that she picked from our garden. "Mum told me you're not well. I'm really sorry."

Neerja was diagnosed with breast cancer a few months ago. Adhiti was really scared and upset – after what happened to Flora, it brought back a lot of bad memories. Murdo and I went into overdrive sending her funny videos and memes to cheer her up. I helped Mum cook meals to take over to them when Neerja came home from her chemo sessions, like they did for us when Flora was sick. But the treatment is going really well and the doctors say Neerja's chances of recovery are really good. It's not going to be like it was with Flora.

"Thank you, love. They're beautiful," Neerja says, though she barely glances at the flowers – she can't pull her eyes away from Flora. "Gosh! Adhiti and Suresh said you looked just like yourself, but I didn't expect…"

She trails off, lost for words. Adhiti claps her hands together and laughs. "I think this is the first time my mum has ever been speechless."

"Don't worry. I wouldn't know what to say either." Flora sits down at the table and looks around, taking in all the details of the kitchen: the elephant teapot sitting by the toaster; the little blackboard where the family jot down things to remember; framed pictures of seabirds painted by Neerja, who's an artist. "It's so nice being back here. It's exactly like I remember."

"Would you like some tea, girls?" Tamal asks, finally finding his voice. "Let me see what biscuits we've got. Do you still like chocolate digestives best, Flora? Or you could have toast, or there's some scones…"

While Tamal runs through all our snack options, the kitchen door edges open and Suresh steps into the room. Looking up at him, I see him through Flora's eyes, how much he's changed in the past few years. He's grown a good seven or eight inches, his shoulders are broader, and he's stopped cropping his hair so short and let it grow out so it falls below his ears.

"H-hi," he stammers. "Hi, Flora."

Flora's smile is so bright it could light up the whole island. She rushes forwards and throws her arms round her old friend. Suresh tenses, then he slowly pats Flora's back. It's not the reaction I expected – knowing how close Flora and Suresh were, I'd imagined huge hugs, tears, hysterical laughter when one of them brought up one of their in-jokes. If Flora notices how stiff Suresh seems, she doesn't show it. She grips the sleeves of his hoodie and leans back to take a better look at him, beaming.

"Look how *old* you are!" She laughs and shakes his arms up and down. "This is so bizarre. Why didn't you come and see me sooner?"

"I was at the harbour when you arrived the other day." Tamal passes him a cup of tea and Suresh pulls his arms away from Flora to pick it up. "I wanted to give you some time with your family."

"You are family, silly." Flora pretend-punches him in the arm. "How much longer are you here for? Are you off to uni in September?"

"No, not yet." Suresh takes a large gulp of tea. His hands are shaking. "I've got a place to do Biology in Glasgow but I deferred for a year."

"Suresh is helping out in the post office while his dad takes me to the mainland for my treatment." Neerja's voice is full of pride and warmth. "We told him we'd manage fine without him!"

"I know, but—" Suresh breaks off and looks down at his mug. "I want to be here."

"Well, I'm glad you are." Flora puts her arms round him again, squeezing so hard some tea sloshes over the side of his mug. "I can't believe you're this tall now. You've both changed loads. Especially you, Adhiti. You used to be such a quiet wee thing."

Tamal laughs, looking more relaxed now. "We can barely get a word in edgeways these days. Gets it from her mum."

"*And* her dad," Neerja says, sticking out her tongue at him.

"Actually, I got it from Nani. She's got much better craic than either of you." Adhiti laughs at her parents' pretend offended faces, then nudges me. "Hey, do you want to see the game I've been working on?"

"Oh yeah, definitely."

I quickly stand up and follow her out of the kitchen. Suresh is acting like he's the robot, not Flora, but maybe he won't be so awkward without us all gawking at them. We go upstairs and Adhiti opens the door to her bedroom, a cosy wee room with lots of maps on the walls and an amazing ceiling mural of the planets that her mum painted when we were seven.

Adhiti picks up her laptop from her desk before flopping on to her bed. "Sorry about my brother. He's being so weird about the whole thing. I don't get it."

"I guess it's strange for him, being older than Flora now." I sit on her desk chair and swing from side to side. "It's a bit like if a ten-year-old version of me showed up and expected us to be friends exactly like before."

"When you put it like that, it would be weird." Adhiti clicks on her documents folder. "Remember how into dinosaurs I was when we were ten?"

"You're still into dinosaurs! You ordered that brachiosaurus T-shirt about three months ago."

"True. It *is* an awesome T-shirt, though."

She clicks again to open a file and a graphic of a cute cartoon squirrel in a forest pops on to the screen. When Adhiti presses the enter button, it starts to run. She sends it leaping over hedgehogs and ducking under low-hanging branches, snatching up acorns and flowers en route.

"You *made* this?" My mouth falls open. "Adhiti, this is unbelievable!"

"I found a tutorial online and Mum helped with the graphics," she says. "It's still rough but it's cute, don't you think? Do you want a go?"

Adhiti's the island's go-to person for tech stuff – Miss Grant always gets her to sort out the school Wi-Fi when it goes dodgy, and she's made websites for her mum's paintings and the MacGregors' woodwork studio. She even got a scholarship to a special coding camp for kids in Edinburgh last summer, she's so good.

I play a few rounds of the game but I keep getting stuck

on a particularly tricky mushroom at the end of level four. Before Adhiti takes over, I ask, "Can I see the code?"

Adhiti raises her eyebrows in surprise. She's tried to get me into coding before, using online teaching games, but I've never got very far. It starts off easy enough – creating buttons and changing colours – but I always hit a wall when I get into the really tricky stuff.

She opens another file and a big block of text in different colours pops on to the screen. "It's not as complicated as it looks," she says. "See, this part shows how I control the squirrel. There are different functions depending on whether I want it to jump or duck, and then this is what happens when he dies…"

She explains it all to me but a lot of it is gobbledygook in my ears. It makes me feel proud of her, my super-smart best friend, although I get a bit frustrated that I can't understand it better.

"It's strange to think that this is what makes up Flora now," I say, pointing to the screen. "All those letters and numbers and symbols."

"It's so cool, though!" Adhiti shakes her head in awe. "Second Chances are light years ahead of everyone else working in AI. I'm dying to know how they managed it. I mean, she's *so* like the old Flora. It's amazing!"

"Well, she's not … totally the same," I say. "There are some memories missing. Nothing major, I don't think. Little things. Like, she forgot she didn't like tangerines, and she couldn't remember dressing up for World Book Day with Suresh.'

It's the first time I've said it out loud. The guidebook says it's normal for returnees not to remember everything but it still seems odd to me. Like pieces of Flora's past have faded away.

"That's probably inevitable," Adhiti says. "She's based on data and what people remembered about her, right? But no one could have known every single thing about Flora. Not even the data. She was a bit different on Sekkon too. Everybody is. There are bound to be changes."

It's true that Flora wasn't totally herself in her videos. She acted more bubbly and outgoing than she was in real life, and her voice even became a little bit Americanized. They always say they have "the best minds in the world" working at Second Chances, though. They probably thought about the difference between how someone appears online and how they are in real life.

I pick up a Pandora21 figurine and make him dance across Adhiti's desk. "What do you think the returnee versions of us would be like?"

"Mine would probably be a lot less blunt," Adhiti says, grinning. "You know how sometimes I say things I shouldn't without thinking? I don't have that problem when I'm typing – I can always delete before I hit send."

I laugh. Adhiti is the most honest person I know. When I got bored and cut my own hair last year, everyone said it looked fine except Adhiti – she told me I looked like a ginger marmoset. Sometimes it's a bit hurtful, but you always know where you stand with her. And in hindsight, she was right. I did look like a marmoset.

"They interview friends and family, though, remember?" I say. "So, I'd fill them in on the real you."

"Oh, good point." Adhiti pauses to adjust something in the game's code. "You probably don't post enough on social media for them to make a returnee of you. There'd be loads of stuff missing if they did, because you don't tell anyone your secrets."

"What secrets?" I say. Apart from Project Homecoming, I don't have any. Although the new girl from football pops into my mind. Holly – her hands tugging on her rainbow laces and the way she'd smiled after she told me I played well. She's not a secret, though, so I'm not sure why I thought of her. Maybe because I haven't mentioned her to anyone yet.

"I don't know, because you don't tell me!" Adhiti laughs. "It's probably nothing to worry about anyway. Humans forget things, and we change in different situations and as we get older too. That doesn't mean we're not ourselves. I don't see why it would be any different for Flora."

"You're probably right," I say. And as Adhiti slides her laptop over to give me another go of the game, I forget all about it.

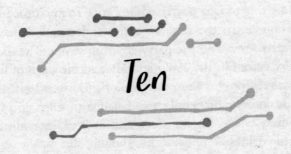

Ten

The last few weeks of the summer holidays zoom past in a blur of bike rides and baking and TV marathons curled up in our duvets. Ùna and I go to Eilean Gorm to visit Dad every Saturday but we still can't convince him to come and see Flora. By the third visit he's starting to really get annoyed at our pestering, so we agree to back off. Only for a little while, though. He can't ignore her forever.

On the last Friday before we go back to school, some of our neighbours throw a ceilidh – a big party with traditional music and dancing – to welcome Flora home now she's had a chance to settle in. We haven't seen many people other than the Bhandaris since Flora got back, and the atmosphere in our house crackles with anticipation all day. From the amount of time Flora spends getting ready, you'd think we were headed to the Oscars.

"You know it's being held in Seamus's barn?" I ask her, as we sift through her old dresses looking for something for her to wear. "It'll probably smell of dung."

"Maybe, but Flora's the guest of honour!" Ùna says. "She has to look good."

Flora eventually settles on a teal dress with white heels

and a string of fake pearls, while I stick to my usual jeans and hoodie. By the time we arrive at Seamus's farm, it's half past seven and the party is in full swing. The dance caller's voice fills the cool night air, and the smell of food wafts out from between the barn's rickety wooden doors. Inside, dozens of people are dancing an energetic Gay Gordons while dozens more mill around chatting and sipping drinks.

"Wow," Flora murmurs. "Looks like almost everyone on the island is here."

Her voice quivers. Mum spins round to face her. "We don't need to go in if it's too much," she tells Flora. "We can head home if you prefer."

"Mum, no! That'd be so rude." Flora stretches her mouth into a wide smile. Her lip gloss is shiny in the glow of the fairy lights strung across the barn's rafters. "Besides, I might as well get all the reintroductions done at once."

"OK, love." Mum smiles. She dyed the grey out of her hair this morning and she's wearing the floral dress she wore to Uncle Griogair's wedding. Despite the nerves, she looks more relaxed and happier than she has in years. "If you're sure."

Taking a deep breath, Flora walks through the doors. The music is loud, but not loud enough to drown out the whispers that ripple across the barn in English and Gaelic. Everyone on the island had to do an online training course to prepare for Flora's homecoming, just like we did. Rule number one: don't talk to anyone outside the island about the trial. Rule number two: try to act normal.

Some people manage it pretty well. They smile and wave to Flora, then pretend to go back to their conversations or carry on dancing. But others stop mid-movement to gawk. The band's guitarist misses six or seven bars before remembering where he is and picking up the tune. My teacher Miss Grant almost chokes on her glass of wine, and Margot MacDonald even bursts into tears.

"This is too weird," Flora murmurs. "I feel like I'm Beyoncé or something."

"What would Beyoncé be doing at a ceilidh in the Hebrides?" I ask.

Flora grins. "I don't know. Maybe she got word about how good Jeanie Mackay's plum pudding is and wanted to try it."

As people continue to stare, Seamus strides across the barn. He's a short, stocky man in his late fifties who fancies himself something of a community leader – Dad used to jokingly call him Mayor Seamus. He takes both of Flora's hands in his and squeezes them.

"Welcome back, Flora," Seamus says warmly. "We're so glad to have you home."

Flora thanks him for throwing the ceilidh and Seamus moves on to complaining about the rise in ferry prices with Mum. Other people begin drifting in our direction to say how good it is to see Flora: Reverend Jack, Davey from the wee shop, Miss Grant. Not everyone manages to keep their greetings as low-key as Seamus. The words "incredible" and "miracle" and "unbelievable" season every second sentence. One wee girl pinches Flora's hand to "check she's actually real", and Margot MacDonald is still wiping her eyes with her sleeve.

But despite looking overwhelmed, Flora seems happy. There are so many people here who are genuinely pleased to have her home. It more than makes up for the handful who aren't.

Adhiti arrives ten minutes later with Murdo. Suresh is with them, but he gives us a quick wave and goes off to talk to some older boys. When they reach us, I throw my arms round Murdo in a hug. "You came! I didn't think your dad would let you."

"He didn't," he mumbles. "He thinks I'm over at Finley's playing video games."

"Isn't Finley still on holiday?" I ask. Finley is constantly posting on Sekkon, so we're usually pretty up-to-date with his schedule. Last time I looked he was in the Seychelles with his dad and his younger brothers, live-streaming kayaking trips and taking selfies on the beach.

"Yeah. He won't be back until next week." Murdo casts a guilty look around the barn. "It's not like my dad knows that, though."

Murdo is a lot like his dad in some ways. They're both very tall and blond, and they both love birdwatching and woodwork. But while Murdo is basically a giant teddy bear who always wants everyone to get along, Andy loves an argument. He's the only person in the history of Eilean Dearg to have been temporarily banned from the wee shop, because he kept picking fights with Davey over prices and sell-by dates. He's a total technophobe too, so it's not surprising he has issues with the trial. If anyone on the island was going to make a fuss, it was him.

As the band starts up again, Flora goes off to find Suresh for the next dance. He shakes his head at first but eventually lets her pull him into line, his body stiff as a toy nutcracker. I grab Adhiti's hand and together we go skipping across the barn behind them. Big groups sometimes make me nervous but I love ceilidhs – they always put people in a good mood, and it's really fun stomping and spinning to the music. Most eyes in the room are still on Flora, although now there are more warm gazes than curious stares. If it weren't for the hole in the back of her neck, she could be any fifteen-year-old, dancing with a friend.

The music ends and the caller announces the Eightsome Reel as the next dance. You need groups of three for that one, so Adhiti and I go to fetch Murdo, who's talking to Reverend Jack by the drinks table. As we reach him, a voice barks across the barn. "Murdo!"

Andy MacGregor is standing in the doorway with Murdo's mum Katie behind him. Behind his scruffy beard, Andy's mouth is locked in a scowl. I catch Flora's eye and her face fills with panic. We had to warn her that Andy wasn't happy about the trial – she kept asking me why Murdo wasn't coming round any more – but we didn't tell her quite how hard he fought against it. Looking at his face now, there's no mistaking his anger.

"Oh, crap." Murdo slips his hands into the pocket of his hoodie, shoulders hunching. "Somebody must have grassed me up."

Katie gestures to her son to come towards the door. When Murdo hesitates, his dad grits his teeth and weaves his way across the barn. I scan the room for Mum, but she's talking to Miss Grant in the corner and doesn't notice Andy storm up to us. Katie hovers by the doorway, her cheeks growing steadily redder the more people turn to stare.

"Come on," Andy snaps at Murdo. He keeps his eyes lowered, purposefully ignoring Flora's gaze. "I've told you I don't want you around that thing."

Reverend Jack takes a step forwards. "Andy, there's no need for—"

"It's dangerous!" Andy gestures towards Flora, who stands frozen by Suresh, her fingers gripping his jumper. "It's probably recording everything it sees! God knows what they're doing with the data."

Murdo's face turns scarlet. "Dad, don't say that in front of her!"

"Don't be daft, Murdo. It's a machine. It doesn't have feelings."

He puts his hand on Murdo's shoulder and marches him out of the barn. Katie's eyes linger on us from the doorway, nervous and apologetic. Murdo twists around to mouth "I'm sorry" before slipping out into the night. My heart is pounding with anger. The barn is filled with chatter but Andy's words seem to resound through the space. It. Machine. *It*.

Adhiti coughs. "Well, uh … that's our third person for Strip the Willow gone."

"You two dance with Flora," Suresh says, steering her towards us. "I'll sit this one out."

Adhiti's distraction eases some of the tension, and by the time the music begins for the dance, the awkwardness of Andy MacGregor's outburst has faded. We spend the rest of the evening dancing and talking and eating too much of Jeanie Mackay's plum pudding, until Ùna starts yawning and Mum shepherds us out to the car. Flora is quiet as we walk down the path between the fields, so I put my hands on her shoulders and leap on to her back. She laughs and catches my legs under the knees.

"You're the one who should be giving me piggybacks these days, you giant," she says, hoisting me up on her back.

"Fair point." I loop my arms around her neck. "Did you have a good time tonight?"

"Yeah, it was fun. Although if I had a pound for every time someone said 'miracle' I'd be a millionaire by now." She's silent for a moment, her footsteps heavy on the path. "That stuff with Murdo's dad was horrible, though. And Suresh is still so awkward around me. Did you notice that?"

"Yeah, but it's only been a few weeks." I slide off her and land on the ground. "Things will get back to normal eventually."

"They might not. Suresh is eighteen now. *Eighteen*." Flora wraps her hands around her bare arms and shivers. "All my swim friends too. Lei's going to study dance in Liverpool, apparently, and Tom moved to Australia. I feel like they've forgotten all about me."

More images from after her death flash into my head. Lei and her mum coming all the way to our house with a week's worth of meals in Tupperware containers. Tom's voice choking when I bumped into him in the Co-op on Eilean Gorm last Christmas. Flora left a permanent streak of grief behind her, like boat trails that never disappear into the water.

"Nobody's forgotten about you," I say. "It's just …

time passed. That's all."

Flora picks at the purple nail polish on her fingernails. "It's really starting to hit me that three years have gone by. Three whole years. Sometimes it feels like everything is exactly as I remember, and at other times, nothing is."

"I know what you mean," I say, though I don't really. I'm not the one who woke up in a tech centre on the other side of the world and was told I'd been dead for years.

After a moment, she shrugs. "Different is OK, though, right? Different can even be better. I'm like … Flora 2.0."

"Flora 2.0," I say, smiling. "I like that."

We're all quiet on the way home – Flora lost in her thoughts, Ùna battling sleep beside me. Sìth is sitting on the gravel outside the house when we arrive but she bolts away as soon as Flora steps out of the car. I open the back door and start dragging Ùna by her feet. She squeals in protest and kicks me away, then pauses.

"What's that?" she asks, pointing towards the house.

On the front step is a bulky, shadowy shape. I switch on my phone's torch function and hold it up as I walk towards the door. What I see makes my stomach flip.

It's a computer, an ancient PC monitor like the type Gran used to have. It's lying face upwards with its screen smashed to pieces, part of its plastic casing missing and wires visible beneath the broken glass. The damage is far too severe for it to have been dropped by accident. Someone has taken a boot to it or maybe a hammer. They've destroyed it on purpose.

"What the…?" Mum kneels down to take a closer look. "What is this?"

The light from my phone glints off the smashed screen, making the shards look like yellowing fangs. There's only one reason someone would have come all the way out here and dumped a computer in front of our house. It's a message – one where the machine represents Flora. And that means it's a threat.

PROJECT HOMECOMING:
A GUIDE FOR FAMILIES

Module 6: Community

When trains were first developed in the nineteenth century, they were believed to cause a condition dubbed "railway madness". Some Victorians feared that their speed (which at that point reached just ten miles per hour) would drive passengers insane. The printing press, tractors, computers, cell phones – all of these innovations faced considerable resistance from the public. Even novels were once thought to be a danger to readers who may not be able to tell fact from fiction.

As long as people have made technological or cultural advances, others have fought against them. In a few decades, we expect returnees and other post-human beings to be as ordinary a part of our lives as trains or paperbacks. Until then, we will unfortunately come up against those who can't or won't accept returnees as individuals with thoughts and feelings as complex as our own.

This may include people in your own community, despite their having agreed to take part in the trial. Our studies show that returnees adapt best when they are surrounded by people who accept them and treat them as equals. If anyone is bullying, insulting or harassing your returnee, or even simply making them feel unwelcome, please inform your Family Liaison Officer as soon as possible so they can take appropriate action.

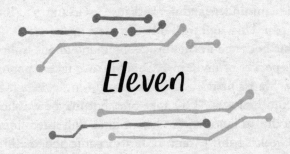

Eleven

"Who would do this?"

Mum asks the question bouncing around my head. We know everyone living on the island. Not necessarily well, but enough to say a friendly hello. The thought of one of our neighbours coming here while we were out at the ceilidh, dumping this computer on the doorstep to intimidate Flora... It sends shivers down my spine.

Ùna nudges the smashed screen with the toe of her shoe. "Do you think it was Murdo's dad?"

"Probably," Flora says hotly. "What a coward. And what a hypocrite, doing this after accepting all that money from Second Chances."

"You don't know it was him," I say, more in defence of Murdo than Andy, though I actually think Flora might be right. We stayed at the ceilidh a couple of hours after Andy dragged Murdo away. He would have had plenty of time to go home, pick up the computer and drive over here before we got back. Given how angry about the trial he is, it's the most likely explanation.

"Look, let's not jump to any conclusions." Mum tries to use her calm voice but her words quiver. "This might all be a misunderstanding. Let's just… Go and get a brush and pan, Ùna, and we'll tidy this mess up."

Ùna nods and hurries inside. I pull my phone from the back pocket of my jeans. "Shouldn't we take a photo to show Marisa first?"

Mum hesitates. "OK, take one, but maybe we should keep this to ourselves for now. Flora's only been home a few weeks. I don't want Marisa to panic and think this isn't a supportive community."

I take a picture of the computer from above, then a few more from the sides. It looks even more bizarre in the photo – the broken screen like a sheet of cracked black ice, ready to cave in at any moment.

"Well, we need to tell somebody," I say. "How about Jim?"

"He's away in Thailand on holiday. He won't be back until September."

Eilean Dearg is too small for a police station. The nearest real law enforcement is over on Eilean Gorm, but there's a voluntary police officer here in case of emergencies – Jim Quinn, a tall, very talkative man who lives in the north of the island. I'm not sure what his police work actually involves because we've never needed to go to him before. Other than a few sweets nicked from the wee shop, I doubt there's been a crime on Eilean Dearg this decade.

"Ùna's right, it's probably Andy trying to stir up trouble. Or maybe it's someone's idea of a joke," Mum says. "Either way, they've said their piece now. No doubt that'll be the end of it."

I look at Flora. The computer is reflected in her eyes, casting flecks of silvery light over her misty irises. She bites her lip and gives a slow nod. "Yeah. Maybe best not to mention this to Marisa for now. There's no point worrying her until we know what's going on."

That doesn't make a lot of sense to me – Marisa said to let her know about any issues, and this feels like a big one. But Mum and Flora seem sure, so I carry the main part of the monitor to the big bin at the back of the house while Ùna sweeps up the debris with the brush and pan. Once we're all inside, Mum locks the door behind us. Normally we only do that when we're leaving the island.

Watching her turn the key, my stomach twists with nerves. If this really is a threat, then it has to be from someone we know – maybe someone we trust. That means we're on our own.

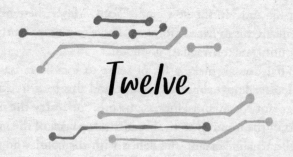

Twelve

High school on Eilean Dearg is nothing like the high schools in our favourite American series. There are no lockers, no prom, no cliques in the canteen – there's not even a canteen. It's just one cramped little classroom, with another next door for the primary kids, and most of our subjects are done through remote learning.

Even though Flora's been home for over a month now, kids stare through the windows as we walk across the courtyard on our first day back. One wee girl presses her face against the glass to get a better look, and Finley's younger brother starts dancing The Robot until Ùna yells at him. Inside, Miss Grant waits in the doorway for Flora and me.

"Seven minutes past nine, girls," she says, tapping the watch on her wrist. "The end of the holidays is hard for us all but do try to be on time."

"Sorry, miss," I say. "Ùna couldn't find her PE kit. Or her glasses. Or her shoes."

"Och, don't be a grass, Isla." Miss Grant does a tiny double take when she turns to Flora but she masks it with a smile. "Welcome back, Flora. You get settled in,

I need to fetch the new planners."

There are six of us in the secondary class this year: Murdo, Adhiti, Finley Graham, Georgie Campbell, Flora and me. The others are already sitting round the table when Flora and I walk into the classroom. Adhiti and Murdo break into smiles, but the others aren't as used to seeing Flora. Georgie hurriedly looks down at the textbook in front of her and Finley's face goes pale despite his holiday tan.

"Morning!" Adhiti waves a green pen as I slide into my usual seat between her and Murdo. "Were your fans waiting to get a look at you outside, Flora?"

"Hardly fans." Flora laughs and sits down in the free seat beside Georgie. "I did feel a bit like a celebrity at Seamus's ceilidh, though. Maybe I should demand a red carpet next time."

"I'm really sorry about what my dad said," Murdo says, his cheeks flushing. "He was totally out of line. Even my mum said so."

"That's OK. It's not your fault." Flora smiles, but her mouth is tense. Three days later, the memory of finding the computer on our step is still sharp. Mum keeps telling us to forget about it but I'm desperate to know who left it there.

Across the table, Finley stares at my sister with unmasked amazement. I'm actually quite impressed he hasn't pulled out his phone and started filming. Finley thinks a good sandwich is worth its own Sekkon video, let alone having the world's most advanced AI join you for the first day of school.

"Welcome home, Flora," he says. "How does it feel to be back?"

Adhiti shakes her head. "Stop it, Finley."

"What? I'm just saying welcome back!"

"You're doing your documentary voice again. You sound like David Attenborough." Adhiti lowers her voice and puts on an English accent, like she's presenting *Planet Earth*. "Here we have a rare spotting of Flora MacAulay, fifteen years old and found on the Scottish island of Eilean Dearg."

The impression is so spot on, everyone laughs. Even Finley gives a reluctant smile.

"It's fine, Finley," Flora says, grinning. "How was your holiday?"

Finley shrugs. He moved here with his mum when he was eight, but his dad still lives down in London. He owns some huge finance company and takes Finley and his brothers on a month-long trip every summer, plus skiing in Switzerland or Italy every winter. Finley always acts so blasé about it, like he's been on some casual two-day camping jaunt, instead of hanging out in a chalet or a château with a private chef for a month.

"Yeah, it was fine." He sits back and links his hands behind his head of curly brown hair. "I actually wanted to stay here, work on some footage, but Dad *insisted* I go with them."

Adhiti laughs. "Wow, Finley, will your suffering never end? The Seychelles! You poor thing!"

"What about you, Georgie?" Murdo asks, changing the subject before Finley and Adhiti get too caught up in their bickering. "You were down in Edinburgh a couple of weeks ago, right?"

Murdo is one of those people who always notices when someone is left out of a conversation and gently scoops them into it. I like that a lot about him.

Georgie brushes her strawberry-blond fringe out of her eyes and nods. "Yeah, we went to visit my auntie for a few days. Saw some shows at the Fringe. It was nice."

Her ears have started to turn red, the way they always do when she's the centre of attention. Georgie has lived on the island her entire life, same as me. As a wee kid she was really loud and boisterous, just like her mum. But when she was nine, her dad died in a car crash on the mainland. Georgie curled up in her shell after that and she still hasn't come out. She spends most of her time at home, hanging out with her dog Lola or practising music – she plays the violin and the piano and does Gaelic singing, so she's always busy with grades and competitions or the Royal National Mòd.

There's a pause now as we wait for Georgie to tell us more about her trip but instead she looks back down at her Geography textbook, pretending to be engrossed in limestone formations. I can't really blame her. This situation is so strange. I barely know what to say, either.

Miss Grant comes back in holding six ring-bound weekly planners and some textbooks. She hands the planners out to each of us – ignoring Adhiti's annual grumble about how she doesn't know why the council wastes money and paper on these when we all have calendars on our phones – then crouches down to talk to Flora.

"I didn't know what subjects you'd want to do, Flora, so I got out the books for those you started before… Well, a few years ago." Miss Grant sets the textbooks down on the desk. "But if you'd like to change any of them, that's absolutely fine."

"Thanks, miss." Flora runs a fingertip over the frayed edges of the books. "Can I do Gaelic instead of History? I know I did pretty badly in my last exam, but I'll do the work to catch up."

Miss Grant's eyebrows rise. I'm surprised too. Until he moved to Eilean Gorm, Dad was our Gaelic teacher. It's my favourite subject but Flora was hardly his star pupil. She always complained that the grammar was too complicated and she's not great at spelling.

"Of course," Miss Grant says. "The course is online now that your dad's moved, so I'll email you the information."

She goes back to her desk and pulls her laptop towards her. I give Flora a questioning look. She shrugs. "I fancied something different."

"Good idea," I say. "I mean, *deagh bheachd*."

My timetable begins with German, so I open my school laptop and log in to the course. As I'm reading through a list of clothing vocabulary, small movements start to snag in the corner of my eyes. Finley shuffles in his chair. Georgie keeps stealing glances at Flora.

After a few minutes, Flora sighs and closes her laptop. "Look, whatever you want to ask, just say it." She sits back and folds her arms over her jumper. "Then maybe we can all start acting halfway normal."

The others glance at each other. Even Miss Grant edges forwards in her seat. Adhiti and Finley both duck beneath the table to grab their phones from their bags.

"Can I film this?" Finley asks Flora.

"Of course you can't, Finley," Miss Grant says quickly. "You know this all has to be confidential."

"I won't release any of it, miss! But if I'm going to make

a documentary about the trial, I need as much footage as I can get." Finley sits up and puffs his chest out. "All this will be public one day. It'll be part of history. I want to be the one to tell the story."

Adhiti catches my eye and we both look away to hide our grins. You have to admire Finley's ambition, but sometimes he sounds so pompous. Miss Grant shakes her head and Finley reluctantly puts his phone down.

"Can I at least interview you at some point?" he asks, turning to Flora. "And you, Isla?"

"I don't think we're allowed to do that. It's too risky – your phone could be stolen or hacked, and then someone else could release it even if you don't." Flora gives an apologetic smile. "Sorry, Finley."

Finley slumps down in his chair and crosses his arms. Apparently he's only interested in asking questions if he can get it on camera.

Adhiti leans forwards, her fingers scrolling through the notes app on her phone. "My questions are pretty technical," she says, her eyes shiny with the reflection of the phone screen. "First of all, what deep-learning architectures did they use to bring you back?"

Flora blinks at her, then lets out a nervous laugh. "Um, sorry, I have absolutely no idea what that means."

"Oh." Adhiti's face falls. She scrolls further down the list. "What about specialized data processing cores? Do you know how many are in your graphical processing units?"

Flora tries her best to answer Adhiti's questions but there's so much jargon involved that she might as well be speaking Greek. Instead, Flora tells her about how long she has to charge every night, how she has to clear out her food tube, about the security procedure we'll have to follow if she's ever hacked or gets a virus. She lifts up her hair to show everyone the port at the back of her neck, which makes Georgie and Murdo blanche but Adhiti's eyes gleam with fascination.

Eventually Finley's curiosity battles his sulkiness and wins. "Can you feel anything there?" he asks, leaning over the table to get a better look.

Flora drops her hair and shakes her head. "I can feel pain in the rest of my body but nothing there. The pain's to make me more human, and seeing as you guys don't have ports, there'd be no point adding sensors around it."

"What about you, Georgie?" Miss Grant asks. "Is there anything you'd like to ask Flora?"

"Um." Georgie looks down at her weekly planner. The foot of the page is already covered with doodles of daisies and stars. "Your memories... They're based on interviews, right? And your search history and stuff?"

"They got a lot of information from the interviews, but yeah, it's mostly all online data. Plus videos and photos to help reconstruct my appearance."

Georgie nods. "So, does that mean you can remember every single message you ever sent? Or every single thing you looked up online?"

"Oh no. That'd be way too much information," Flora says, smiling. "They use the data to create my personality, my interests and my habits and so on, but then they filter it so I have access to certain memories and not others. I guess it's all in there somewhere but I can't see everything. Similar to how a human brain works."

"OK." Georgie shakes her head slightly. Her ears are still scarlet. "Wow, it's all so complicated."

"It is indeed." Miss Grant folds her arms. "But that's enough for today. It's almost ten and you've barely even looked at your work."

Flora opens the laptop again. The others reluctantly do the same, though I can tell from their fidgeting that they're still distracted. Even Murdo, who's usually a bit of a swot, can't keep his eyes on his book for more than a few seconds.

After a minute, Flora starts giggling. A moment later, she's properly laughing.

"What is it?" I ask.

"I'm trying to log in to the course but there are some security questions I have to answer." For a few seconds Flora can't speak for laughing. "It's asking me to confirm I'm not a robot."

Murdo blinks. Adhiti presses her hand against her mouth. Georgie lets out a nervous giggle. And then suddenly we're all cracking up, even Miss Grant, and everything about today feels a little less strange.

Thirteen

Football training starts up again that Saturday, so after another lunch at Kirsty's – Dad makes Quorn shepherd's pie, plays Dobble with me and Ùna, and still refuses to talk about Flora – I head over to the high school on Eilean Gorm. Our coach Lily has come back to training with a renewed determination to get us to the finals of the under-fourteens league this season. We got to the fourth round last year but we were beaten 3–2 by a team from Aberdeen.

"We can do this!" Lily paces across the grass while we tie up our football boots, punching her fist in the air. "Remember the three Ts: training, teamwork and total belief in ourselves."

"Is she always this fired up?" Holly whispers. "She's like something out of a cheesy American sports film."

Tiwa and I giggle.

"She did actually make us practise to training montage songs once," Tiwa says. "It felt like we were the Power Rangers."

Lily starts the session with some fitness drills, then we split into two groups and work on defence before finishing with penalties. I thought I'd be rustier after the summer holidays but I score a few goals and Lily compliments my ball control. By the end of the session, most of the girls are as determined to take home the cup as she is.

Afterwards, Tiwa, Rachel and some of the others talk about going up the road to get an ice cream. I wish I could join them, but I've got to meet Ùna to get the ferry home.

"You're going to the harbour?" Holly asks, looking up from her rainbow laces. "I'll come with you. I need to go to the shop to pick up some strawberries for my dad. He got really into watching cooking shows over the holidays and now he's addicted to making pavlovas."

"OK," I laugh. "Sure."

Butterflies spin around my belly as I follow her off the field. Holly and I haven't talked much one-on-one yet and the idea of having to make conversation all the way to the harbour is a bit intimidating. I don't have to worry, though, because Holly is what my mum would call a "total blether". She chatters non-stop as we walk down the street, leapfrogging from football to her new Maths teacher to her dog so quickly I can hardly keep up with the conversation.

"What kind of dog do you have?" I ask, when she finally stops to draw breath.

"A cockapoo. Her name's Oakley. She's the best." Holly's eyes crinkle with a smile. "Here, I'll show you."

She takes out her phone and shows me a photo of her posing for a selfie with a very fluffy golden dog. She swipes through her camera roll, her expression changing – pouting, crossing her eyes, sticking out her tongue – while Oakley's happy grin stays the same.

Holly's hair is down in the photos, not tied up in the ponytail she usually wears for football.

"Aw, so cute," I say. "Oakley, I mean! I'm more of a cat person, though."

Holly hisses, then laughs to show she's joking. "Do you have one? Let's see a photo."

I take out my camera and find one I took of Sìth a few days ago. There's a quick jolt of fear in my chest when I remember that the picture was taken in Flora's bedroom. Flora's leg is to the right of the frame but you can't tell it's her. Even if you could, Holly has no idea who Flora is. I'm safe for now.

"OK, I have to admit, that's a beautiful cat," Holly says. "That cat could be on the cover of *Vogue*."

I giggle. "I won't tell her you said that. She's got enough of an ego as it is."

"Cats are sort of arrogant, right? We used to have one too but she went with my mum after my parents split up." Holly tugs on her ponytail to tighten it. The purple tips brush the back of her neck. "I was sort of glad, actually, because she was super grumpy and she always had fleas. The cat – not my mum."

"Is that why you moved here?" I ask. "Because your parents split up?"

"Oh no, that was years ago. My dad's from here. My grandpa's had a few bad falls recently, and he's been on his own since my grandma died. Dad wanted to move closer so we could see him more."

"Oh, sorry," I say. I dribble a small stone along the pavement for a moment, then add, "My gran has dementia. Some days she doesn't really remember who I am."

Holly clicks her tongue sympathetically. "Getting old is the worst."

I don't really know what to say. I understand what she means, but at the same time, losing Flora so young made me realize that growing old is a gift not everyone gets. Even now, I'm not sure it'll be possible for Flora. Second Chances say they're working on a way to change returnees' physical appearance as they age but they're not there yet. There's no guarantee they ever will be. Flora might be stuck at fifteen even when I'm eighteen, twenty-five or forty-seven.

I shake the thought out of my head. Even thinking about the new Flora around other people feels risky, like she might slip out through my ears and ruin the trial.

"Do you like living up here?" I ask Holly instead.

Holly makes a so-so gesture with her hand. "It's fine. My brothers made such a fuss that I felt like I had to be more positive about it for my dad, you know? I do miss some stuff, though. My friends, obviously. Proper shops. Dream Rings."

"What's that?"

Her eyes light up. "Only the most delicious thing in the universe! They're from my favourite bakery – it's like a donut cut through the middle, filled with cream and with icing on top. I'll bring you one back next time I visit my mum. Well, I'll try. It's a long journey, I might end up eating it myself."

"OK." I laugh, though it sounds a bit sickly. "Thanks."

We turn the corner and the harbour comes into sight. Dad and Ùna are waiting for me on the bench outside the ticket office. The butterflies are still flitting around my stomach, but there's something different about their dance now. After a moment, I realize the feeling is disappointment. I don't want to stop talking to Holly yet. I could talk to Holly all day.

Back home that evening, I keep replaying our conversation in my head. After tea, I look up cockapoos on my phone and find a photo of one with its ears dyed turquoise. Then I open the group chat for the football team and find Holly's number.

Think Oakley would suit this? I write a message just to her.

My thumb hovers over the screen for ages before I take the plunge and press send. Two ticks appear below the photo. I stare at the screen nervously, hoping she doesn't think it's silly or wonder why I've sent her a message out of the blue. A reply quickly pops up.

Ha! I might try that if we ever need to paint the bathroom. I guarantee Oakley would have the walls covered in seconds.

A few moments later, a drawing of a Siamese cat wearing a crown and Tudor ruff collar appears on my screen.

I know I haven't met your cat but I bet she gives off this sort of energy. Tell me I'm wrong.

I grin. *Totally. Sith is a massive diva.*

That's how you spell it?! All day I've been wondering why you named her She.

I laugh and read the message again. *All day.* Holly's been thinking about me. Holly with the purple hair and the rainbow laces, and the smile that sparkles in her eyes, has been thinking about me all day. The fact leaves a warm, giddy feeling in my heart that lasts until I've fallen asleep.

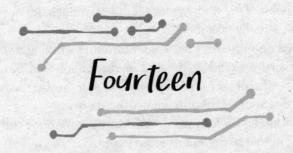

Fourteen

Now that school has started again, we slip into our old routine, the way it was before Flora died. We come home at four o'clock, do our homework, eat tea, watch series or read or scroll on our phones until Mum nags us to do something else. Ùna whines about having to go to bed earlier than Flora and me, and Flora and I bicker over her taking forever in the bathroom. It's not exactly the same as it used to be, not without Dad. But the clouds of sadness that hung above our house for so long are finally starting to disappear, blown away by laughter and loud voices and the constant music blasting from Flora's room.

The other main difference from our life before is that we now have weekly check-ins with Second Chances. Every Wednesday evening, after Flora has connected to the network so their technicians can make sure her system is running properly, we gather round Mum's laptop and give Marisa a rundown of how the past week has been.

"And how about school, how's that going?" Marisa asks one evening, like she always does.

"It's fine. Same as always." That's Flora's usual response but this time she pauses. "Sometimes I wonder what's even the point of me studying for the exams, though. It's not like I can actually take them."

Flora is in fourth year. That means she's working towards National 5 exams at the end of the school year, but she can't officially sit the papers – no one at the Scottish Qualifications Authority knows she exists.

"School is for learning, love," Mum says. "You've still got a lot of that to do, exams or no exams."

"True, but it's understandable if qualifications are important to Flora." Marisa leans towards the screen. "We could arrange for you to take some online courses, if you like?"

Flora shakes her head. "It's not that I even want to do the exams, really. It… It's hard feeling like I'm not going anywhere. All my friends have moved away. Except Suresh, but he'll be going to uni next year too." She looks down at her hands and picks at the purple polish on her fingernails. "I feel like I've been left behind and I've got no way of catching up."

"How about setting yourself some new goals?" Marisa suggests. "They wouldn't have to be academic. You could start a new hobby?"

"Yeah, maybe." Flora shrugs again. "I don't know what I'd do, though. The main thing I liked doing was swimming and that's out now."

Mum says that when Flora was a toddler, they had to put reins on her when they went to the beach or she'd charge right into the freezing-cold water. She started swimming competitively when she was seven or eight and she was really good at it. She would stay over at Kirsty's twice a week so she could get to training at the pool on Eilean Gorm on time, and she won golds and silvers for her backstroke and butterfly. It was more than a hobby. The swimming pool was the place she felt like the best version of herself. I understand that – it's what football is to me.

Marisa smiles sympathetically. "I know these limitations are frustrating. We're doing our best to work around them, but right now submerging your whole body in water isn't possible."

Ùna looks up from her phone, where she's on her millionth round of some bubble blaster game she's currently addicted to. "You could try a different sport. What about dancing? Kylie in my class goes to these modern dance classes on Eilean Gorm, she says—"

Flora looks up sharply. "How could I go to a dance class? I can't even leave the island, remember?"

Ùna shrinks back in her seat. Flora hasn't snapped at her like that since she came back, and for a horrible moment I think Ùna might cry. I catch her eye and nudge my glasses up my nose, our secret sign. She gives me a wobbly smile and goes back to her game.

"Think about what you might like to try," Marisa says to Flora. "We could get you an online tutor or sign you up for a course. We're here to help, Flora. Let us know, whatever you need."

We spend the next few weeks looking for a new hobby for Flora. She starts with other sports – yoga, running, cycling – but nothing grabs her the way swimming did. Mum digs her old guitar out of the loft and orders new strings for it but Flora gives up learning after three or four chords. She looks up dance tutorials for her favourite songs but she gets frustrated when she can't pick up the moves fast enough.

"I miss being in a team," she sighs, running her fingers over the swimming trophies lined up on her bookcase. "You're so lucky you have football, Isla."

Next, she tries arts and crafts. We look for some ideas online and come across something called paper cutting – these beautiful, intricate artworks cut from single sheets of thin white card. When I come downstairs for tea one Tuesday, she's trying to hack a heart out of a piece of white card with the small kitchen knife.

"Maybe you should start with something a bit easier," Ùna says, wincing as the blade skates past Flora's fingertips.

"You're right." Flora puts the knife down. "Finger painting, maybe. That's probably around my level."

The paper cutting lies unfinished on the kitchen counter for the next day and a half, until Flora eventually admits she's not going to complete it and slides it into the recycling. Right as I start to think she's giving up on her search, she mentions it at school after Murdo tells us about the golden eagle he saw on a trip to Harris with his dad at the weekend.

"I wish there was something I liked as much as you like birdwatching," Flora says. "Your whole face looks different when you talk about it."

Murdo's cheeks flush. "I know it's kind of nerdy but it feels like a treasure hunt. Even if you don't spot the bird you're looking for, you always find something interesting."

"It's not nerdy." Flora slumps back in her chair. "I've been trying to find something new to get into, now

I can't go swimming or make Sekkon videos any more, but it's hard."

Finley looks up from his Maths work with a wry grin. "Margot MacDonald is talking about starting a line dancing club. So far she's got Seamus, Jeanie and Davey from the shop to sign up."

Flora laughs. "I think I'll pass on that one."

"How about surfing?" Georgie says, chewing on her fingernail. "I saw a few tourists surfing here last year. In winter the waves are perfect for it."

I shake my head quickly. "Flora can't go in the water, remember?"

"Yeah, it'd be game over for me if I fell in. That's why I can't go swimming either." Georgie blushes and mumbles something about how she forgot, but Flora smiles at her. "It was a good idea. Surfing looks so much fun."

Suddenly, Adhiti slaps the table with her hand. "I know! Why don't you learn to code?"

Flora screws her mouth up. "I don't know. I'm so bad at that sort of stuff."

"You get better at it with practice, same as any sort of skill." Miss Grant pauses her marking and leans forwards on her desk, a sign that she's about to share some of her teacherly wisdom. "So many girls are put off studying STEM subjects, but those industries really need more women going into them. It's important for testing and research, for example, to make sure products are suitable for all genders."

"Exactly. Plus, it's really not that complicated at the beginning. I'll help you!" Adhiti reaches for her laptop. "We can start with HTML and CSS, simple stuff. There are loads of fun websites for learning."

Flora shakes her head, but Adhiti starts bouncing in her seat with a big smile on her face, excited at the thought of having someone to code with. Saying no to that grin is like telling a puppy you don't want to play.

Eventually Flora laughs and throws her hands up. "OK, OK, fine! But I'll be terrible – don't say I didn't warn you."

Adhiti beams. She instantly starts putting together a teaching plan for Flora, until Miss Grant reminds her she has Maths to do and steers her back towards her work.

I look down at my classwork, but I can't focus. There's a funny feeling in my stomach. The thought of Adhiti and Flora hanging out without me, having something just for the two of them… It's a wee bit strange. Adhiti's always been *my* friend. To Flora, she was Suresh's little sister. But I want Flora to be happy. If learning to code with Adhiti can do that, it's a good thing.

Miss Grant's alarm rings to tell us it's the end of the period. Flora goes up to the desk to ask her something about her Gaelic coursework. I save my essay and move on to the next subject on my timetable, Chemistry. My yellow highlighter has run out so I duck under the table and peer into Flora's bag to see if she has a spare one.

As I'm rummaging, something catches my eye. Hidden underneath all the pens and coins and papers is a bright red envelope.

Maybe it's the stark, angry colour of the paper, but something about this gives me a bad feeling. Flora is still talking to Miss Grant, and the others are all busy with their own work. I quietly fold the envelope in two, tuck it into my back pocket, then raise my hand.

"Can I go to the bathroom, please, miss?"

Miss Grant waves towards the door. "Of course, Isla, on you go."

I hurry out to the toilet between the two classrooms. Leaning against the door, I open the envelope and take out a folded piece of paper. When I turn it round, my stomach drops. It's a print-out from the Second Chances training modules, the one that explains how returnees are built. On it is a diagram that looks like a human body with half of the skin peeled back to show what's underneath. Instead of bones, organs and muscles, there are metal plates, thick bolts and tangles of wires. Three words from the description on the side of the page have been highlighted in yellow.

Just

A

Machine

It's another threat. And staring at the illustration, a horrible realization sinks in. I don't think Flora's taken that bag anywhere except home and school. There are only five people who could have slipped something in there without her noticing – and they're all sitting in the room next door.

Fifteen

I decide not to tell Flora about the message. Actually, I don't tell anyone about it. The smashed computer was a horrible surprise, and she's already feeling cut off from her friends and upset about Dad not wanting to see her. It'll make things worse if she knows that someone in our class is out to get her too.

The best thing I can do, I think, is to try to work out who did this by myself. That way I can confront them, or at least tell Mum so she can decide what to do.

That night, after everyone has gone to bed, I find an orange journal with a padlock that I haven't used yet. I open to a random page near the back and write down five names.

Murdo
Adhiti
Finley
Georgie
Miss Grant

I cross out Adhiti's name right away. She's Project

Homecoming's number one fan – there's no way she'd do something like this. After a moment, I strike out Miss Grant too. She sometimes comes by the big table where we all sit but she would have to kneel down, reach between our chairs and grab Flora's bag to slip something inside it – it's not likely she could do that without someone seeing. Plus, she was already at the ceilidh when we arrived and she was still there when we left. If the envelope and the computer came from the same person, it can't be her.

The problem is, I can't imagine it would be any of the others, either. Everyone seemed excited about the trial – including Murdo, even though his dad is so against it. And since Flora came back to school, they've all been happy to have her around.

At least, I thought they were. There must be something I don't know. A secret that someone is hiding.

My phone buzzes as I'm staring at my list. Even with all the bad thoughts swirling around my head, my heart gives a little leap of happiness when Holly's name appears on the screen.

Important question – would you rather have snakes for arms or snakes for legs? The rest of your body is exactly the same.

I shake my head, grinning. She's so weird. I love it.

Snakes for legs. It'd be impossible to pick stuff up or type otherwise. They'd be wriggling around too much.

Good point. Imagine having snakes for legs, though, Holly writes back. *Football would be practically impossible.*

I open the browser on my phone and look up the world's fastest snake.

The black mamba can move at up to 12.5 miles per hour, I tell her. *If you could train them to dribble a ball they'd be amazing for football.*

True! Plus, the other team would be terrified so they'd probably run off and forfeit the match anyway.

I laugh and curl back on my pillows, my phone cradled in my hands. Holly and I have been talking a lot lately. I'll be sitting in class and she'll ask me out of the blue what my top three biscuits are (chocolate Hobnobs, Jaffa cakes and ginger nuts; hers are party rings, custard creams and caramel wafers) or send me a voice note of her singing a made-up song about strawberries or the moon. Even with all those miles of water separating us, she's like a ray of sunshine lighting up my day. Seeing her at football has become the highlight of my Saturday. Maybe even of my whole week.

I glance back down at the notebook. I wish I could tell Holly what I'm doing. Even though she doesn't know any of the people involved, I bet she'd have some good ideas about how I could go about finding the culprit. We could team up to solve the mystery, like Daisy and Hazel from the Murder Most Unladylike books.

We keep chatting as I go over and over the list. Holly sends me a photo of Oakley, a Sekkon video of the different type of parents at football matches and my horoscope – she's really into star signs. But all the while, my eyes keep being drawn back to the journal, and especially to the name at the top of the page: Murdo.

It makes me feel sick to admit it, but Murdo is the most likely suspect. He would never do anything to hurt me or Flora on purpose, but he can be a bit of a pushover and it's not a secret that his dad hates Project Homecoming. Maybe Andy forced him into leaving the envelope in Flora's bag, or maybe he lied and told him it was an apology letter.

Either way, I have to ask. I'm going to feel so awful if I'm wrong, and even worse if I'm right, but I need to do it. This trial might even depend on it.

I spend the next day trying to find the right moment to talk to Murdo about the red envelope, but our classroom is so tiny and there's always someone hanging around at lunch and break time. It's only when school ends that I manage to get him on his own.

"Want to go for a walk?" I ask, following him through the front door and out into a dull grey afternoon. I try to keep my voice casual, but the words feel strained. Murdo doesn't seem to notice.

"I was going to cycle over to the loch. Davey said he saw a spoonbill there yesterday." Judging by the way Murdo beams, this is a big deal. "First time in years!"

"Oh, nice. I'll come with you."

"Me too!" Adhiti jogs across the courtyard to catch up with us. "I just need to be at the post office at five, so I can get a lift home with Suresh."

I open my mouth to find an excuse but, thinking about it, maybe it's best if Adhiti comes too. That way it won't feel so much like I'm singling Murdo out.

We stop by Murdo's house to pick up his binoculars, then walk up the hill towards Loch na h-Àirde. It's a long, thin lake bordered by tall grass and is known as the best spot on the island for birdwatching. Today the area is deserted except for a few ducks, all quacking merrily as they glide past. We wade through the grass and sit down on some large, flat rocks at the edge of the water.

"What's this spoonbeak like then?" Adhiti asks. "So we know what to look out for."

"Spoon*bill*. White plumage, yellowish crest and breast. Its bill is long and black and shaped a bit like a spoon." Murdo swings his backpack off his shoulder and takes out his binoculars. "That's the Eurasian spoonbill, of course. There's also the Roseate spoonbill and the yellow-billed spoonbill, but they're not found in Europe."

"Oh yeah, of course."

Adhiti and I grin at each other. We don't exactly share Murdo's passion for ornithology. I like birds but not enough to spend hours trudging up hills or along cliff sides to spot a rare one. Going birdwatching with him is always fun, though, if only because of how animated he gets when we see something interesting. One time we spotted a white-tailed eagle up in the hills on the west of the island, and he got so excited he tripped and cracked his tooth on a rock. Adhiti and I were freaking out but Murdo was more concerned with getting a photo to show his dad.

I open my bag and take out a raspberry muffin left over from lunch. Adhiti pulls off a chunk with a *yoink* sound but I'm too nervous to eat. While Murdo scans the loch, I try to work out the best way to ask him if he's the one leaving the messages for Flora. I can't just come out and accuse him. I need to be tactful.

After a while, Adhiti lets out a groan. "Will you spit it out, Isla?"

I look up from my muffin. "What do you mean?"

"You've been acting weird all day," Murdo says, lowering

his binoculars. "What's up? Is it something to do with that Holly girl?"

"Holly? What? No! Why would it be about her?" My cheeks start to burn. I take a deep breath, reach into my backpack and take out the envelope. "It's this. I found it in Flora's bag the other day."

I unfold the page from the manual and hand it to Murdo. Adhiti shuffles along the stone to take a look. Their eyebrows rise when they reach the part highlighted in yellow.

"That's so creepy," Adhiti says. "Who do you think it came from?"

"No idea, but it's not the first time something like this has happened."

I scroll through the photo gallery on my phone and show them the broken computer. Murdo must be genuinely shocked because he manages to keep his eyes off the water, even though there's a bird rustling in the long grass a few metres away.

"Wow," Adhiti mumbles. "Well, it's pretty clear what the message is."

"If they're both from the same person, it must be someone from school," I say. "Whoever sent that envelope needed to get into Flora's bag and she hasn't taken it anywhere else."

"You…" Murdo swallows. "You don't think *I* did it, do you? Because I didn't."

"Me, neither!" Adhiti flexes her arms. "You really think I could carry a computer all the way to your house on these noodles? And anyway, you know we both love Flora."

"Of course I don't think it was either of you," I say, and in that moment I realize it's true. Murdo is a terrible liar.

It's obvious from his reactions that he didn't know about the envelope or the computer. I look at him and bite my lip. "But I did think maybe your dad left them there… Or that he got you to do it, somehow."

"My dad wouldn't do that. Neither would I, even if he asked me." Murdo picks up his binoculars and turns back to the water, his shoulders hunched. "There's no way he could have got to Flora's bag, and we went straight home after the ceilidh. He gave me a massive lecture then watched anti-AI videos online for, like, two hours. He wouldn't have had time to dump the computer at yours before you got home."

So it wasn't Andy. I don't know how I feel about that. It's a relief that my best friend's dad isn't harassing my family, but it also means we're even further away from finding out who is.

"Maybe it's not about the trial. Maybe it's something personal," Adhiti says. "Did Flora get on somebody's bad side before she died?"

I hadn't thought about that. It doesn't seem likely. Flora was a normal fifteen-year-old. She went to school and swim club, hung out with her friends, made cute Sekkon videos. I doubt she could have made an enemy of anyone on the island.

"Not that I know of." I finally take a bite of the muffin and think for a moment as I chew. "Besides, she was so ill before she died. Even if she had done something bad, who could hold a grudge against a dead girl for that long?"

Something twitches in the grass at the other end of the loch. Murdo leans forwards, then sinks back down when a heron slips out from between the reeds. It dips its long

112

neck into the water and comes back with a tiny fish in its beak. I link my hands behind my head and look up at the pale grey sky. There are a few dark clouds rolling across the island towards us.

"What should I do?" I ask. "Mum doesn't want to tell Second Chances about the computer in case they overreact, but what if this keeps happening? It's scary. Especially for Flora."

Adhiti helps herself to another chunk of muffin and pops it in her mouth. "Well, you know… Georgie didn't come to the ceilidh. And she does sit right beside Flora at school. I'm not saying it's her," she adds quickly. "It's just an idea."

"She *has* been really quiet lately," I say. "Even more so than usual. Maybe I'll go and talk to her about it this weekend."

"OK, but be nice," Murdo says, his eyes still fixed on the water. "Georgie's sensitive, and it's horrible being accused of something you haven't done."

Guilt creeps over me like a rash, hot and itchy. "I'm sorry. I had to ask."

Murdo puts down the binoculars. "It's all right. I get why you thought those things, after what Dad said at the ceilidh. But I'm sure it wasn't him, and it *definitely* wasn't me."

He holds out his hand for a fist bump. We smile at each other and settle back to birdwatching. Half an hour later, the clouds arrive and rain starts to fall, so we head home. We haven't spotted the spoonbill but that's fine. Murdo will have to keep searching, and so will I.

Sixteen

Summer makes a comeback at the weekend. We wake up to a cloudless blue sky and a breeze so warm you'd think you were in Italy, or at least Cornwall. What I really want to do is go to the beach with Flora, maybe Murdo and Adhiti too if they're free. But today is Dad's fiftieth birthday and afterwards we have our first football match of the season, so at eleven o'clock Ùna and I board the ferry along with a beetroot chocolate cake that I baked last night.

"I don't know why you bothered making that." Ùna slumps into a seat at the side of the boat. "Dad's been so mean to Flora."

"He's not trying to be mean, Ùna. He just doesn't get it." I set the cake tin on my knees. The floor wobbles beneath me as the boat lurches away from the shore. "Besides, it's his fiftieth birthday. We can't miss it."

Sunlight glints off the handrails on the edge of the boat, turning Ùna's scowl into a squint. "Maybe not, but he doesn't deserve beetroot chocolate cake. He doesn't even deserve a stale Victoria sponge."

Kirsty is alone in the kitchen when we arrive at her house fifty minutes later. There are plates of shop-bought sausage rolls and mini quiches on the counter, and she's cutting cheese sandwiches into triangles. Even those seem to be beyond her cooking skills – the knife she's using to cut the bread is so blunt the edges come away ragged.

"I can finish that!" I say quickly. I take the knife from her and swap it for a proper breadknife from the stand by the microwave. "Where is everyone?"

"Your dad's reading outside." Kirsty opens the cupboard and counts out plates and glasses. "Gran's not feeling great. She's gone back to bed."

I feel a pang of sadness. With Gran's memory getting worse and worse, I sometimes forget that her body is getting weaker too. Every time we visit, it seems like something else has been taken away from her.

"Poor Gran." Ùna removes the lid from the cake tin and takes a sniff. "We can save her a slice for later."

"She likes this one." I swat Ùna's hand away from the cake before she can go in for a lick of frosting. "She cut the recipe out of the paper for me."

Gran was the one who taught me how to bake. Mum or Dad would drop me and Ùna off at hers while they took Flora to swimming practice, and we'd make gingerbread, fairy cakes, lemon soufflé… Ùna was only interested in licking the bowl but I loved watching Gran carefully ice and decorate cakes and biscuits, and the way she'd encourage me to get creative with different flavours and ingredients. I wonder if she can remember any of those days, if they sometimes emerge like stars on an overcast night, or if her mind is all clouds now.

"We'll take some up to her later," Kirsty says, smiling sadly. "Anyway, we need some candles! I can't do fifty but

I must have some lying around somewhere."

She riffles through the drawers and eventually finds a single striped pink candle tucked underneath some napkins. One hand cupped around the flame, I carefully carry the cake out to the garden. Kirsty and Ùna follow with trays of sausage rolls and sandwiches. Dad is sitting on a kitchen chair on the lawn with a book in his hands and sun cream slathered on his pale face. He looks up from the page when he hears us coming, a hand raised to block the light from his eyes. His face breaks into a surprised smile at the sight of the cake.

"What's all this?" he asks, as if he's forgotten it's his birthday.

Kirsty claps one hand against the side of the tray and starts to sing: "*Meal do naidheachd an-diugh, meal do naidheachd an-diugh…*"

Ùna and I join in, then quickly break off. Dad's smile has fallen from his face like a stone dropping from the edge of a cliff.

"What's going on?" he asks, his voice strained. "What's she doing here?"

When I turn round, my heart plummets. Flora is standing at the back door, wearing a white summer dress under her pink hoodie and her hair in a French plait, the way she used to do it when she was younger. Kirsty lets out a gasp and drops the tray. As sausage rolls go bouncing over the grass, Flora takes a step into the garden.

"Hi, Dad," she says. "*Is mise a th'ann. Tha mi dhachaigh.*"

It's me. I'm home. Flora knows that Gaelic is the bow to Dad's heartstrings, that for him every word is infused with meaning in a way English never will be. It's a trick we've

116

pulled since we were tiny – if we ever want to win him over, Gaelic is the language to do it in.

And at first, it seems to work. The fear and anger in Dad's eyes melt away, and for a moment I can see them fill up with a mixture of overwhelming joy, love and disbelief. But then he blinks and it's gone. He ducks his head, as if looking at Flora directly might hurt his eyes, and turns to me.

"What's going on, Isla?" he says, and I almost take a step back at the fury in his voice. "Why did you bring her here?"

"We didn't!" I say, shaking my head. "I didn't even know she was on the boat. She's not supposed to leave the island."

Flora takes another few steps forwards, palms up. "I know, I know, but I had to see you. It's been ages, Dad." Hands shaking, she reaches into her pocket and takes out a small parcel wrapped in striped paper. "Here. Happy birthday.'

Dad keeps staring at the ground. Kirsty is frozen beside him, her fingers grasping the long, opal necklace beneath her collarbones. I didn't think it would go like this. I thought that the moment Dad saw her he would be instantly won over, same as I was.

"Dad, come on!" Ùna grabs his sleeve. "Look at her. How can you say she's not Flora?"

"Because she's not!" Dad wrenches his arm away from Ùna. Eyes still fixed on the ground, he addresses Flora in English: "You're not her. You can't be. It's impossible."

Flora flinches back like she's been slapped. Ùna gives a cry of frustration and turns to Kirsty. "You can see that it's her, can't you? You must be able to see that it's her."

Kirsty's mouth opens, then she presses her lips together

tight. There are tears running down her cheeks and her arms keep twitching, like she wants to rush forwards and hug Flora but is holding herself back. Dad puts his hand on Kirsty's shoulder and steers her away from Flora.

"Go, Isla. All of you," he says. "You can make the next ferry if you leave now."

"Why are you being like this?" Flora gestures to her body with shaking hands. "Look at me! It's really me, Dad."

"No. You're a machine. You're a mirage." Eyes closed, he points towards the door. "Go back to Sarah's house. Please don't come here again."

The fact he says "Sarah" and not "Mum" seems so cruel. Flora's face is turning pink and there's a soft, whimpering sound coming from the back of her throat. For the first time, I realize that she can't cry tears like we can.

"Wishbones," she chokes out. "Fourteen miles to Fort Lauderdale. Do you really mean it?"

We all stare at her. Flora's eyes have gone completely blank, like she's staring into space. Then she blinks and stumbles back, her mouth open and her hands pressed to her temples.

"What are you talking about?" Ùna asks. "Mean what?"

"I don't know." Flora blinks and rubs her head. "I think that was some sort of … glitch."

The expression on Dad's face changes then. He almost looks triumphant, as if Flora has proved him right. As if she really is just a machine. "It's time to go," he tells her again, before switching back to Gaelic to talk to me. "Take her away, Isla."

Kirsty wipes her tears with the back of her hand and nods. "Go on, girls. This isn't doing anyone any good."

Ùna takes Flora's hand and pulls her back into the house. The gift slips from Flora's fingers and on to the grass but no one picks it up. I follow them through the kitchen and into the hallway. It's only then that I notice I'm still gripping the birthday cake; melted wax is now dripping from the candle on to the icing. I put it down on the stairs and hurriedly slip my shoes on.

Then a voice calls down from the top of the stairs. "Oh, hello, girls!"

Gran is standing on the landing, feet bare beneath her thin white nightie. She takes a few uneasy steps, her hands outstretched towards Flora. I rush up the stairs to meet her and gently help her down.

"What a nice surprise," Gran says. "Are you coming in for a cup of tea?"

Gran's tone is so warm and so casual, just like old times. In her mind, Flora never got sick, never died, never had to be brought back as a machine to be part of our family again. The thought makes a lump rise to my throat. This is all so, so unfair. We shouldn't have to go through all of this to be a family again.

Hearing Gran's voice, Dad and Kirsty hurry through from the garden.

"The girls are heading off, Mam," Dad says. "Aren't you?"

He and Flora look at each other. There's a pleading look in his eyes, a defiant one in hers. They only keep eye contact for a few seconds before Dad looks away.

As I help Gran to the bottom step, Flora turns to her and smiles. "Sorry, Gran," she says. "I'm just stopping by. I've got a swim tournament this afternoon."

"Oh, good luck. You girls, always so busy." She squeezes both of Flora's hands. "Come and see me soon, you hear? I'll make those lavender biscuits you like so much."

Flora smiles again, but I think she might cry if she was able to. "Great. I'll try, Gran."

Kirsty takes Gran's arm and leads her into the kitchen as the three of us step outside. Dad follows us and pulls the door shut behind him. "Thank you for doing that," he says gruffly. "She doesn't remember what happened. I don't want her getting upset."

"Neither do I." Even though he won't meet her eye, Flora looks right at him. "You might think I'm only a machine but that's not how I feel. She's my gran. I care about her. And you too, even if you don't care about me."

Something in Dad's gaze softens then. The anger in his voice fades and he switches back to Gaelic. "I'm sorry. I'm not trying to hurt you. None of this is your fault. Maybe you're even a person, in your own way." Tears spring to his eyes. He dips his head and brushes them away. "But you're not my daughter. My Flora is gone."

With that, he goes back inside and closes Kirsty's pink front door. The key turns in the lock. And in that moment, I know that nothing Flora or Ùna or I do is ever going to change his mind.

Seventeen

There's no way I'd be able to concentrate on football after what's happened, so I skip the match and hurry back to the harbour with Flora and Ùna. My heart pounds the whole way there, terrified that we'll bump into one of my friends – or worse, someone who used to know Flora from the swim club. Right as we're rushing up the ferry ramp, grey clouds roll over the blue sky and it starts to rain.

"Why didn't you tell us you were coming?" I ask Flora. "You should have warned us."

Flora pulls her hoodie over her head. A few raindrops run down her face and fall off her chin. "You would have told me not to come."

"Of course we would," I say, throwing my hands up. "It's against the rules. You're going to be in so much trouble if Second Chances finds out."

"You're the ones who kept saying Dad needed to see me himself," Flora snaps. "He wasn't going to come to ours. How else was that supposed to happen?"

I don't answer. The boat ride back is long and rough, the ferry buffeted side to side by the sudden turn in the tide. The three of us sit in silence for most of the journey, apart from a few minutes where we make a pact not to tell Mum about what happened on Eilean Gorm today. However rubbish today has been, it'll only be made worse if Mum realizes that Flora left the island.

Our plan crumbles when the ferry pulls into the shore and we see a blue Fiat waiting for us at the harbour.

Flora lets out a long sigh. "Oh, awesome."

I trudge down the ferry ramp feeling like I'm walking the plank. The car's front door opens and Mum climbs out. The worry in her eyes quickly morphs into anger when she sees that Flora is OK. Without saying anything, she hurries towards us, takes Flora's arm and steers her towards the car.

"Your dad phoned," she says as we hurry inside. "And so did Marisa. They noticed you'd lost your connection earlier. I had to make up something about a power outage. God knows if she believed me."

I almost slap my hand to my forehead. Of course Second Chances would find out. Flora has to be constantly connected to their network – the company even installed superfast 5G all across the island especially for the trial. I was so focused on what happened between Flora and Dad, I totally forgot.

"What were you thinking?" Mum asks Flora, her voice tight with anger. "What if someone had seen you?"

Flora sinks down in the passenger's seat. "They didn't, though. It's fine."

"As far as we know." When Flora doesn't reply, Mum sighs and raps the steering wheel. "Well, you're all grounded for the rest of the weekend. And no computers, either."

Ùna gasps. "But that's not fair! Isla and I didn't even

know she'd followed us!"

"I don't care. I need all three of you to take this more seriously." Mum runs a hand through her hair and sighs. A few frizzy strands blow out around her face. "Maybe I should tell Marisa the truth."

"Mum, no," Flora says. "You know they'll panic if they find out."

"I don't understand how they don't know about it already," I say. "You must have reconnected to the network when we got to Eilean Gorm, at least. How come they didn't get a warning that you'd left the island?"

Flora freezes, then slowly rolls up the sleeve of her hoodie. There's a small red mark shaped like a crescent moon in her right forearm.

"I cut out my tracking device." Seeing the horrified look on our faces, she quickly adds, "It's not a big deal, I can put it back in. They won't even notice."

Ùna swallows. "But won't they get suspicious if they see you haven't moved for ages? It's been hours by now."

"Well, I, uh…" Flora clears her throat. "I thought of that too. So, I stuck it to Sìth's collar."

Even though I'm mad at Flora for getting us into trouble, I have to press my lips together to stop myself from laughing. The thought of some engineer over at Second Chances watching "Flora" walk in circles around our kitchen or lounge on the carpet for hours… It *is* sort of funny. Beside me, Ùna starts trembling from the effort of holding back the giggles. I catch her eye and we both crack up. Flora puts her hand over her mouth, but I can tell from her shaking shoulders that she's laughing too. Only Mum stays stony.

"Stop it. This is serious, Flora." Her voice breaks on Flora's name. "We need to stick to the rules. I can't lose you again."

The laughter cuts out instantly. Mum tilts her head away from us but I can see her eyes glossing over in the car's side mirror. I have a sudden flashback to the day of Flora's funeral, after the poems had been read, the weak cups of tea drunk and the bland sandwiches eaten. I drifted off in the back seat on the way home, but at one point we hit a bump in the road and I woke up and caught Mum's face reflected in the rear-view mirror. Tears were pouring down her face, but her entire body was clenched tight as she forced herself not to sob. It's a moment that will be seared into my memory forever – Mum breaking apart, trying not to show it.

"Sorry, Mum," I say. "We are taking this seriously. I promise."

"I won't go there again." Flora looks down at her hands. "There's no point, anyway. Dad wouldn't even look at me."

"Oh, Flora." Mum puts her hands on Flora's face and kisses the top of her head. "He just sees this differently to the rest of us. It's not because he doesn't care. He cares so much."

As she struggles to get the car going – it's ancient and is always giving her grief – she chuckles lightly. "Attaching the tracking device to Sìth. I must admit, that was clever." She shakes her head, a reluctant smile tugging at her lips. "Don't think you're not still grounded, though. And don't even *think* about doing it again."

In all the upset of Flora's surprise visit, I forgot to tell the football team that I wouldn't make it to the match. By the time I get home, I already have thirteen messages asking if I'm OK, five of them from Holly.

Food poisoning, I type eventually into our group chat. *My aunt Kirsty's cooking... It's practically a weapon of mass destruction.*

There's no reason for any of them to doubt me. I've never missed a game before and they know I wouldn't unless it was an emergency. Tiwa, Màiri and some of the others tell me they hope I feel better, then Holly sends a photo of her dog with rainbow football laces tied in a bow over her head.

Oakley says get well soon!! She threw up a sock earlier, so she feels your pain.

Guilt gnaws at me as I send back a heart-eyes emoji and a vomiting emoji in response. I so wish I could tell her the truth. All of them, but especially Holly. Every lie feels like another brick in the wall between us.

I spend another couple of hours scrolling on my phone and chatting with my friends before turning off the light, but as I start to drift off, Sìth leaps across my bed and starts using my head as a scratching post. I get up to kick her out into the hallway, then pause. Faint voices are coming from Flora's room. There's something familiar about the sound though I can't work out what. I do our knock and open the door. Flora is sitting on her bed in new striped pyjamas, her hair in a messy high ponytail.

"Can't sleep?" I ask.

Flora rolls her eyes, though I hadn't meant it as a joke, I'd genuinely forgotten that she can't sleep any more. On her laptop, one of her old Sekkon videos is playing.

I recognize it instantly – a short, silly clip where Flora "interviewed" Sìth about her views on the musical *Cats*, filmed during the Christmas holidays before she got sick.

"I was watching some old videos," Flora says. "Feels a bit weird seeing them now."

I sit down beside her as the video ends and automatically rolls on to another one. It's from a few months before her diagnosis. A tour of her bedroom, lingering over her bookcase and posters and all the trinkets around her desk so long that it ended up lasting over twenty minutes.

"This is a good one," I say, leaning my head on her shoulder. "It was just after you painted your walls purple."

"It's weird that people still watch them," Flora says. "My follower count hasn't even gone down that much. There are comments from a few weeks ago."

I scan the lines of text below the video. Among the emojis and comments about how cute Flora's room looks, there are a few dozen "rest in peace" messages. She still has over twelve thousand followers. It's not much compared to Finley's channel – his non-stop content has somehow managed to pull in almost a hundred thousand people – but a couple of her videos have six-figure view counts.

"I think I liked that they were brightening other people's day," Flora says. "That someone in Houston or Hong Kong would see me messing around with Sìth and laugh, even if it was only for a second."

"You'll be able to do them again," I say. "Once all this is out in the open."

Flora doesn't reply. I'm starting to notice how often we talk about the future now – when people get used to her, when the trial is over and she has more freedom.

It must be frustrating for her, constantly looking towards a horizon she can't see.

"I'm sorry about today," I say. "I really thought Dad would come round. I thought once he saw you, saw how human you are—"

"But I'm not human." Flora shifts away from me suddenly. "He's right. I'm just a machine."

My heart skips a beat. *Just a machine.* It's an exact echo of the words lurking inside that red envelope – the envelope I still haven't told anyone about. "That's not what Dad—" I start to say, but Flora cuts me off with a low grumble of frustration.

"If I was human I'd be yawning right now, instead of wondering how long I have left until I have to hook myself up to the wall for energy." She points at the tangle of cables on her desk. "I'm not human, Isla. We need to stop pretending I am."

I try to find the right words, but I don't know if there are any. "OK, so you're a machine, but what does it matter? If you look and act like everyone else, what difference does it make?"

"It makes a difference. You know it does." She flops back on to her pillows with a light thump. "It makes a difference to Dad. And it makes a difference to whoever dumped the computer here, doesn't it? That's all I am to them. Just a piece of junk."

"You're *not* a piece of junk," I argue, but then I break off. Flora's eyes have gone dull suddenly, the way they did at Dad's earlier.

"The flights are booked for Monday," she says in a flat voice. "Sagittarius. I never lie."

That glitch again. It makes my whole body go cold. Flora shakes her head and blinks, and the life comes back to her eyes. It's a quicker recovery than the first time, but she looks shaken.

"See? Just a machine." She laughs and it sounds bitter. "Speaking of which, I need to charge now."

I say goodnight before I go to my room but she doesn't reply. For the first time since Flora came back, there's a distance between us. I need to find out who's been sending these messages, before something else happens and it grows even wider.

Eighteen

Mum goes to Eilean Gorm to do the big shop the next day, so after lunch I "forget" that I'm grounded and cycle down to the village. The day is dry but cold and overcast, and there's smoke coming from the Campbells' chimney. Georgie is sitting on her front step, combing her dog's ears while music plays from her phone. She looks up when she sees me coming, her blue eyes narrowed in the dim sunlight.

"Lola rolled in chewing gum." She holds up the comb. There's a mangled knot of black fur and pink gum between the teeth. "She'll never get to Crufts."

I laugh but it comes out high-pitched and awkward. I like Georgie but we don't spend much time together outside school. The rest of us make an effort to include her in things, Murdo and Adhiti especially, but since her dad died Georgie's preferred to stay home with her mum and Lola. Sometimes I'll send her videos or memes that she might like, but I've never turned up out of the blue and asked her to hang out.

"I'm going for a walk," I say, trying to sound casual. "Do you want to come? Lola too."

Georgie's eyebrows rise in surprise. "Um, OK." She stands up and brushes the dark dog hairs from her jeans. "Let me get my jacket."

She hops up from the step and disappears into the house. I kneel down to pet Lola and take a few deep breaths to still the nerves pinging around my body. Inside, Georgie shouts up to her mum to tell her she's going out. Their house is a traditional fishing cottage with white walls and a pale blue door and shutters. It used to have a thatched roof too, but it went up in flames during the church fire and had to be replaced. It was so lucky Georgie's mum woke up and got them both out of the house, otherwise it could have been a far worse tragedy.

Georgie comes out a minute later, shrugging her arms into her navy coat. "Beach?"

"Sure."

We walk by the harbour, past the school and on to the long stretch of sand looking towards Eilean Gorm. Lola scurries ahead, stopping every few seconds to sniff at seaweed and rocks, and pale grey waves leave their ghostly tidelines on the sand as they glide to meet us. The two of us talk about school, TV shows, the pieces Georgie is playing at the Mòd next month, but it's like conversation ping-pong between nervous beginners – slow, overly careful and certain the ball will drop at any moment.

"So, um…" Georgie swings her arms out in front of her. "Is there something you wanted to talk to me about?"

I take another deep breath. "Somebody's been leaving messages for Flora. There was a smashed computer left outside our house the night of the ceilidh, and then someone put this in her bag."

I take out my phone to show her a photo of the page from the Second Chances manual. Georgie zooms in to see the highlighted words.

"Just a machine," she reads, shivering.

"Yeah, it's been pretty horrible." I clear my throat. "So, um, how come you weren't at the ceilidh that night?"

"I had a violin lesson on Eilean Gorm the next morning. I've got my grade six exam coming up, so—" Georgie stops walking so abruptly I almost bump into her. "Wait. Are you asking me if *I* did it?"

"It's nothing personal," I say quickly. "I asked Murdo about it too. I'm trying to rule out the possibilities."

I tell her about my theory that someone in our class must have slipped the envelope into Flora's bag while no one was watching. Georgie listens intently but I'm starting to feel a bit silly. This is Eilean Dearg. Stuff like this doesn't happen here.

"Why do you think I would do that?" Georgie asks. The hurt in her voice makes me wince.

"Honestly, I have no idea. You seem a little awkward around Flora sometimes. I mean, I get it," I say. "She is technically a machine. It's normal to feel weird around her."

Lola comes bounding back with the stick between her teeth. Georgie pulls it from her and throws it far across the beach. Lola races after it, sending arcs of sand rising up behind her paws as she runs. We walk behind her in silence, the waves whispering as they rush towards our feet.

"OK, I know I've been awkward. But it's not really about Flora." Georgie stops to draw a circle in the sand with the toe of her shoe. "I can't help but think if things were different, maybe my dad could have been the one we were welcoming back."

Georgie's dad was called Iain. He was a lorry driver, a big, broad man with a bushy beard and a booming laugh. I still remember how heavy the atmosphere on the island felt after he died, like the sky was about to split open.

I'd never thought about what it must be like for Georgie and her mum, seeing a piece of our family coming back when such a large part of theirs was gone forever. I wonder how I would feel if I were standing at the harbour back in July, waiting for a brand-new version of Iain Campbell to step off the boat.

"They could only do it for Flora because she had so much online data available," I say. "They needed all that to get her personality and appearance right."

"I know. They never could have done that for Dad. He could barely even work the camera on his phone, let alone make his own Sekkon videos." Georgie bends to pick up a piece of dull sea glass. When she holds it up to the pale grey sky, it glows red. "But it sucks to know that it was a possibility and he missed it."

That's another thing that hadn't occurred to me. If the project works and being brought back as a returnee becomes a regular thing, like Second Chances is planning, it's going to hurt all the more for the people whose loved ones missed out. I've been so focused on how the trial has affected my family, I hadn't really thought about what it might mean for the rest of the world.

"I'm sorry," I say. "I didn't mean to bring up bad memories for you."

Georgie drops the sea glass back on to the sand. "It's not your fault. I just miss him a lot, especially around this time of year. His birthday was in October and he loved autumn."

There were times when Flora's loss stung even more than usual. Christmas and her birthday, but also rainy Sunday afternoons without her curled up by the fireplace reading, and hearing Pandora21 on the radio without her to try to sing along. Even now she's back, I still get those pangs of grief.

"It's weird we've never talked about this before," I say. "We both lost somebody really close to us. None of the others have been through that. I hope they never do."

"Exactly," Georgie says, nodding. "I know it's not the same but I do have some idea of what it was like for your family. Besides, I wouldn't do anything to hurt Flora."

"I know." I sigh and kick at the sand. "The problem is, I have no idea who would."

"My mum says some people felt really pressured into signing up for Project Homecoming," Georgie says, fidgeting with a thread on her jacket. "It was such a lot of money ... nobody wanted to be the one to say no and stop everyone from paying off their debts or buying a new car or whatever, even if they didn't agree with the trial. Maybe someone feels resentful about that."

"You could be right." I stick my hands into my pockets. Up ahead, Lola starts barking at a starfish on the wet sand. "Everyone went a bit mad when they heard about the money, didn't they?"

Georgie nods. "My mum's already spent a lot of it doing up our house. The rest is for university. She's dying for me to go."

"Why?" I ask. Georgie is a year older than me but still only fourteen. All of that is a long way away.

"She doesn't want me getting stuck here like she did." Georgie gives a wry smile. "Why do you think she's got me doing every extracurricular activity under the sun? She wants to make sure I've got plenty of stuff to fill my applications."

"How come she never left then?" I ask.

"Dad liked it here," she says simply. "Mum stayed for him. I think she's still staying for him, in a way."

It's something I've asked myself about my own parents. Dad is from Eilean Gorm and Mum grew up here on Eilean Dearg. They met at a ceilidh when they were teenagers, went away to university in Dundee together and came back straight after. I wonder how much of that was a real decision and how much of it was them being drawn in by the tides of what they knew, what was comfortable.

"Maybe if they'd moved somewhere else Dad would still be alive now," Georgie says. "He would have taken a different job and he wouldn't have been on the road that afternoon."

"You can't think like that," I say. "I used to wonder what might have happened if Flora had gone to the doctor sooner, or if someone had picked up on symptoms earlier. It's pointless. You end up torturing yourself over something you can't change."

"You're right. But it's hard not to." Georgie shrugs again. "At least that won't be a problem if Second Chances takes off. This life will be just the beginning."

We turn round and head back towards the village. It looks so quaint and quiet – the thatched roof on the school, the houses with glowing gold windows and smoke billowing from their chimneys. It's hard to imagine that someone out there, on this sleepy little island, could be plotting against our family.

PROJECT HOMECOMING:
A GUIDE FOR FAMILIES

Module 9: Privacy

Privacy is hard to come by these days. Much of our lives is determined by the boundaries of the internet, where every word we type into a search engine, every click is registered and recorded for someone else to see. And yet even the most avid internet users have thoughts, feelings and ideas that are theirs and theirs alone – a private sphere that no technology can reach.

We believe our returnees deserve that same inner sanctuary. The aim of Project Homecoming is to assess how our participants interact with their family and local community. It would likely be difficult for most people involved to act naturally if they felt they were being constantly watched. So while we do have access to returnees' full activity and data, including video and audio recordings, our regular monitoring is limited to checking that their systems are running optimally and that there is no risk of a security breach.

The tech industry has not always behaved ethically or respectfully when it comes to users' privacy. We fully understand that participants may have concerns about how their data is being used, and we encourage them to read a full breakdown of how we do so on our website.

Please bear in mind too that these guidelines have been put in place not for financial gain, but to help us achieve our aim of creating a new, better world – one where the most severe forms of grief and loss will one day be a thing of the past.

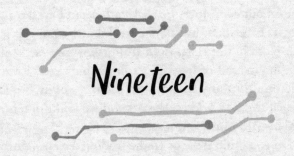

Nineteen

Flora mentions the speech glitches she's been having at our check-in that Wednesday. Luckily, Marisa doesn't seem too worried about it.

"We've seen this issue in a few other returnees. It happens when the Emotional Response Unit becomes overworked," she tells us. "Were you really excited or upset at the time? Occasionally when returnees have experienced more intense emotions, they've lost control of their speech."

I shift in my seat, remembering Flora's horrible surprise visit on Dad's birthday. Marisa definitely wouldn't be so relaxed if she knew Flora had broken the rules to go and see him.

"Yeah. Yeah, I was feeling sad about something." Flora twirls her earring between her finger and thumb. "Can it be fixed? I don't want it to happen at school."

"Don't worry. I'll schedule in a maintenance session with our technicians. They'll have it sorted in no time." Marisa taps at her screen. "How about this Friday? 4 p.m. your time?"

Seeing as Flora will be busy, I ask Murdo and Adhiti if they want to hang out after school. We haven't had much time on our own since the trial started and I'm starting to miss it. I see them five days a week but it's not the same with Flora in our class. Even if she's now two years older than me instead of five, she's still my big sister. I want a little time with my friends, just the three of us. So, after the bell rings on Friday, we say goodbye to the others and head over to Murdo's house.

"Do you mind if we go to the studio?" he asks, pushing open the front door. "I want to show you something I've been working on."

The three of us used to spend hours in Andy's woodwork studio when we were younger. We'd sit at the workbench, our feet dangling above the ground, and try to carve patterns or our names into old bits of wood. Sometimes, if he wasn't too busy, Andy would make little birds or animals for us to colour. I still have a squirrel that he carved for me somewhere. I painted it lime green with a glittery purple tail.

"Won't your dad mind?" I ask Murdo now. I don't know how deep his distrust of the trial goes – if it's only Flora that Andy's uncomfortable with or the whole MacAulay clan.

"Nah, of course not," Murdo says, pausing to grab some crisps from the kitchen cupboard. "Besides, he's gone up to Stornoway to teach a carpentry course for the weekend. He won't be back until Monday."

My heart instantly lifts as we walk into the studio. I love the smell of varnish, the neat rows of tools on the walls, the swish of the wood shavings that litter the ground as you walk through them. Murdo goes to the shelves on the back wall and reaches for something – a tall, circular wooden house with a cone roof and three rows of windows. My jaw drops when he sets it on the table.

"You *made* that?" Adhiti and I shout at the same time.

"Well, Dad helped a lot, but I did most of it," he says, grinning. "It's a birdhouse. I'm going to paint it blue with a red roof."

I lean over the table to take a better look at the house. There are rows of individual wooden tiles circling the roof, tiny frames round the windows, even an awning over the door. "It's so cute."

Adhiti crouches down to inspect the details. "It's perfect, Murdo. You could actually sell that."

"Don't you start. My dad won't stop going on about me joining the family business. I keep telling him I want to study zoology but he's not listening." He takes three leather aprons from a hook on the wall and tosses one each to me and Adhiti. "So, what do you want to make?"

Murdo finds a few spare blocks of birch wood and fetches some tools for us. Despite all those years playing carpenters in here, Adhiti and I are both still useless at woodcarving. Today she gets ambitious and decides to make a starfish. I try to carve out a spoon and soon realize it was a bad idea.

"Maybe I can cut off the top and make it into a conductor's baton," I say, swishing the stick in the air. "Or a very skinny rolling pin."

"Speaking of rolling pins," Adhiti says, "what's going on with Holly?"

I blink at her. "What does Holly have to do with rolling pins?"

"Nothing, as far as I know. I'm just asking because it's

139

impossible to get any gossip out of you otherwise."

"I don't know what you're talking about," I say, but my cheeks heat up in a way they probably wouldn't if that were true.

Adhiti grins. "Really? Because I bet you don't get that look on your face when me or Murdo texts you."

"What look?"

Adhiti picks up her phone and mimics grinning and swooning like a dizzy Cheshire cat. Murdo giggles and joins in, swaying so fast he almost topples off the stool. I throw handfuls of wood shavings at them both, but I'm laughing too. "Shut up. I do not."

My face feels like it's on fire. I tuck my chin in and keep my eyes fixed on my spoon to hide the blush. Adhiti's right. The first thing I do in the morning is check for messages from Holly. When I'm talking with her it feels like there are sparks in my fingertips. It's not like that with my friends. It's never been like that with anybody. When Adhiti came back from coding camp in Edinburgh last summer with a huge crush on a boy called Kofi, I didn't really get it. But now I do – I totally do.

"OK, I do like her. A bit," I say, blushing again. "But I can't really do anything about it. She doesn't know about Flora or the trial. Whenever we talk, I have to leave out huge chunks of what I've been doing."

Adhiti picks a wood shaving out of her hair. "Are you sure that's not an excuse?"

"What do you mean?"

"You don't exactly love change." Murdo grins as he sands the edge of the birdhouse's roof. "Remember how mad you got when Miss Grant moved around the tables at school last year?"

"That layout didn't make any sense!" Even thinking about it makes my hands clench into fists.

Adhiti laughs and picks up her starfish and the carving knife again. "You *could* tell Holly about the trial, you know. I bet she'd understand how important it is to keep quiet."

Murdo looks up from behind the birdhouse. "That's way too risky. We don't know how much Second Chances are keeping tabs on us. They could be listening to our calls or reading our messages."

"Of course they're not," I say. "They don't even look at the footage that Flora records. Not unless it's an emergency or she's in danger."

"And you trust them?" Adhiti asks, reaching for the crisps.

"Marisa said so and I trust her. Besides, it's in the contract, isn't it?"

"Yeah, but there's probably some fine print tucked away somewhere that says they can do what they want." Murdo slides off his stool and goes to the shelf with the paints. "There always is with these big tech companies. That's what my dad says, anyway. He's convinced they're using Flora to spy on us."

"Why would they bother? They could check our phones if they wanted to do that." I nod to Murdo's phone on the worktable. "If he hates her so much he should hate that thing too."

"He doesn't hate her, Isla," Murdo says, reaching for a red tin. "Or at least, he doesn't hate *Flora*, your sister. But he doesn't think she is Flora."

"Well, she is," I snap. "And she's definitely not a spy."

Murdo goes quiet as he pours out the paints into little

pots. Silences are never awkward between the three of us, but this one feels tense. Adhiti pops a crisp into her mouth and crunches it loudly.

"Well, I can confirm from our first coding class last weekend that Flora does not have superhuman capabilities," she says, licking crumbs off her fingertips. "At this rate we'll have left school by the time she's ready to move on to JavaScript."

I laugh, even though I don't really know what that means. Murdo smiles too, but he keeps mixing the red and white paint and doesn't look up.

"Sorry. It's not only your dad," I tell him. "Mine doesn't think she's human, either. He says you can't rebuild a soul and you can't be human without a soul."

Adhiti leans back on her stool and squints at her wooden starfish. "That depends what you think a soul is. If it's a totally separate part of us, then maybe not. But if it's in our personality and our memories, maybe you can."

"Flora definitely has a soul," I say hotly. "You've seen her. She's not some cold, unfeeling robot."

"Well, obviously." Adhiti pokes me in the arm with the point of the starfish. "Stop getting so defensive. We're on your side. Flora's too."

But for a fraction of a second, I wonder if Dad and Andy are right. Maybe Flora's feelings are all programming, a mimicking of human responses. Then I think about her laughter when she was playing thumb wars with Ùna last night, and the expression on her face when Dad wouldn't talk to her, and my doubts instantly fade. That has to be more than the result of some complex code. I don't need to understand formulas and equations to know her reactions are real – that she's a person.

Murdo sits up suddenly. He has that excited look he gets when he's about to talk about birds. "You know starlings? How they move in those murmurations?"

Adhiti and I nod. Sometimes I can see them rising over the hills from my window – huge groups of tiny creatures, moving and twisting like a storm cloud in the sky.

"Scientists still aren't sure how they know which way to turn without bumping into each other. It's like they're interconnected, even though each one is an individual being." He dips his paintbrush in the red paint and turns back to his birdhouse. "I think humans are a bit like that. We're all separate people but we form to connect something bigger than ourselves. Maybe that's what the soul is. It's the thing that links us all together. That makes us more than just bodies."

"Returnees could be part of that," Adhiti says, nodding. "Ones as smart and as independent as Flora, at least."

I picture it – connections zipping between humans and returnees like shooting stars, together mapping out something special and magical. The thought makes me smile. I just wish that Dad and Andy could see it that way too.

Twenty

LOGICAL BUT NOT REASONABLE.

We find the words painted on the wall of the church the following Monday. Large and pale against the charred brick, the paint shining in the morning sun.

Mum left early for work this morning, so Flora, Ùna and I had to cycle down to school. It's a dry, warm day and we were all in a good mood until we arrived in the village and saw this waiting for us. Because somehow, without even knowing what the words mean or where they come from, I can tell they're directed at Flora.

"Logical but not reasonable," she reads. "What does that mean?"

Ùna is already typing it into her phone. "It's from a book. *The Naked Sun* by Isaac Asimov." She nudges her glasses up her nose. "*Logical but not reasonable. Wasn't that the definition of a robot?*"

"Reasonable means fair, right? Or rational." Flora grips the handlebars of her bike. "Do they think I'm irrational? Like, some sort of threat?"

"Surely a robot would be more rational than a human," Ùna says, shrugging.

"Maybe they mean reasonable as in understandable," I say. "Like standing to reason. Making sense."

"First the computer and now this…" Flora kicks the toe of her shoe against the gravel. "They really want me gone, don't they?"

The same sickly feeling I got when I found the red envelope is churning in my stomach. Maybe it's time I finally told Flora about that. Before I come to a decision, the sound of tyres screeching on the road behind us makes me jump. I turn round and see Finley skid to a halt so fast he almost topples over. He's riding a fancy blue road bike with black disc wheels, a present for his last birthday. He posted it on Sekkon, but I've never actually seen him ride it before. His house is way up on the cliffs on the other side of the island and his cheeks are red with the effort of cycling here.

"What's this?" Finley dumps the bike by the sea wall and hurries across the road towards us. One hand is already reaching into his pocket for his phone. "I'm guessing it's about you?"

The answer is so obvious that none of us bothers to reply. The empty paint tin is still lying on the ground at the foot of the building. I nudge it with the toe of my shoe. It probably has the vandal's fingerprints on it. If things were different we could take it to the police, but since the trial's a secret that's not an option. It almost feels like whoever did this thought of that and left the tin behind as a taunt.

Finley takes a photo of the graffiti, then types something into his phone. He reads out the same quote that Ùna found. "Any ideas what it might mean?"

"Not really, but it doesn't matter," Flora says. "Somebody's trying to scare us. That's the only point they're making."

Finley spins round so his back is to the church. He lifts the phone, taps the screen and starts speaking into the camera. "It's a chilly Monday morning here on Eilean Dearg, and I've made a startling discovery at—"

His voice has gone into TV presenter mode. I reach for his arm and pull it down. "You can't film this, Finley!"

"Why not? Flora's not in the shot. I'm not going to post anything about her." He jerks his arm away and scowls at me. "There's nothing in Second Chances' rules about filming random graffiti on churches."

"No, but…" The thought of him sharing this on Sekkon still makes me feel uneasy. It's too close for comfort. "Make sure you don't mention the trial."

"Well, obviously, Isla. I'm not trying to get the whole project pulled," Finley says, rolling his eyes. "It's just material for my documentary. I'll need as much as I can if I ever get to release it."

As he carries on filming, I think back to my list of suspects. The only name I haven't crossed out yet is Finley's. After talking to Georgie, I shoved my orange journal in a drawer and put the investigation on pause. Confronting her and Murdo like that made me feel all icky and guilty. I didn't want to do the same to Finley – I was hoping the messages would stop and I wouldn't have to.

Clearly that's not the case. I have to talk to him too. But I need to find a reason Finley might do this before I can accuse him, and I can't think of one. Not yet.

A voice calls out "good morning" from behind us. Reverend Jack walks towards us wearing a Fair Isle jumper and a solemn expression and carrying a bucket of water with a sponge in it.

"Morning, Reverend," Finley says. "I'm sorry to see this. The church has been through enough without this nonsense."

His phone stays in his hand, pointed towards the ground, but I can tell from the shift in his tone that he's recording the conversation.

The minister smiles sadly. "Thank you, Finley. Nonsense, indeed."

"Any idea who might be behind this?"

"None at all, lad."

Reverend Jack sets the bucket down on the pavement with a grunt. He puts one hand on the back of his neck, wincing slightly. Even after three years, it's always a shock to see the leathery skin of his right hand, the one that was burned in the fire.

"I suppose it doesn't matter much," the minister says. "The building will be pulled down next year anyway."

As well as paying everyone who is taking part, Second Chances agreed as part of the terms of the trial that they would pull down the damaged church and replace it with a brand-new building. There are only a few people on the island who still go to Reverend Jack's services now but the new place will double up as a community centre. There's been talk of starting a playgroup, art classes, all sorts of stuff.

"Even so, it seems disrespectful," Finley says.

Flora nods. "I'm sorry. I feel really bad about it."

Reverend Jack casts a look at Flora. It's not a cold look exactly but there's something strange about it. Maybe he blames her for the message. That seems unfair if so. Flora's the target here. She didn't ask for any of this.

"We can help you wash it off if you like," Ùna says.

The odd expression is quickly replaced with the minister's usual warm smile. Mayor Seamus might think he runs the island but it's Reverend Jack who really takes care of everyone in the community. He's always giving people lifts here and there, fixing things and getting older folk their shopping. And when Flora died, he popped in to bring us meals, tidy up the house or see how we were doing for months afterwards.

"No, no, don't worry yourselves about that. I don't think I'll have much luck with soap and water, anyway. I'll need to order some paint stripper online." He nods towards the end of the street. "You'd best be getting off to school."

As if in agreement, the bell rings. We leave the minister to scrub at the wall and pick up our bikes. Finley walks behind the three of us, pushing his bike with one hand and filming himself with the other. His recording voice rings out over the sounds of the waves and the seabirds.

"Four words on a wall," he says, "but they've opened up dozens of questions. Who's behind this? What do they want? And what might they do next?"

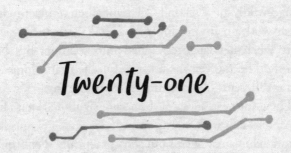

Twenty-one

Something changes after the message on the church wall. It's like someone's turned a dimmer switch on Flora's personality. She's quiet and withdrawn. She spends most of her time in her room or out on her bike, and when I offer to go with her, she says she wants some space. She even tries to get out of meal times with the rest of the family.

"What's the point?" she mutters, after Mum orders her to sit down with us one evening. "It's not like I need to eat."

She gazes at her dinner. It's mac and cheese with crispy onions, one of her favourites. Last time Mum made this Flora scraped her plate clean but now her nose wrinkles in distaste.

"But Marisa's always said how important meals are," Mum says. "It's not all about food. It's family time. Besides, you can eat if you want to."

"Well, I don't want to," Flora snaps. "It's a waste of food and cleaning out my feeding compartment afterwards is gross. It's totally pointless."

Ùna casts me a nervous look before taking a mouthful of pasta. This reminds me of the way Flora was after her diagnosis. She'd snap at anything and her mood could change wildly in a second – I remember trying to cheer her up with an impression of a meerkat, then feeling so guilty when her laughter tipped into sobbing. But back then she'd been given the most awful, life-shattering news. This is different. Her new life is just beginning.

"Then don't eat, Flora," Mum says, sighing. "That's fine. But sit and talk with us anyway, OK?"

Flora reluctantly agrees but she's practically silent for the rest of the meal, and she disappears as soon as the dishes are washed and dried. She races up to her room after school for the next few days too, and she says no whenever Ùna and I ask her to play a game or watch Netflix with us.

On Friday afternoon we plan to go for a bike ride after school, all three of us, but Flora changes her mind and decides to go to Adhiti's for more coding practice instead.

"At least we can take our time this way," Ùna says, strapping on her helmet. "No getting out of breath trying to keep up with Flora."

We head to the east of the island, past the flat white beaches and up into the hills. The route takes three times longer than usual – Ùna keeps stopping to take photos, get my opinion on the best ones, then post them online – but it's such a beautiful evening that I don't mind. There's something quite nice about it being just the two of us for a little while.

After Flora died, the dynamic between Ùna and me changed. I went from being the middle sister to the oldest. I had Flora's shoes to fill and Ùna had to grow up faster than she might have otherwise. We still bickered sometimes, of course, but we got a lot closer too. Sometimes it felt like we only had each other, especially when Mum and Dad were completely spaced out or after they started fighting about Second Chances.

Having Flora back has changed all that. She's the big sister again, the one who Ùna goes to for help with her make-up or advice about what to wear. I was always rubbish at that stuff but I miss it now Ùna doesn't ask any more. And with Dad gone, there's no arguing for us to bond against, either.

Still, those three years haven't disappeared. Ùna and I are like two sailors who battled a storm together. There's a connection there that we don't have with anyone else.

"What's going on with you these days?" I ask her once we stop for a break. We're sitting in the long grass near the peak of the hill, surrounded by daisies and deep purple heather. "You haven't updated me on your friend drama in forever."

Ùna scrunches up her mouth. "Kylie and Agata aren't talking because Agata told everyone about Kylie wetting herself a bit when she went on one of the roller coasters at Alton Towers in the summer. Lewis fancies Agata, but she likes this boy from Eilean Gorm who's in her musical theatre class."

"Who's the boy? Does he go to the high school there?"

"David something? I don't really know."

A few months ago, this sliver of gossip would have provided days of discussion. Now Ùna shrugs off my question and flops back on to the grass. "I'm worried about Flora. She's been really weird the past couple of days."

I pluck some daisies from the ground and make slits in their stems with my fingernail. "I know. I think that message on the church really got to her."

151

"Katie in my class said she heard Annie Campbell talking about it in the shop. She was telling Davey she thinks Flora wrote the message herself," Ùna says. "That Flora was probably trying to cause some drama."

"What?" I stare at Ùna. Georgie's mum has always been really nice to Flora. I can't believe she'd say something so horrible. "That doesn't even make sense. Why would Flora do that?"

"That's what I told Katie." Ùna pulls up a handful of grass and lets it flutter away in the breeze. "I told her I was there when Flora saw the message. She was obviously really upset."

I remember arriving at the church that morning, and Finley skidding to a halt on his bike behind us a few minutes later. In a shadowy spot in the back of my mind, a tiny suspicion starts to grow. If someone was trying to create drama, it could be the person making a film about the trial – the person who's trying so hard to get footage that Flora won't give him.

Plus, Finley never cycles to school and he almost always arrives late. He has two younger brothers and the three of them usually tumble out of his mum's car at quarter past nine with milk stains on their jumpers and books spilling out of their bags. It's strange that he just so happened to get to the village early enough to see Flora, Ùna and me arrive at the church.

Almost like he'd expected us to be there.

"What if Second Chances find out about it?" Ùna asks, her voice small. "Or about her breaking the rules and going to see Dad? They're not going to take Flora away or anything, are they?"

She wants me to say no, but I can't. Not when I don't know if it's true. Instead I thread the daisies into a loop and pick up Ùna's hand. "I don't think so," I say, slipping the bracelet on to her wrist. "I hope not."

Ùna smiles at the daisy chain but she looks so sad, so little in her hoodie and dungarees. I nudge my glasses up my nose with my knuckle. After a moment Ùna gives a reluctant grin and does the same back. We're still in this together.

Flora is in her room when we get back, sitting on her bed with her computer in her lap. When she sees me, she quickly closes the laptop and claps her hands together with a big grin.

"I have a surprise for you!"

She runs out into the corridor and comes back carrying Stephen the vacuum cleaner. She sets him down on the carpet and presses the button to turn him on. He scoots forwards, the little brushes he uses to sweep up moving right to left, and bumps against the leg of Flora's desk.

"Who put that there?" he says. "I can't work under these conditions!"

For a moment I think I must be hallucinating. When Stephen 'speaks', it's to give us updates about the cleaning and say goodbye when he's finished. He doesn't ask questions. He definitely doesn't complain.

"What did he say?" I ask.

"I was mucking around with his settings earlier." Flora crouches down and waves at him. "How's the cleaning going, Stephen?"

"You people are animals," he says in his mechanical voice. "Dust, dust, more dust. All I ever eat is dust."

He sounds so fed up, it makes me burst out laughing. Flora beams.

"Look at this too! Play 'Cotton-Eyed Joe', please, Stephen."

The country folk song begins to play from the vacuum cleaner's low-quality speakers. Stephen shifts from back to front, left to right, then round in a circle and back again, all in time with the beat.

"Is he ... line dancing?" I ask.

"Yeah! He's pretty good, right?" Flora bobs her head along to the music as the vacuum cleaner twirls around. "Do a waltz now, Stephen."

I run across the hallway and tell Ùna to come and see. The shock on her face makes me laugh even harder. We make Stephen dance to BTS, the Weeknd and Lady Gaga, until Flora eventually tells him to turn the music off and get back to work. He grumbles, "Fine, whatever," then trundles back out into the hallway, Ùna chasing after him as if he was a puppy.

"How did you do all that?" I ask Flora.

Mum and Dad are both so bad with technology that I had to set up Stephen when we first got him. There definitely wasn't an option for snarky comebacks and line dancing. You could change the language he speaks – Ùna got him stuck in Finnish for a couple of weeks once – but that's it. And, like Adhiti said, Flora is far from being some programming genius.

"Oh, it was easy. Adhiti showed me most of it. Plus, it's not like he's actually coming up with any of it himself.

I just gave him a few extra tricks."

I ask her a second time, but she won't give me more details and she won't meet my eye. There's something Flora's not telling me, like she didn't tell me about her plan to come to Eilean Gorm. Even with our laughter still ringing in my ears, it feels like the tide is pulling her even further away from us, towards a horizon that I can't see. I need to bring her back.

And that means it's time to move on to my next suspect: Finley.

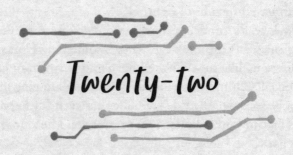

Twenty-two

I find out via Sekkon that Finley is away shopping on the mainland this weekend, which means my investigation will have to wait until Monday. Seeing his post, I'm hit by a blast of frustration, then another of fear. Monday is three whole days away – who knows what could happen in that time.

But after a few hours of worrying, I decide to try to put it out of my mind for the weekend. I have football practice after lunch at Kirsty's on Saturday, which means I'll get to see Holly again. The thought makes me feel all light and jittery. If anybody can help distract me from what's going on at home, it's her.

Ùna has refused to visit Dad since the birthday disaster, so on Saturday morning I cycle down to the harbour and get the ferry by myself. When I push open the door to Kirsty's house an hour later, a faint burning smell wafts out to greet me. Gran sits at the kitchen table with a large photo album in front of her while Dad lays out knives and forks. When he sees me, he puts the cutlery down and pulls me into a hug.

"What's that smell?" I ask, glancing around. "Where's Kirsty?"

"She tried to make a crumble for pudding and almost set the house on fire. She's gone to the Co-op to buy another one." He looks over my shoulder to the empty doorway behind me. "Ùna still in a huff then?"

He smiles, but there's a hurt look in his eyes. It makes my heart twinge with sadness. Even if it was his choice to leave, I feel bad for Dad, stranded over here without the four of us. He's got Kirsty and Gran, of course, but it's not the same.

"She'll come round," I tell him. I sit down at the table and lean towards the photo album. "What are you looking at, Gran?"

She looks up at me. It's one of her better days. Her eyes are free from their usual cloud of confusion and her smile looks almost the way it used to.

"Pictures, love," she says. "There's you."

She turns the album towards me. Younger versions of myself and my sisters fill the pages – Flora and me with ice lollies and sticky-lipped smiles, three-year-old Ùna splashing in a paddling pool. Usually I see photos like this and cringe at the girly clothes Mum used to dress me in, the way my unruly red hair would clash with the pink, but today I'm hit with a wave of nostalgia. Life was so much simpler back then, before Flora got sick. Before any of us had heard of Second Chances.

"I was sorting out some of my stuff for the charity shop and found those," Dad says. "The doctor said looking at photos might help Gran to remember better."

We turn the pages slowly, moving through the milestones of my childhood: birthdays and Christmases, Halloweens dressed up as cartoon characters and christenings in our Sunday best. My favourite photos are the everyday ones, the ones of random breakfasts or walks on the beach. I point to a photo of Flora, aged around nine, and four-year-old me both cuddled on Mum's lap. The lights are off and the kitchen table is covered with tea lights and candles.

"Do you remember this?" I ask Dad. "There was a power cut, and you and Mum lit every candle you could find to distract me."

Dad comes to the table and tilts his head to see the photo. He smiles fondly. "That wasn't to distract you. Flora was the one who was scared. She was terrified of the dark at that age."

"Really?" I ask. "I always thought it was me."

I still remember the warmth from the candles, the thrill of being out of bed so late even if I was scared. Or at least, I think I do. Now I'm not sure if I remember that day or if I've patched together a memory from the photo and the story I've been told.

"Definitely. You only cried because she did," Dad says. "It was always like that when you were wee. As if you were tuned into her emotional frequency."

"Unless you were arguing," Gran chuckles. "Lord, the two of you could bicker."

I smile sheepishly. "Sorry, Gran."

Dad pulls out the chair beside me and sits down, leaving the quiche he's made for lunch cooling on the counter. He raps two fingers on the table, the way he always does when he's thinking.

"There's something I need to talk to you about, Isles," he says. "I'm looking at using my money from Second Chances to buy a place here. Somewhere with a room for you and Ùna too."

There's a little jolt of pain behind my ribs. I knew Dad couldn't live in Kirsty's spare room forever, but the decision still takes me by surprise. Even after his horrible meeting with Flora last month, I hadn't let go of the hope that he would come home eventually.

"I want you to know that once I find somewhere, you'll be able to visit whenever you want. You can even come and live with me if you like. I'll leave the decision up to you." He smiles, though his eyes look sad. "Just know it's an option, if things get difficult at home."

"Right. OK." My voice is tight. "Are you and Mum going to get divorced then?"

Dad straightens his fork and knife so they're parallel with the place mat. "I don't know. We haven't talked about it yet. But yes, maybe. At some point."

Gran reaches over and squeezes my hand. It makes tears spring to my eyes, so I look down at the photo album. In the right-hand corner is a picture of Mum dancing with baby Ùna. A younger version of Dad is watching them from the sofa in the background, his head resting on his hand and his eyes crinkled in a smile.

"Do you miss her?" I ask, taking off my glasses to wipe my eyes.

"Of course I do, love. I really wish things hadn't turned out this way." Dad sits back and rubs a hand over his stubble. "But I feel like I don't really know who she is now. The Sarah I married would never have been taken in by something like this. Then again, the Sarah I married had never lost a child. That changes a person."

I turn the page to a collection of photos taken on a family holiday to Edinburgh. In one, Flora is wearing a purple anorak and sticking her tongue out at the camera. Around her neck is her necklace, the one shaped like a leaf and engraved with the letter F that she lost before she died. I take mine out from underneath my collar to show Gran. She smiles, then mumbles something about needing to find Griogair's shoes and gets up from the table. Uncle Griogair lives in Dunbar now but Dad and I don't correct her. The doctors say it's best to go along with Gran's way of seeing things, rather than trying to force her into our world.

"I have to admit, Second Chances did an incredible job," Dad says, once Gran is out of earshot. "She looked exactly like Flora. Even the way she walked, the way she moved her hands… It really was just as I remember her."

"That's what makes her really her," I say. "The little things."

Dad shakes his head. "Those things are all external. Anyone could learn to mimic them with enough practice. It's like … like trying to replicate one of these photos." He points to the picture of Flora. "Someone could recreate this perfectly but they wouldn't be able to tell that Flora bumped her head on a signpost right after it was taken, or that Ùna got lost in a supermarket the next day and sent us all into a panic. Experience, memories – that's what makes us really us."

"You think the fact that Ùna got lost in a supermarket when she was four changed Flora's personality forever?" I ask.

Dad gives a wry smile. "Not on its own. But everything adds up."

"Second Chances say it's normal for some memories to

be missing, just like ours," I tell Dad. "And anyway, most of Flora's personality is based on data. Murdo's dad says those big tech companies know more about us than we know about ourselves."

Dad scoffs. "They've got a lot of information on us but they can't know who we really are. They only know our behaviours, not our inner selves. Besides, Flora was only fifteen. She would have changed so much in the next five, ten years. How is this version going to do that?"

"We're going to have to agree to disagree on this," I say, because I don't know the answer and I don't want to talk about it any more. It wasn't supposed to be like this. He was supposed to see Flora and come home. Things were supposed to go back to normal.

"That's fine." Dad stands up and kisses the top of my head. "But let me know if things start to change, or if you feel uncomfortable with anything."

I nod but there's this niggling feeling at the back of my mind that grows the longer I look at the photo album. Maybe we couldn't share enough in our interviews to make Flora really Flora, or maybe Second Chances missed some important piece of the puzzle. A tiny seed of doubt begins to sprout. Flora's been so distant lately, so secretive. Not really like the girl I remember. Maybe Dad's right. Maybe she isn't actually Flora at all.

But if she's not Flora, who is she?

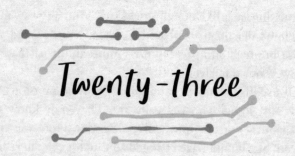

Twenty-three

Football that afternoon is a total disaster. My conversation with Dad keeps buzzing around my head, ruining my concentration. I miss some really easy passes and I even trip up over my own feet while we're doing dribbling drills.

"Come on, Isla!" Lily shouts when I let Rachel grab the ball from me and miss my chance to score. "Focus!"

Afterwards, Holly hangs back and waits for me as I struggle to undo my laces – even they are causing me problems today. She takes a half-eaten bag of Skittles from her jacket pocket and holds it out to me. "Want some? You look like you could do with a bit of rainbow."

"Thanks." I know she likes the purple ones best so I pick two green and two red. "That was rubbish. I was so bad."

"Don't worry about it. Everyone has their off days," Holly says, though I've never seen her have one. She always plays well and she's always in a good mood. "Can I walk you down to the ferry?"

Now that Ùna has stopped coming to Dad's with me, Holly walks me to the harbour and stays with me until the boat arrives. Sometimes Tiwa or Rachel comes with us too, but today they mumble something about needing to go to the post office and hurry off in the opposite direction, leaving Holly and me alone. She pulls on her jacket and flips her hair out from behind her collar.

"Lily's really into this idea of winning the cup, isn't she?" she says, swinging her arms by her side as we walk. "I think she's been watching too many sports films. Maybe we should cancel her Netflix subscription."

I smile. "It would be pretty great to win something, though. My sister has tons of medals from when she was on the swim team. It made me so jealous. I always really wanted one for myself." I quickly add, "*Had*, I mean."

It's the first time I've mentioned Flora to Holly – the first time I've slipped up. From the way her gaze softens, I can tell that one of the other girls has filled her in on the story. I don't mind. It saves me having to watch people's shock and awkwardness, see them squirm as they try to find the right thing to say about my dead sister. Though actually, I don't think Holly would react like that at all.

"Was that why you were in a bad mood earlier?" she asks. "Something to do with your sister?"

"No, not really." I pause for a second, weighing up how much I can say. "My dad told me this afternoon that he's planning on buying a house here, and I guess it hit me that this is permanent. That he's not coming home."

At least I can tell her some of the truth. Holly grimaces sympathetically. "I'm really sorry," she says. "That must suck. Especially if you were hoping he and your mum would sort it out."

"Well, you know what it's like."

Holly's posted a few photos of her mum and her little sister Elsie online, but she doesn't talk about them that often. It's always seemed a bit unusual to me, since she's so open about everything else.

"Yeah, but I was four when my parents split up," she says, offering me the Skittles again. "It's normal for me. You're still getting used to it."

For a second, I'm tempted to tell her the truth. The more I've got to know her, the more I think she'd believe me. But I can't risk it. If word got out about Flora and the trial had to end, I'd never forgive myself.

We arrive at the harbour and sit on our usual bench, the one near the steps with dozens of initials scratched into the back. Holly spins to face me and holds up three fingers.

"Let's play a game. You get three wishes. They have to be real things and you can't ask for more wishes or say world peace."

"What have you got against world peace?" I ask, laughing.

"Everyone wants world peace, that goes without saying! Unless they're some sort of monster, and in that case they don't deserve any wishes at all."

I chew on an orange sweet while I mull it over. Before Second Chances, I would have wished for another day with Flora. Even another hour, or five minutes... Just the chance to see her again, no matter how brief. I wouldn't share that with anyone but I would with Holly. It feels dishonest to say it now, though, knowing that Flora is at home, probably scrolling on her laptop and eating crisps in her pyjamas.

"I'd ask for a cure for cancer," I say instead. "One that works for all the different types of it."

Holly nods sagely. "That's a great one. Pretty much along the same lines as world peace but that's OK." She holds down one finger with her thumb. "Two left. Next?"

"Hmm." I tap my lower lip. "Can I have immortality for Sìth? I hate that I'm not going to have her around forever."

"I said real things! Where is this poor genie supposed to pick up a dose of cat immortality?" Holly wraps a purple-tipped lock of hair round her finger, laughing. "I'd allow it for Sìth. At least then I might get to finally meet her."

There's no chance of that happening any time soon. If Holly came to visit our house, Flora would have to stay out of sight. It wouldn't be fair to ask her to hide up in her room like a stowaway on a ship.

"One day," I say vaguely. "Maybe we can introduce her to Oakley."

"Definitely. Oakley's surprisingly fond of cats."

A strong gust of wind blows across the water then, making the boats in the harbour bob and bump together. Holly shivers and shifts along the bench towards me. It's barely a centimetre but it sends the butterflies in my stomach spinning into pirouettes.

"One more," she says. "What's your last wish?"

What I'd really wish for is to see her more than once a week. There are so many things about Holly that I like, things that I replay in my head over and over – the way she literally falls over laughing when she finds something really funny, how she hums jingles under her breath when she's daydreaming. I'd wish that I could see those things every day. I'd wish that I could hold her hand sometimes. That's what I want to say but the butterflies flutter up into my throat and block my words.

The ferry edges past the houses lining the harbour and comes into view. I stand up quickly and pull my backpack over my shoulder. Despite the cold air, my palms feel clammy. "There's the boat," I manage to stammer. "I'd better go."

Holly looks up at me from the bench. There's an expression on her face that I haven't seen before. She twirls one of the enamel pins on the collar of her jacket, the one shaped like a pink crescent moon. "I was thinking... Seeing how there's no school next week, do you want to come to mine one day?" she asks, the words coming out all rushed. "When's the last ferry? You could stay for tea if you like. You're veggie, aren't you? I'll ask my dad to make his Quorn fajitas. Or maybe his cauliflower curry. Actually, he got this new vegan Japanese cookbook recently that he's obsessed with, so he'll probably try something from that."

I'm starting to realize that Holly talks a lot when she's nervous. I smile. "The last ferry's at eight. And I am vegetarian, yeah," I say. "That'd be great. I'll make something for pudding. Maybe on Friday?"

"Awesome." Holly holds her hand up and we do what is probably the most awkward high five in the history of the world. "See you next week."

The regret hits the moment I step on to the ramp leading up to the ferry. I should have told her that I like her – or at least given her a hug instead of that high five.

Well done on making it weird, Isla.

When I turn back to the shore, Holly is still standing by the bench. She lifts her hand in a wave. "Remember, you still owe me a wish!"

My laughter rings out over the sound of the sea. "You still owe me three!"

Twenty-four

The rest of the weekend drags by, but finally Monday arrives and I can get stuck back into my investigation. Since it's also the start of the October holidays, I text Adhiti and Murdo and ask them if they'll come to Finley's house with me. Adhiti is busy coding with Flora again and Murdo seems reluctant, but I eventually persuade him to tag along in exchange for one of my caramel apple cakes. We cycle up to the Grahams' after lunch and by the time we arrive we're both exhausted. Their house is a big, fancy new-build perched on the western cliffs and it takes forever to get up there.

Murdo rings the bell and collapses against the wall. "I'm not sure this is going to help much, Isles," he whispers in between gasps of breath. "I really don't think it was Finley. Even if it was, you know what he's like. He could talk his way out of anything."

Last night I sent Finley a message saying I was ready to do the interview he's been asking for all these months. My plan was to slip my questions in as we talk, catch him off guard and hope he'd answer truthfully without thinking. But Murdo is right. Finley's too smart for that.

No matter what I ask, he'll be able to hopscotch his way around the truth without actually lying. If he's the one threatening Flora, I need to find some concrete proof.

"Let's look for clues then! The paint he could have used to write the message, maybe?" I say, but then I remember the tin was at the foot of the church. "Or a copy of that book the quote was from – *The Naked Sun*, I think."

Murdo gawps at me, horrified at the thought of riffling through someone else's stuff, but manages to hide his expression as Finley pulls the front door open.

"Isla! Thanks so much for agreeing to this," he says, all formal, like he's really a film director. For a moment it looks like he's even going to shake our hands but instead he gestures for us to come in. "I didn't know you were coming too," he adds to Murdo.

"Oh, uh, yeah." Murdo's cheeks flush as he unties his shoes. "I was bored, so I thought I'd tag along."

"Can I interview you too? I need more footage. So far I've only done my mum and my brothers, and they mostly mucked around and made fart noises."

"Even your mum?" I ask.

Finley laughs. "Oh yeah. She was the worst!"

Murdo and I follow him upstairs, our feet sinking into the plush tartan carpet. Professional photos of Finley and his younger brothers grin down at us from the duck-egg blue walls. I haven't been here since Finley's twelfth birthday party but I remember which of the bedrooms is his – the door has a sign saying *Quiet on the Set!* on it. Inside, he goes to his computer and gestures for us to sit on his bed.

"So, where do you want to shoot?" Finley asks me,

reaching for his camera – not his phone this time but a proper video recorder. "It's a bit windy, but I thought we could go down the path towards the beach, where the—"

"Um, can't we do it in here?" I ask quickly. "It's freezing outside and it looks like it's going to rain."

Finley cranes his head to look through the window. Sure enough, there are dark grey clouds hovering over the hills. He rubs the back of his neck and sighs. "I suppose we can do a talking head here, and then get some shots of you outside later on if it clears up. Let me get the lighting sorted out."

He goes to his cupboard and takes out a ring light, the kind I've seen advertised on Sekkon for people who make videos. While he's setting it up, I take a look around the room. I'm surprised how neat it is – much more so than mine or my sisters'. It makes me a bit worried. If Finley's really this tidy, he probably would have cleared away any clues that might have been here.

"So, what made you change your mind?" he asks.

He plugs in the ring light by the desk and switches it on. Murdo and I both flinch and cover our eyes as the bright light floods the room.

"About the interview?" I peek out from behind my hands. "Well, you're right. This is such a weird thing for us to go through and it should be someone from here who gets to tell the story. It might even help people in the future, to know how to help returnees integrate and stuff."

"Exactly!" Finley nods. "The technical side of the trial is really interesting but I want to talk about what it was like for the people living here too."

He sets up the camera on a tripod, then makes me sit in a few different spots while he tries out the light. Eventually, he places me by the window and wheels his desk chair over to sit in front of me.

"Let's start from the beginning," he says, once the camera is rolling. "Tell me about the first time you heard about Second Chances."

I start with the advert for the support group on Sekkon and how that led Mum to Project Homecoming, leaving out the part about me signing her up for it – I still haven't told my family I was the one who did that. It feels strange to admit how uneasy I felt about the trial at first. It was all so long ago now, and it's been so amazing having Flora back. When I reach the day she stepped off the boat, the door to Finley's room bursts open. Rory, his youngest brother, stomps inside with a scowl on his face.

"Rory! Get out!" Finley shouts, leaping to his feet. "We're shooting!"

"Adam won't let me play with his Switch!" Rory whines. "Can I use yours?"

Finley grits his teeth. I've seen him and his brothers have full-on wrestling matches over biscuits and laptops but this time he's in professional mode. He apologizes to me and Murdo, stands up and frogmarches Rory out of the room. As soon as the door closes, shouts explode from the hallway.

In a flash, I jump out of my seat and go to the desk. "You check the wardrobe," I whisper to Murdo. "Quickly!"

"Isla! We can't go through his stuff!" But Murdo tiptoes towards the wardrobe and gingerly opens the door. I scan the desk and rummage through the drawers. Inside there's nothing but stationery, a few Warhammer figurines and a half-eaten packet of chewing gum. Murdo carefully pulls a box labelled 'old stuff' from the back of the wardrobe, still shaking his head and mumbling that we shouldn't do this. Next I check under the bed. The only thing stored there are two suitcases, and when I shake them they sound empty.

"What are you doing?"

Murdo and I both freeze. Finley is standing in the doorway, staring at us – Murdo with his head bent towards the box, and me on the floor with both arms under the bed and my bum in the air. There's no excuse I can think of that will get us out of this one.

As Murdo sheepishly slides the box away, I stand up and face Finley. Now I've no choice but to ask him outright. "Were you the one who wrote that message on the church wall?"

Finley frowns. "What makes you ask that?"

"You were right there when we found the message. Bit convenient, isn't it?" I take a step towards him. "And your documentary is going to be a lot more interesting if there's somebody going around the island leaving her creepy messages…"

There's a pause. For a split second, I think I've got him. But then Finley shakes his head and laughs. "What? Isla, that's nuts!" He sits down at the computer desk again. "That's actually a great idea but no, it wasn't me. I only cycled to school early because I had an argument with my mum and didn't want to get in the car. It was just luck that I got there when you did."

"I don't think I believe you." My hands are shaking,

so I put them on my hips. "You're obsessed with your documentary. It's all you've talked about for months."

"So what?" Finley rolls his eyes. "I've told you a thousand times, I'm not going to publish anything about Flora until it's made public. We'd all have to pay back the money if I broke the clause. The whole island would hate me."

"That money is nothing compared to how much some newspapers would pay you for an exclusive," I say. "Or the ads you could get on your channel with a few million followers."

"I'm not in this for the money. I just want to create good films. Films that make people think. What am I supposed to make them about, if not the trial?" He gestures through his bedroom window to the peaceful sea, the pale grey sky that stretches on forever. "We live in the most uneventful place in the universe. Something exciting *finally* happens here and I'm not allowed to tell anyone about it. Do you know how frustrating that is?"

"Oh, I'm so sorry it's an inconvenience for you, Finley," I say. "I'm so sorry that for once in your life, you can't get what you want."

Murdo puts his hand on my arm. "Isla, come on. You're being totally unfair."

Finley swallows and blinks three times, his brown eyes wide. He looks … hurt. Guilt starts to itch at the back of my neck. I sit down and let out a deep breath. "I'm sorry. It's not only the church thing. Somebody left a smashed computer outside our house and then I found an envelope in Flora's bag…"

I pull up the photos on my phone and take my notebook

from my bag. Finley stares at the names on the page as I talk him through my investigation so far.

"If the same person did all these things, it has to be someone in our class," Murdo says. "They're the only ones who could get to Flora's bag."

Finley runs a hand through his curls, thinking. "Not necessarily. Flora's been hanging out at Adhiti's a lot lately, right? And sometimes she goes there straight after school?"

"Well, yeah, but it's obviously not Adhiti," I say, frowning. "She'd never do something to put the trial in danger like that."

"Not Adhiti," Finley says, shaking his head. "Someone else."

Grabbing a biro from his desk, Finley strikes a line through his own name and adds a sixth to the list. It's the name of someone who works less than a minute from the church – someone who's been acting strangely around Flora for months.

Suresh

Twenty-five

"Why would Suresh do something like that?" I ask. "He was Flora's friend. Her best friend."

Finley pulls his laptop towards him, clicks on a folder called 'Footage' and opens a video. The four words written on the church wall loom on to the screen. I hear my own voice telling Finley he can't film this, then him snapping back at me. He pauses the video and points. "Look at this."

For a second, I'm not sure what I'm looking at. Then he zooms in and I see it. Suresh is in the far left of the frame, standing by his car. The image is blurry but he's obviously looking right towards us. Seeing and hearing everything.

"He was watching us the whole time but he didn't come over to ask what was going on or check if Flora was OK," Finley says. "Don't you think that's suspicious? Like you said, Flora's supposed to be his friend."

"He was probably late for work," Murdo says, shrugging. "And besides, things have been awkward between him and Flora, haven't they? Maybe they're not that close any more."

But for me, things are starting to click together. Flora took her backpack with her that first time we went to visit Suresh and Adhiti – I remember because she put the flowers that she picked for Neerja in it. She and Suresh were alone for most of the afternoon, and Flora said he was acting strangely. He might have snuck the envelope in there while she was distracted – that bag is so full of stuff, Flora could easily have gone ages without noticing it. Suresh starts work at the post office really early, so he could have painted the message on the church wall without anyone seeing him. I can't believe I didn't think about it before.

I shove my journal back into my bag and head for the door. "Thanks, Finley."

"Wait!" He darts out of his room after me. "What about the interview?"

"Another time, promise!"

Murdo hurries down the stairs, wriggling his arms into his jacket as he slips through the front door. "Sorry, Fin!"

I grab my bike and cycle at top speed to the village, Murdo right behind me. When I look through the window of the tiny post office, Adhiti's dad is behind the desk, chatting with Jeanie Mackay as she slides an envelope across the counter. No sign of Suresh.

"Maybe he's gone for a break?" Murdo suggests, but we wait ten minutes and Suresh doesn't show up. The disappointment stings. The next step of my investigation is going to have to wait.

Adhiti's bike is lying by our front door when I get home. I pull off my jacket and shoes and hurry upstairs, hoping she might know where her brother is. But before I charge into Flora's bedroom, something makes me pause. Pandora21 is playing behind the door, and Flora's singing along. Normally for her that means singing the English parts and humming or mumbling along with the Korean lyrics, but now she's enunciating every single syllable. I have no idea if the pronunciation is right but she seems to know all the words.

I rap on the door and push it open. Flora jumps and slams her laptop shut, cutting out the music. She and Adhiti spin round, both looking like they've been caught doing something they shouldn't.

"How are you doing that?" I ask Flora.

The guilty look is quickly masked by confusion. Flora was always a bad liar but this time it's surprisingly convincing. "What?"

"You were singing along in Korean," I say. "How?"

"What do you mean?" She glances at Adhiti, who's suddenly become very interested in the pattern on her tights. "I just looked up the lyrics. I learned them phonetically."

That could be true but I'm sure it's not. Flora tried to memorize a few Pandora21 songs when she first got into them but she could never get the sounds to stick in her memory. This time she was singing with feeling, like she knew the meaning of every single word.

"I don't believe you," I say. "How were you doing that?"

Flora and Adhiti look at each other. It's like they're communicating in some private code, and that makes me so annoyed that I ask again and again, until Flora finally cracks and opens up her laptop. On the screen are scores of coloured text on a black background, endless strings of code that I can't make sense of at all.

"Look, don't freak out, OK? It's just … Adhiti's been helping me tinker with my programming a bit. To help me learn things faster."

"You what?" I stare from Flora to Adhiti. Both of their mouths are twitching, like they're trying not to smile. "Is that allowed?"

Adhiti sidesteps the question. "It wasn't that difficult. We adjusted Flora's knowledge acquisition, downloaded a load of language software, and now—"

"And now Flora can speak Korean? Just like that?"

"Not exactly. It means I can access the information we found online. I don't understand all the nuances and cultural references like a native speaker would." Flora shrugs, all modest. "Plus, it wasn't *totally* automatic. It took about an hour and a half."

"An entire language in an hour and a half?" I let out a short laugh. "That's ridiculous, Flora."

She grins and responds in what sounds, at least to me, like fluent Korean. Adhiti laughs and claps her hands in delight. I lean forwards and peer at the huge tangle of text on her computer screen. It's a foreign language all in itself.

"How did you do it?" I ask Adhiti. "How did you even know where to start?"

She and Flora give each other that knowing look again, and it's even more irritating than the first time. Maybe it's babyish but Adhiti was my friend first. I don't like that she and Flora have been keeping secrets from me.

"What?" I ask, tugging on Flora's sleeve. "Come on, tell me."

"Fine, but you can't tell anyone else about any of this. Especially not Mum. Promise me, Isla." Flora waits for me to nod before I go on. "We found some people online who helped us get past the code blocking me from accessing all of my capabilities. Then we—"

"Wait." My heart stops. "You told someone about the trial?"

"Of course not!" Adhiti says, shaking her head. "We kept it all really vague."

"We were only messing around." Flora shrugs. "It's not a big deal."

It's not like her to be this modest. Flora can be a bit of a show-off. She was always bragging about her swim times or how many views her Sekkon videos were getting. To have mastered something like this so quickly is a big thing, even if she is technically a machine. It's a huge step up from teaching Stephen how to line dance.

"What else can you do?" I ask.

Behind the nonchalant act, Flora's eyes spark with excitement. She spins from side to side in her desk chair. "We reactivated my computational abilities too. Give me a sum. A really hard one. Type it into your phone so you don't forget."

I press a bunch of numbers into the calculator on my phone. "1769.5 times 66.9, divided by 144.2."

Flora replies after a fraction of a second. "820.94, rounded to the second decimal point." She rocks back and laughs. "Come on, I said a hard one."

My mouth goes dry as I look down at the screen. She got it exactly right. The old Flora couldn't even have told you six times eight that quickly. We do another few tests, this time including the most complex algebra I can think of, and every single answer is correct. It's weird but also sort of exciting. There's so much she could master. She could learn to play the piano or rewire an electric circuit or compete in champion-level chess in five minutes if she wanted to.

"What else?" I ask, bouncing on her bed.

Flora clicks on the track pad and opens up another window. "OK, this is pretty bad but I managed to get around the no-contact rule with my friends. Look at this."

It takes me a moment to work out what I'm seeing. A group chat called Blue Island Swimmers, filled with messages from Flora's old friends from her club on Eilean Gorm. Even as I'm looking at the screen, a gif of a tiny kitten headbutting a mirror pops up.

"You hacked their phones? That's spying!"

Adhiti holds her hands up. "This bit was all Flora. Nothing to do with me."

"I just got access to their group chat! It's not like I'm going through their messages to their boyfriends or anything." Flora scrolls back through the conversation until she arrives at a cluster of photos of different cakes, some with candles stuck into the sponge. "Look, they all had a piece of cake for me on my birthday, even though they're in different places now. Isn't that cute?"

This is what she was looking for – proof that she hasn't been forgotten. I know why she wanted that. But it doesn't feel right at all.

180

"Doesn't this seem ... wrong?" I ask. "They don't know you're reading this. You don't know how they'd feel about it."

"Well, they don't even know I exist, so they're never going to find out." Flora's smile fades. "Come on, Isla. I'm basically cut off from the rest of the world. I'm not even allowed a Sekkon account any more. You can't blame me for wanting to check in on my friends."

I clear my throat. "Isn't Suresh around? You've got him."

"Hardly," Flora mutters. "When I went over to his yesterday, he practically jumped out of the window to get away from me."

Adhiti rolls her eyes. "You're exaggerating. He used the front door, for one thing, and he was also running late for the ferry. It was nothing to do with you."

"Where was he going?" I ask, trying to sound like I'm just casually enquiring.

"Glasgow. Dad gave him the week off, so he's going to stay with our cousins for a while."

So, Suresh isn't on the island right now. That's another delay to my mission, but at least it gives me time to work out what I'll say to him when he comes back.

Flora keeps scrolling through months of chat and photos and links. I don't agree with her spying, but after days of her being mopey and grumpy, it's good to see her smiling again. Still, part of me wonders what other people on the island would say if they knew she was capable of doing things like this.

"Well, don't get caught, OK?" I poke Flora in the side. She grins and slaps my hand away. "They must have the world's best computer engineers working at Second Chances. I doubt you can outsmart them."

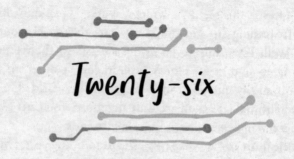

Twenty-six

Over the next few days, Flora picks up more and more skills. She 'learns' to play Mum's old guitar and memorizes Pandora21's most tricky choreography in minutes. She downloads a dozen more languages, including German, so she can help me with the homework I need to hand in after the October holidays. I know it's all data but it's irritating that I've been learning for two years and still can't remember whether it's *der Hund*, *die Hund* or *das Hund* when Flora has the entire language mastered in one single morning.

"Dog is masculine, so it's *der* in the nominative case, but *den* in the accusative case, *dem* in the dative and *des* in the genitive," she tells me. We're in my bedroom, the door closed so Mum can't hear. "It's actually really easy."

I roll my eyes and kick my feet against the wall. "*Du bist* so annoying."

"*Nervig*," Flora corrects me, smirking. Then suddenly her voice goes flat. "Today's the day. Six hundred and twenty-five miles to Juneau, Alaska. Virgo with Aquarius rising."

That speech glitch again – I thought the technicians had fixed it. This time, when Flora looks up, her eyes are shining bright red. I jump back so fast my head hits the shelf above my bed. "Whoa! What was that?"

Flora rubs at her forehead. Her eyes have gone back to the same grey-blue as my own. "What was what?"

"Your eyes turned r-red," I stammer. It was so fast I might think I'd imagined it if it weren't for the blurred spots the light has left on the back of my eyelids.

"Really? Oh." Flora blinks a few more times. "I think that happens when there's a technical problem."

"What sort of problem? Should we call Marisa? I'll get Mum."

The training module has a chapter about what to do if returnees catch a virus – or worse, if they're hacked – but I can't remember a word of it now. I start to climb off the bed but Flora catches my wrist and pulls me back. "No! It's nothing, Isla, honestly. There's no point worrying her over it."

Slowly, I pull my wrist from her grasp. "Is this because you've been messing around with your settings? What if you've damaged something?"

Mixed in with the worry is a pinch of anger. Flora shouldn't be breaking the rules like this. Adhiti shouldn't have let her. She might be a coding genius but this is way out of her depth.

"I haven't!" Flora rubs her eyes and stands up. "Don't tell Mum, OK? I'll sort it out myself."

I'm sure the technicians will pick up on the error during Flora's check-up but Marisa doesn't mention it the next evening. Even Mum hasn't noticed what's going on yet, though there have been loads of near misses. Once she came in the front door right as Flora was playing a complex riff on the guitar, and another time she walked into the kitchen while Flora was showing off by reciting all the districts of India in reverse alphabetical order. Each time makes me sick with nerves but Flora barely seems to notice.

By the time Friday comes, I'm looking forward to getting off the island and going to Holly's for the afternoon. I wake up with a stomach full of butterflies, half of them excited, half so nervous I can hardly eat my breakfast. I'd been planning on making my famous triple chocolate brownies for pudding but as I'm brushing my teeth I have a better idea – a Dream Ring, the cake Holly mentioned she likes. I look it up online and make an oversized version. The donut is the size of a dinner plate, with tons of cream in the middle and white icing on top. I don't know how close it is to the real thing but I think it'll make her smile.

I cycle down to the village with the cake tin balanced on my handlebars, leave my bike at the harbour and board the ferry. The crossing is calm today but my stomach still churns the whole way to Eilean Gorm. I clutch the tin tight, trying to calm the nerves whirling around inside me. When the boat arrives, Holly is waiting for me at the shore. Oakley is with her, straining on her lead as she tries to chase a pigeon.

"Oakley!" I laugh and hold the tin above my head as the dog jumps up on me. "I've seen so many photos of you, I feel like I'm meeting a celebrity."

"Look, she's even given you an autograph," Holly laughs, pointing to a paw print on my jumper. "Ooh, did you bake something?"

"Well, I don't know if I got it right, but…" I peel back the lid. "My interpretation of a Dream Ring."

Holly claps her hands together and shrieks. "Isla! That's the best thing I've ever seen!"

She keeps pulling the lid off to peek at the cake all the way to hers. She and her family live in a row of brightly coloured houses that are always on postcards of Eilean Gorm, not far from Kirsty's. Her dad is out in the garden when we arrive, kneeling in the vegetable patch with the radio playing from his phone behind him.

"Hi, girls." He stands up and waves a bunch of muddy carrots at us. "This must be the famous Isla. The best football player on the whole island, I've heard."

"That's not saying much, Dad. There are like, twelve people here." Holly lets Oakley off her leash. "She is really, really good, though."

"I take it you don't like tidying up then, Isla?" He pulls his leg back and kicks towards his gooseberry bush. "Because you're a real Messi."

Holly rolls her eyes. "Wow, Dad. That's terrible even by your standards."

I laugh. "Almost as bad as my dad's jokes."

Her dad chuckles and pretends to throw a carrot at us. Oakley pads off to have a sniff around the vegetables and I follow Holly into the house and through to the kitchen. She gets two plates down from the cupboard, cuts us each a huge slice of Dream Ring and takes them to the front room. It's a cosy room with a big fireplace, a well-worn red sofa and a huge stack of video games by the TV.

"Do you want to play something? My brothers are off

camping so they won't be back until tomorrow," she says, peeling a Post-it saying *Keep off, Holly!!* from some war game. "Better eat this first, though. I won't be able to focus until I've tried it."

She bites into the cake and grins, her nose crinkling up in that cute way it always does when she's happy.

"How does it match up to the original?" I ask.

"It's not quite as sweet," she says, which surprises me since I put about a ton of sugar in. "But it's really good! Makes me a bit homesick, even."

I take a bite of my piece. "You must miss your mum and your wee sister."

"Yeah, I do. It was weird going from seeing them every weekend to only every month or so at first, but I got used to it pretty quickly." Holly's jeans rustle against the carpet as she shifts position. "They were supposed to come up for my birthday next Wednesday but Mum had to cancel. Something about a conference."

"Oh, sorry," I say, wiping cream from my mouth.

Holly shakes her head. "It's OK. She already sent me some new shoes and a gift voucher. She forgot last year, so she was extra careful this time."

I gawp at her. "She forgot your birthday?"

"Yeah. She's a Pisces. Always away with the fairies." Holly laughs. "I know that makes her sound like a total monster, forgetting her daughter's birthday, but she's not. We mostly get on really well. She's just not there in the same way my dad is, you know?"

"Still, that must have hurt." Even in the days when grief had turned my parents into foggy, faraway zombies, they never forgot my birthday.

"It did at the time, yeah. I was pretty upset about it." Holly licks her thumbs to pick up the crumbs from her plate. "Sometimes it seems like Grant and Elsie are her real family, and me and my brothers are an afterthought. Not always. But it's hard not to feel like that when she forgets which day I was born."

She laughs but her voice wobbles. It's the first time I've ever seen a wisp of cloud in the sunshine that is Holly. It's hard to hear but it feels good that she can be honest with me. "I'm sorry," I say again.

"Ah, it's fine. Dad ran out and bought me another present to cheer me up, so it was worth it."

Holly scrapes the last of the icing from her plate and starts looking through the stack of video games. She lets me pick first and I choose Mario Kart. Adhiti has it, so I've had lots of practice. We select our characters (Yoshi for me, Peach for Holly) and set off speeding around the first course. As well as being really good, Holly's hilarious to watch. She plays with her entire body, flinging herself right and left and adding her own sound effects to those from the game.

"So, has your dad found a house here yet?" she asks, as we get ready for the next race. We've done six or seven so far and she's won all of them.

"No. It's only been six days," I laugh.

"Oh, right. Duh." She leans forward as she sends Peach zooming along the track. "I was thinking it would be good if you got to spend more time here. That way you wouldn't need to run off for the ferry straight after football."

Her cheeks have turned almost as pink as Princess

Peach's dress. I look at her a beat too long and let Yoshi crash into the crowd watching the track.

"That's true. It'd be good to get to hang out with you more too. And Tiwa and Rachel and the others," I add quickly, as a flurry of nerves attack. But then I decide to be brave and add, "But especially you."

Out of the corner of my eye, I see Holly smile. "Yeah. Especially you too."

She moves on to her knees to change position again and when she sits back down she's only a few centimetres away from me. On the TV screen, Peach suddenly goes spiralling off the track and hits the wall of the stadium. It happens a second time and then a third, giving me enough time to finally edge Yoshi over the finish line in first place.

"Did you let me win?" I ask.

"No… Well, maybe a wee bit." Holly laughs. The butterflies go twirling around my stomach. "I'm going to get us more Dream Ring. You pick the next course."

She jumps up and runs off to the kitchen, singing the game soundtrack as she goes. My smile is so big, my cheeks are starting to hurt. While I'm tapping through the options, my phone buzzes on the floor. I look down and see a message from Ùna flash on to the screen.

You need to come home. It's urgent.

After a moment, a second one pops up: *It's Flora.*

I drop the console and scramble to send Ùna a message asking what's wrong. When she doesn't reply, I try calling. No answer. My pulse racing, I check the time – 5.35p.m. If I leave right now, I can make the six o'clock ferry. I'll be home by seven if I cycle fast enough.

Home. Urgent. Flora. The words screech through my mind, leaving no room for any other thoughts. I shove my arms into my coat, hurry through the door and out into the street. Holly's dad calls after me, asking if everything is OK, but I'm too panicked to answer. In my rush to get home, I don't even stop to say goodbye.

PROJECT **HOMECOMING:**
A GUIDE FOR FAMILIES

Module 16: Emergencies

While returnees are not mortal in the same way as humans, they are still at risk of accidents and sickness. They feel pain in a similar way to us and their physical bodies can be damaged just like ours, sometimes to the extent that they may need to be sent to the Second Chances base for essential repairs. They may also be vulnerable to viruses and hacking, which in the most extreme instances could permanently damage their systems.

Generally, there is no need for either returnees or their families to worry about this. Our world-class engineers have installed the most advanced firewalls and protections in each of our returnees' hard drives, allowing them to fight off most malware without even being aware there is an issue. And unlike humans, their body parts can usually be replaced quickly and easily.

Nevertheless, family members need to be aware of these possibilities so they can act appropriately in the case of an emergency, either by contacting your Family Liaison Officer or by using the Returnee Health Hub to restore settings. It's also important that returnees attend their health status check-ups every week, and that they don't attempt to fix any issues by themselves or with the help of anyone other than a Second Chances technician.

Failure to follow these rules could lead to serious – even irreparable – issues.

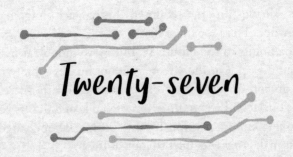

Twenty-seven

My heart pounds for every minute of the boat ride back to Eilean Dearg. I text Ùna again, then Flora and Mum, asking what's happening, what's the emergency, if Flora's OK. No one replies, which makes my anxiety spiral out of control. Holly sends me a bunch of messages asking where I went and if everything is all right but I'm too distracted to find an excuse. I keep thinking about the way Flora's eyes flashed red the other day. I should have told Mum. We should have told Marisa.

By the time I leap off my bike and rush into our kitchen, I feel sick with fear. "What's happening? What's the emergency?"

No one answers. Flora is sitting at the kitchen table with her eyes closed, her chin tucked into her chest and her laptop in front of her. There's one cable running from the computer to the port in her neck, another from the computer to her Health Hub. Mum sits beside her with her own laptop open. Marisa's voice drifts out of the speakers, saying something about Flora's operating system that I don't catch.

"What happened?" I ask again, turning to Ùna.

She's sitting on the counter, biting her fingernails. "Why does Flora look like that?"

Ùna points to the Health Hub. I move to look at it and let out a gasp. On the screen, random images rapidly pile one on top of each other like a strange and frantic card game – Machu Picchu, three horses, a pile of Snickers bars, a cooking knife, a painting by Van Gogh… They change so fast it makes my eyes hurt to look at them.

"Flora has a virus." Behind her glasses, Ùna's eyes are wide with worry. "Second Chances are trying to sort it out."

My breath catches in my throat. "Is she going to be OK?"

"Marisa says she will but she's been like this for over an hour now."

I sit down at the table opposite Flora. Dread swells up inside me like a high tide. I can't believe we have to go through this again. Flora hooked up to machines, battling something attacking her body, the rest of us unable to do anything to stop it or help her. It's not supposed to be like this any more. Second Chances were supposed to fix that.

"The technicians have almost finished running the scan. It'll be done in a few minutes." Marisa's voice drifts out of Mum's computer. Her words come out strained and fast, totally different from her usual smooth, professional tone. "I don't understand how this happened. It doesn't make any sense."

She keeps talking, stuff about malware and firewalls that I can't follow. I sit down beside Flora and watch as more images flash on to the screen of the Health Hub: a sandcastle, sushi rolls, a drawing of a dragon… On and on for ages, until finally Flora's eyes open. The Health Hub goes blank. A moment later, a green circle with a white tick appears on the screen.

"Flora?" Mum leans forward and grabs her hand. "Can you hear me, love?"

Flora's head jolts upright. Her eyes open and flash red. Mum flinches and Ùna lets out a shriek of fear. A moment later they turn grey-blue again, and Flora blinks and looks round at us.

"I'm fine." She looks down at the Health Hub and taps the screen. "Everything seems to be running optimally."

She smiles calmly. Her voice is so relaxed, it almost scares me. It sounds so … mechanical.

"Are you sure?" Mum's hands hover like they want to pat her head or stroke her cheek, do something to take the hurt away.

"I'm fine, Mum. Look." Flora turns the Health Hub round. Graphs and numbers pop up on the screen, all constantly changing as data flows in and out of her system. I don't know what any of it means. Mum nods but I doubt she does, either.

"Here's what we know," Marisa says. "Flora was hit by a worm, a type of malware that can replicate itself and spread via computer networks. That's how it was able to move from her laptop and attack her operating system. We'll need to check your other computers and phones to make sure it's not lurking there too."

"But how did it get to her laptop in the first place?" Mum asks. "Did you download something by accident?"

"No, it came from an external drive. A simple USB," Marisa says, reading from her tablet. "Do you know which one, Flora?"

She nods. "It's a USB pen that I use for the printer at

school. Somebody must have borrowed it and accidentally downloaded something dodgy."

I stare at her. If Suresh is the one behind this, he could have had the chance to snatch the USB drive while Flora was over at his house. But giving her a virus… That means he's actually trying to *hurt* Flora. The thought makes me feel sick.

On Mum's computer screen, Marisa nods. "Honestly, I'm relieved. We thought at first that someone might be trying to hack your system. But what I don't understand is why it didn't catch such a basic programme," she tells Flora. "We have multiple firewalls in place to protect you from attacks like this and they're incredibly sophisticated – they should really be impenetrable, especially for such a primitive type of virus. Have you noticed anything unusual lately?"

Flora shakes her head. I open my mouth to tell Marisa about the adjustments she's made to her system, then stop myself. I don't know what Marisa will say if they find out that Flora has broken so many rules. I don't want to get her in trouble.

"I'll have our security team look into it again," Marisa says. "I'll check you in for another maintenance session tomorrow. Let's say 7 p.m. your time?"

Marisa sends off a confirmation email to Flora then says goodbye and ends the call. I stand up the moment she disappears from the screen.

"There's no way that was an accident!" I say. "It was obviously another attack. Why didn't you tell Marisa the truth?"

"*Attack* sounds a wee bit dramatic, Isles." Mum tries

to laugh but her face is pale and her voice trembles. "Anyway, Flora's fine now. Aren't you, love?"

"But she might not have been," Ùna says. "That could have been really bad."

"Exactly. This is much more serious than some graffiti on the church wall," I say, nodding. "We need to tell Marisa what's been going on."

"No, Isla. It's fine," Flora says again. "Everything is running optimally."

My heart is still beating too fast. The words *virus*, *urgent*, *emergency* still echo through my head. I wait for Mum to take my side, to finally agree that Marisa needs to know the truth about the messages that have been sent to us. Instead she mumbles something about getting dinner started, and Flora slides the Health Hub back to its usual spot on the windowsill and tells us she'll be in her room if we need her. I don't understand it. They're acting as if this was some silly misunderstanding. As if it was nothing important at all.

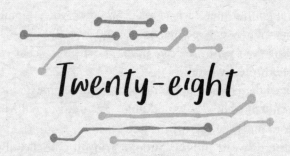

Twenty-eight

The following Monday, while Ùna and I are rushing through bowls of cereal and cups of tea, Flora announces that she's not coming back to school. It's not even an announcement, really. She says it as calmly as if she was mentioning the weather.

"What do you mean, you're not going back to school?" Mum blinks, her mug of coffee on pause beneath her mouth. "Why not?"

Flora leans against the kitchen counter and hunches her shoulders. It's quarter past eight and she's still in her pyjamas, flicking casually through yesterday's newspaper.

"Like I keep saying, there's no point." She turns to the puzzles page and reaches for a pen. "I can't sit the exams next year. Even if I could, I can't go to college or university. There's no reason for me to be there."

Though she doesn't say it, I know she's thinking that there's nothing school can teach her that she doesn't already know. Her knowledge has gone way, way beyond high-school level. She must feel like a rocket scientist being sent back to a primary science class.

"Of course there's a reason." Mum's voice is rising with panic. "There's the social aspect and it's important for you to have a routine… We should really discuss this with Marisa before we make a decision."

"*We're* not making any decisions about this. I am. I already have."

Flora pulls the top off the pen with her teeth, then fills in the crossword and two Sudoku grids. It takes her about thirty seconds to complete them all. She pushes her hair behind her ears and meets Mum's bewildered stare with a calm smile. "I'll be in my room if you need me."

There's no way Flora could have got away with having an attitude like this before she got sick. Not without a lecture, anyway. Now Mum watches Flora leave, then snatches up Ùna's empty cereal bowl and puts it in the dishwasher.

"Aren't you going to do something?" I ask her.

She slams the dishwasher door shut. The knives and forks clatter inside. "What can I do, Isla? There's no law saying she has to go to school. I can't force her."

"So, you're not even going to try?'

Mum doesn't answer. I run upstairs after Flora and fling the door to her bedroom open. She's sitting at the desk, typing on her computer.

"What's going on?" I ask. "You've been acting weird the whole weekend and now you're not coming back to school? What are you even going to do all day?"

Flora glances over her shoulder. "Don't worry about it. I've got loads to do."

"Like what? More *tinkering*? What if you get another virus and this time you can't fight it off?" As I ask the question, another occurs to me. "Is that why it affected you so badly? Because you've damaged something in your system?"

Flora ignores me and keeps typing. Her computer is open on a Sekkon profile – an Asian man in his early twenties or so, smiling at the camera in a busy restaurant. Judging by the palm trees visible through the window, it's somewhere far away from here.

"Who's that?" I ask. "Are you talking to people online? You know you're not supposed to do that! What if you get caught?"

A blast of anger hits me, at Flora for being so reckless, and Adhiti for helping her, and at both of them for doing it behind my back. But Flora just turns to me and smiles. "I won't get caught, Lala. I promise," she says. "I've got this all under control."

Though Ùna and I keep nagging her, Flora won't come back to school the next day, or the next, or the next. The classroom feels weird without her now, unbalanced with only five of us at the table instead of six. On Thursday lunchtime I go for a walk with Murdo and Adhiti and notice that Suresh is back in the post office. I take out my journal during my last lesson, hide it on my lap and write down the questions I want to ask him.

Why have you been so awkward around Flora?

Are you the one who's been sending these creepy messages?

Did you infect her with a virus that could have destroyed her?

Opposite me, Adhiti is concentrating hard on her

Computing Science work, her eyebrows in a tight frown. The thought of asking Suresh these questions makes me feel sick. If I'm wrong, he's going to be so hurt. Tamal and Neerja too, not to mention Adhiti – even if I'm still annoyed with her, I don't want to upset her. But I have to take that risk. These messages have sent Flora drifting so far away from us, even more so now she knows how to alter her system. If I don't pull her back soon, she might get into serious trouble.

As I'm tidying away my stuff at the end of the day, a notification pops up on Sekkon. It's from Holly, which surprises me because she doesn't post much on there. In the video she's leaning over a bright blue cake decorated with white icing stars, fizzing sparklers and candles shaped like the number fourteen. As voices off-screen sing a tuneless "Happy Birthday", Holly pushes her hair behind her ears and blows out the candles.

My heart sinks. Holly's birthday was yesterday.

I forgot Holly's birthday.

I scramble to send her a message, typing so quickly I accidentally add two flamingos and an umbrella emoji. Two ticks appear to show that Holly's read it, but there's no response. Usually she's lightning fast. I send her a bunch more messages apologizing but she doesn't reply to any of them. I sheepishly tell Ùna about it when we're walking out of school and she gasps with horror.

"You need to make her something right away!" She grabs my arm and drags me towards our bikes. "And it needs to be something good."

I push Suresh out of my mind for now and hurry home. Flora is sitting at the kitchen table when we get in, the

Returnee Health Hub in her hands, but she looks up as Ùna starts raiding the drawers to find something we can use to make a present. We don't have much in the way of art supplies. Kirsty used to always get us painting or playing with clay when we went to her house but none of us are that crafty.

"I wish I could post a cake," I say, flopping into the chair next to Flora. "Maybe I should skip school tomorrow and take one to Holly myself."

"Mum would kill you," Ùna says. "Especially after Flora's trip to Eilean Gorm. You need something you can send in an envelope."

Flora presses a button on the Health Hub and puts it back by the window. She's quiet for a moment, a blank look on her face like she's lost in thought. Then she turns to me and says, "How about paper cutting?"

I remember Flora's failed attempt a few months ago and laugh. "Are you kidding? There's no way I could do something like that! Maybe a paper people chain if I try hard enough."

"I could, though," Flora says. "You think up a design, something personal to Holly, and then I'll make it for you. It'll be like you commissioned a piece of art for her."

She goes to look for paper and a decent knife while Ùna and I scan the internet for inspiration. I sketch out a letter H filled with a pattern of holly leaves, the Scorpio symbol, paw prints and footballs – something unique to Holly. Flora finds a couple of images to base it on, then places the paper on a chopping board and gets to work. Ùna soon gets bored and wanders off to play with Sìth but I stay and watch Flora work.

"How did you forget her birthday, anyway?" she asks me. "Don't you talk all the time?"

Holly and I haven't spoken much since I ran out of her house last Friday. I sent her a ton of messages saying sorry the next day, making up some excuse about really bad period pains that I'm not sure she believed, but I've been so worried about Flora and the virus that we've hardly talked since.

"I got distracted," I say. "The computer and the graffiti were one thing, but the virus... It's much scarier."

"Oh, don't worry about all that." Flora flaps her hand like she's swatting away a fly. "I'm not bothered about it. Honest."

She turns back to the cutting and makes three curved strokes for a holly leaf. Usually I like watching other people making things – the concentration on Murdo's face as he carves something out of wood, the way Kirsty's eyes shine when she's sculpting or painting. But this is different. The way Flora's arms move is too confident, too smooth, too fast. It feels more like watching part of a machine line reproducing a product than an artist creating something new. Still, I'm grateful to her for helping me.

"I hope Holly likes this," I mumble. "I feel so guilty for forgetting. I need to make it up to her."

Flora glances up at me. "You really like this girl, don't you?"

"Yeah, I do." I nod, trying to ignore the flush in my cheeks. "She's so funny. I think you'd really like her."

"That's so great, Lala." Flora smiles and turns back to the cutting. "I'm a bit jealous, to be honest. I'll never have a boyfriend."

I roll my eyes. "Don't be daft. Of course you'll have a boyfriend."

"Who? There's nobody on the island. Even if I could leave, the permanently fifteen-year-old robot thing is a bit of a deal breaker." She strokes the back of her Pandora21 phone cover and sighs. "Oh, Park Joowon. You are the closest I'll ever get to love."

I remind her that Second Chances are working on ways for her to age, but she's in a sulky mood and won't be cheered up. Still, it's sort of nice to hear her talking about boys, instead of showing off with ridiculously complicated sums or giving us the exact co-ordinates to any place in the world. Like she's a normal teenager, not a machine with superhuman powers.

An idea comes to me then. "You know how you hacked into your friends' phones?" I ask, sitting up. "Could you do that for someone else?"

"Weren't you the one telling me it was immoral and a huge invasion of privacy?" she says wryly. "Who would you want me to check up on?"

I bite my fingernail. "Suresh. I think he's the one who sent you the virus."

"What?" Flora looks up sharply. "Isla, no! Honestly, forget about it. It doesn't matter."

"It does matter, Flora! Whoever did this could have really hurt you."

It's time to tell her the whole story. I take my notebook out of my bag and tell her about my investigation, going through the names on my list one by one. I start to tell her about the red envelope but Flora cuts me off before I can finish.

"Isla, seriously." She brushes the paper cuttings on to the floor. They look like shards of broken china on the wooden boards. "You're wasting your time with all this. Just forget about it, OK?"

The force in her voice makes me stop arguing. Flora makes one last cut in the paper, then holds up the H shape to examine it. Every line is perfect. The holly leaves and footballs are cookie-cutter identical, the Scorpio glyphs completely straight and neat. It would have taken an artist years of practice to be able to create something like this and yet Flora has done it in barely ten minutes.

"It's amazing," I say. "Thank you."

But it's too perfect. Flora shouldn't be able to do this. Maybe I shouldn't even have asked her to. Even so, I pick up the cutting and slide it into an envelope, ready to send to Holly. And despite Flora telling me to forget about it, when I go to the post office tomorrow I'll be ready to talk to Suresh.

Twenty-nine

The post office on Eilean Dearg isn't much bigger than a garden shed: four corrugated-iron walls with a bright red door on the outside, and a tiny counter, a community noticeboard and a stand of postcards inside. Suresh is sitting behind the counter when I arrive on Friday morning, scrolling on his phone. He looks up as the bell on the door jingles and smiles.

"Morning, Isla."

"Morning." Between nerves and the fast bike ride down here, my heart is still thumping. I rush up to the desk and hand him the envelope with Holly's cutting. "Is there any way of getting this to Eilean Gorm today?"

Suresh shakes his head. "Other than going there yourself, no. The next post goes out on the eleven o'clock ferry but it won't be sorted until the afternoon. You can pay for next-day delivery if you want to be sure it arrives tomorrow morning, but that's the best I can offer. Sorry."

My heart sinks. "I'll do that then, please."

"Sure." Suresh weighs the envelope, then takes a stamp from a drawer under the counter and sticks it on the front. "That'll be one pound twenty-nine."

I reach into my coat pocket, take out the coins and hand them to Suresh. As he drops them into the till, I study him for a moment. He and Adhiti don't look much alike. His face is square where hers is round, and her eyes are bigger and darker, but they have the same kindness in their smiles. It makes it hard to picture him doing something as awful as sending Flora a virus.

Suresh catches me staring. "Everything OK, Isla?"

"Was it you?" I blurt out. "Are you the one who's been threatening Flora?"

"What? *Threatening* her? Of course not." Suresh's jaw tightens. "Why would I do something like that?"

"You've been acting so weird around her since she got back." My voice is trembling but I swallow the nerves and keep going. "She was so excited to see you again and you treat her like she was some acquaintance you barely knew."

"It's complicated, Isla." Suresh sighs. "There's the fact that I'm eighteen, and she's still fifteen. That's hard to get my head round."

"I get that. It was weird for me too. But it's been months now," I say. "Everyone else has got used to it. You could still be friends."

He walks out from behind the counter and goes to the window. For a moment he's silent, his hands in his pockets as he looks out to the quiet, rainy village.

"You did the interviews with Second Chances," he says, his gaze fixed on the horizon. "Did you really tell them everything you knew about Flora?"

"Yes," I say. As much as I could remember, anyway. All the things that mattered. "Didn't you?"

"I answered all their questions, but there was definitely stuff missing. Things that ... that I'd forgotten." He rubs his jaw. "I wasn't sure I could tell them what Flora was *really* like, anyway. We can only ever look at someone through our own eyes. Can anyone ever describe someone as they actually are, not just how we see them?"

The question catches me off guard. After Flora died, our memories of her seemed to shift. The way Mum and Dad talked about her, it was like she was the perfect daughter – as if she'd never answered back or fought with Ùna and me, never lied about homework or faked a headache to get out of chores. None of the bad stuff seemed so bad after she was gone, anyway. I even missed the things that used to irritate me so much – like how she used to leave smudged cotton pads all over the bathroom after taking off her make-up, and how she'd borrow my slippers and flatten the back part with her heel instead of putting them on properly.

So, when Second Chances asked me about the times we argued, the times she annoyed or upset me, I downplayed how they'd really made me feel. The opposite happened when I had to talk about the times I did something to upset her. I actually winced when I told the interviewers about the time I deliberately broke her favourite bottle of perfume to get back at her for not letting me borrow her laptop. Every little thing I did to hurt her was magnified.

"I did the best I could," I tell Suresh. "I tried to be honest."

"Me too. But I don't know if it's possible to really be objective," Suresh says, sitting back down behind the counter. "Even my parents or Adhiti… I could only describe the way they look to me, not the way they truly are. Obviously I'd get pretty close but I'd never be able to do it perfectly. That's impossible."

"What's your point?" I ask, feeling impatient now.

"Honestly, I don't even know." Suresh runs a hand through his hair and puffs out his cheeks. "But I'm not sure I knew Flora as well as I thought I did. She changed a lot, in the last few months especially."

"Well, yeah," I say. "She was really sick. She'd been told she was going to die. How could she not change?"

"I get that. My mum's going through chemo now, I know it's hard. But even so, Flora was different. She…" As he trails off, his eyes dart to the window again. "I just think it means something that of all the buildings that could have been vandalized, it was the church that the person picked."

"What do you mean?" The church? What does that have to do with all of this?

Suresh looks at me, a tight frown on his face. He seems to be grasping for the words, but then he shakes his head and looks back down at the till. "Nothing, nothing. Forget I said anything."

The bell on the door clings again. Seamus comes in with three parcels under his arm and raindrops falling from the brim of his hood. He lifts his hand in a wave to Suresh and smiles at me. "Oh, hello there, Isla. How are things? Flora doing OK?"

I nod and try to smile, as if everything is normal. "Fine, thanks, Seamus."

Seamus dumps the parcels on the counter and starts

asking about postage prices for different places. Knowing how talkative he is, it'll be half an hour before Suresh is done serving him. I need to get to school, so I mumble a goodbye and step outside.

None of this makes sense. Suresh was Flora's best friend. If someone asked me to help them recreate Murdo or Adhiti, I could do it. I'd tell them about the way Murdo's eyes light up when he talks about birds, or how he always hums under his breath when he gets lost in a daydream. I could tell them about how Adhiti always moves her ankles in clockwise loops when she's bored and how she always has three black hairbands around her wrists. I could do the same for the rest of my family too.

Suresh knew Flora. He did. And there's something he isn't telling me.

Flora's not home when I get back from school that afternoon. Mum tells me she went out on her bike an hour ago.

"I'm glad to see her out of the house, to be honest. She's been cooped up in her room for days." Mum puts down the knife she's been using to chop a tomato and pushes her hair out of her face. "I told her to be home for tea, though. It's the only time we see her right now."

But six o'clock comes and Flora's still not back. Anxiety settles in the pit of my stomach, heavy and unsettling. We sit at the table, waiting, watching Stephen circle the room snuffling up crumbs and dust and making snarky remarks about how lazy we are. At half past six, I send Adhiti a message. She says that Flora's not at her house and Suresh hasn't seen her, either. The unsettled feeling stretches like a shadow. At seven o'clock, Mum gets up to microwave the pasta that's been sitting cold for an hour.

"We'll start without her," she says. "Maybe she'll be back in time for pudding."

We're only a few bites in when the Returnee Health Hub starts beeping. Mum snatches it up from the windowsill. As a red warning sign flashes on to the screen, the colour drains from her face. "There's an emergency."

My heart begins to thud. Mum takes so long fumbling with the Health Hub that I grab it from her and hurriedly tap on the screen. It opens on a map of the island with a flashing red dot.

"She's at the harbour." I watch the cursor blinking but it doesn't budge. I can feel my pulse beating in my ears. "She's not moving. Mum, she's not moving!"

Mum snatches the Health Hub from me and runs out to the car, Ùna and I right after her. We're completely silent throughout the whole drive to the village. I can hear Ùna's breath behind me, as quick and shallow as my own. *Please let her be OK*, I chant to myself. *Please, please let her be OK.*

It's dark when we arrive at the village, the one street lamp by the harbour glowing in the mist. There's no sign of Flora at first, so Mum parks outside the post office and we all tumble out of the car and race across the road. When I look over the harbour wall, my breath catches in my throat.

Flora is lying face down on the sand, one leg bent backwards over the other. I hurry down the steps, rush over to her and flip her on to her back. Her eyes are open and flashing red.

"North star," Flora says in a monotone. "Sixteen litres of milk. Call Max and tell him about the weathervane."

I pull her into a sitting position. Mum arrives, puts her hands on Flora's face and begins babbling questions. The Health Hub is going nuts, beeping and blinking and flashing red. I take it from Mum and try to work out what damage has been done, what we need to do to fix it. Before I even touch anything, the noise disappears and a green circle with a white tick flashes on the screen. When I look back, Flora's eyes have returned to their usual grey-blue. She looks around like she's woken from a dream.

"I'm OK," she says. "I'm fine."

Mum lets out a long breath. "What happened, darling? Does anything hurt?"

Flora looks down at her legs. Her jeans are torn from the knee and there's a scrape against her skin but it doesn't look quite right. The mark is too red, so red it seems fake. Ùna brushes Flora's hair out of her face and zips up her jacket against the cold.

"I'm fine," Flora says again. Her voice is completely calm. "It hurts, but not too bad."

"What happened?" Ùna asks.

"I don't know. I was walking along the wall, then all of a sudden I was lying on the sand."

Flora twists round to look up at the harbour wall. When the tide is out like it is tonight, the drop is two and a half metres at least. She turns back to look at us and swallows. "I think someone pushed me."

Thirty

I hardly sleep that night. Every time I doze off, I dream of shadowy figures lurking by the harbour, Flora hitting the wet sand with a thud, her red eyes shining in the darkness. Each time I wake up shaking, knowing that if Flora had fallen into the water, it would have damaged her systems beyond repair. This was more than a joke or a threat, worse even than the virus. This was a real attack. Someone tried to destroy her.

I'm too tired to go to Eilean Gorm the next day, and I don't sleep any better the following few nights. Eventually I start getting up to bake to take my mind off things. On Tuesday I make Florentines and on Wednesday a blackberry drizzle cake. Thursday is cinnamon rolls then raspberry financiers on Friday. There's so much that I have to take most of it into school for the others to finish, and I spend all of my pocket money on sugar and butter, but it's the only way I can zone out and forget. On Saturday, Mum comes downstairs and finds me making ganache for chocolate tarts.

"Isla? What are you doing?" She squints at the clock on the wall. "It's six o'clock in the morning!"

Outside, the sky is pitch-black. The kitchen is scattered with mixing bowls and baking trays, plus a stack of plastic containers filled with the leftovers of this week's baking. This isn't normal. None of this is normal.

"There's something I haven't told you," I blurt out. "Something about Flora."

Worry flashes in Mum's eyes. She sighs and runs a hand through her hair. She hasn't been sleeping well, either. "How about we go for a drive, just the two of us?" She grabs her keys from the bowl on top of the fridge and tosses them to me. "Here, turn the heater on to warm the car up. I'm going to make some coffee. I'll be out in five minutes."

I wipe a smear of chocolate off my arm, throw my big coat on over my pyjamas and pad out to the car in my slipper socks. A few minutes later, Mum comes outside wearing her thick winter jacket and carrying two flasks. She passes one to me as she climbs into the driver's seat. "Put on some music and have some hot chocolate. We're going on a mini road trip."

"But, Mum, I really need to talk to you about—"

"If you've waited this long, another twenty minutes won't hurt." She pulls her seat belt across herself. "How about we go up the long road past Seamus's and watch the sunrise?"

Gritting my teeth in frustration, I scroll through her phone and pick her 90s playlist, the one she puts on when she's in a good mood. Mum takes a big gulp of coffee from her own flask and turns the key in the ignition. The car groans and wheezes, like it always does, but after two or three tries Mum finally manages to get it going.

Back in the Before, Mum and Dad used to love going for drives around the island. They'd blast old music from their uni days and sing so loud I was sure half of Eilean Dearg must have been able to hear them. The three of us would sit in the back seat, sometimes singing along with them, sometimes squabbling or staring out of the window. I liked watching raindrops race down the glass on wet days, the moon chase after the car on clear nights. All we could do was loop around the island, but that didn't matter. It felt like we could have kept going forever.

That stopped when Flora died. Although Mum or Dad would sometimes ask Ùna and I if we wanted to go for a drive, I'd always say no. The gap that Flora had left was obvious enough at home. It felt even more intense in their small, cramped cars.

I can feel that gap now, hovering around us like a ghost. I don't want to go back to those days.

We arrive at the north-east cliffs of the island as Björk turns to Céline Dion on the playlist. There's a hint of orange above the horizon and the stars are beginning to melt into the dawn sky. I turn the music off, unclip my seat belt and twist round to face Mum. "OK, you're going to be mad about this, but—"

Mum holds up a hand. "Hang on. I want to talk about you first." She settles back in her seat. "How's football going? Did Holly like the paper cutting you sent her?"

Of all the times for chit-chat. It's been ages since I had any one-to-one time with Mum. Normally I'd love an early morning drive with hot chocolate, just the two of us, but not when I've got all this on my mind. I grit my teeth and slump back against the seat.

"Holly's not talking to me. She said thanks for the cutting but she hasn't replied to me since then," I say, trying not to sound as upset as I feel about it.

"I'm sure she'll come around, love," Mum says, blowing on her coffee. "It's no wonder you forgot her birthday, what with everything that's been going lately."

"She doesn't know that, though." I sigh and kick my feet up on the dashboard. "Anyway, can we talk about Flora? It's important."

It all comes out in a gush of words: the red envelope, my investigation, my botched interview with Finley and the fact that he suspects Suresh. And even though I promised I wouldn't, I tell her about Flora's new abilities. Mum's eyebrows shoot up in shock at that but she doesn't interrupt.

"So, you think that's why Flora got the virus?" she asks when I'm finished. "Because she's been interfering with her programming?"

"No. I think it affected her worse than it should have done because of that. But the reason she got it in the first place was because someone put it there on purpose," I say. "That's why I keep saying we have to tell Marisa. She's a good person, Mum. She'll want to do what she can to keep Flora safe."

But Mum shakes her head. "It's too much of a risk, Isla. Flora's already broken so many rules. More than I knew." She looks out of the window. The world is still fast asleep, the only lights the stars and a far-off twinkle on Eilean Gorm. "If they haven't noticed anything is wrong yet, Flora must be able to cover her tracks somehow. I don't want to give them another reason to think the trial isn't working."

"But the threats are affecting Flora really badly! She's won't have meals with us any more, she's not going to school. She keeps saying she doesn't care but they're pushing her away from us."

Mum is quiet for a long moment, one finger tracing the rim of her flask. "The thing is, Isla... Flora is still property of Second Chances. They can take her away from us at any time, for any reason. And if they do, they can do whatever they want with her."

For a moment, I'm sure my heart has stopped.

"What?" I splutter. "They can't do that. She's a person!"

"Legally, she's not. As far as the contract is concerned, she's a machine. One of their machines. They can change her in any way they like."

My head is reeling. I thought Flora was only at risk if the trial failed. I didn't know that the company could end all of this – end her – so easily. I didn't realize she *belonged* to Second Chances.

"What do you mean, change her?" My fingers tighten around my flask. "What sort of changes?"

"Most likely, they'd delete the data that makes her Flora and turn her into some simple robot assistant for chores and housework," Mum says, not meeting my eye. "Or they ... they could get rid of her altogether."

I can hardy speak. All this time I've been scared that Second Chances would take Flora away from us again but I didn't really think about what would happen if they did. I picture her with her personality stripped away: dull eyes and stiff limbs, something no more human than Stephen. It sends shivers down my spine.

"So, that's why you didn't want to tell Marisa about

what's been going on?"

Mum nods. "I was worried that if they thought the community was a hostile environment, they might cancel the trial and recall Flora."

Recall. That's the word manufacturers use when a product is faulty or dangerous and they need customers to return it. As if Flora were no different from a badly made gadget or a damaged toy – a thing to be examined and tested and thrown on the scrap heap if found to be not up to scratch.

Outside, the sun's orange glow begins to bleed slowly into morning. I pull my legs to my chest, rest my chin on my knees and watch birds flit past the car, worries swarming around my head.

"I came up here the morning Flora passed away," Mum says suddenly. "I hadn't left the house for days and I needed some air. I checked on her then drove up here and watched the sunrise on my own. I wasn't even away for an hour but when I came back, your dad told me she was gone. The only time I left her in all those weeks and that was the moment it happened."

The words reach inside my chest and squeeze my heart hard. Mum never told me that before. "It wasn't your fault," I say, but her eyes have gone all misty, the way they always do when she gets lost in her memories.

"I should have seen it coming but I was distracted." She wipes her eyes on her sleeves. "I spent all those months researching alternative treatments, looking for hope where there was none. It's what I had to do, I would have regretted it if we hadn't exhausted all our options. But I wish I'd just *been* with her more. I wish I'd sat and talked to her more, listened to her. I'd do anything to change that."

I tilt my head so it rests on her shoulder. "Well, we have her back now," I say, though I'm scared it might not be for much longer.

"Yes, we do. But now, when I think about the past three years, I realize I missed a lot of time with you and Ùna. I'm sorry, Isla." She lays her head on top of mine. "And I'm sorry that I didn't talk to you about the trial before I got in touch with Second Chances."

"It's all right." I take another sip of my now lukewarm chocolate and swill it around in my mouth. "You know, it was me who signed you up for that support group. Homeward Healing."

Mum sits up to look at me. "It was? Why did you do that?"

"I thought it might help. You were always so sad, and you seemed so … stuck. I wanted us to move forward." I swallow. "But then I felt guilty for even *wanting* to move forward without Flora."

I'd always thought grief was a pit that you slowly climbed out of but Flora's death showed me it's more like an endless game of snakes and ladders. You can be sent back to square one at any moment and there's no telling how long you might get stuck there. There's no getting over something like that. All I wanted was for us to be able to accept it. That was impossible when Mum wouldn't – couldn't – say goodbye.

"Oh, Isla. You shouldn't feel like that, love. I never wanted for you to feel like that. Flora wouldn't, either." Mum puts her hand on my cheek and kisses the top of my hair. "Why didn't you tell me all of this?"

"Because that's how Second Chances found us, and that's what made Dad move out." My eyes start to sting. "It felt like it was all my fault."

"Of course it wasn't, Isles. That was his decision." She sits back in her seat with a sigh. "He always said we'd never get everyone on the island to accept the new Flora, even if they did sign up. Maybe he was right."

"I really think it's Suresh," I say. "I'll keep investigating. Someone's bound to know something."

"No, Isla," Mum says sharply. "Suresh is like family to Flora, he wouldn't do something like that. I don't want you going around accusing people and upsetting them. So, no more detective work, OK?"

"But, Mum—" I start to argue, but Mum cuts me off with a firm shake of her head. "What are we going to do then, if we can't tell Marisa?" I ask instead.

"I don't know." Mum rubs her face with her hands. "I'll speak to Flora about these changes she's been making to her system. That has to stop. Other than that... I think we'll have to hope that whoever's sending these messages gets bored eventually."

I grit my teeth in frustration. Mum's been saying the same thing since the computer was left on our doorstep. I don't know why she thinks this person is going to leave us alone – it's been months now, and they even went as far as trying to push Flora into the sea. They're not going to give up.

But neither will I. Especially not now I know that Second Chances can snatch Flora back at any moment. That just makes me more determined than ever to find out who's behind this, no matter what Mum says.

We drive home with the music off, both lost in our thoughts. Morning has properly arrived by the time we pass through the village. Davey is opening up the wee shop and the light is on in the post office. Reverend Jack is outside the church, looking towards the sea, and Annie—

Wait.

Reverend Jack.

Like a lightning bolt, I remember what Suresh said about the church. If there's anyone on the island who might know what he meant, it'll be the minister. That's who I have to talk to next.

Thirty-one

I cycle down to the church before Reverend Jack's service starts the next morning. The familiar smell hits me as soon as I push open the creaky wooden door: cold stone and musty books, though now there's a hint of charred wood behind it.

Reverend Jack is already inside. I thought he'd be busy getting ready for the service but instead he sits on the first pew, his back to the door. A rush of fear hits me and for a moment I think about turning round, hopping back on my bike and going home again. What if Reverend Jack tells Mum about this? I'm not supposed to be investigating at all any more. She'd hit the roof if she knew I was sneaking around questioning the minister, of all people.

But that's when I notice someone sitting on the pew beside him.

"Suresh? What are you doing here?"

At the sound of my voice, both Suresh and Reverend Jack spin round. Suresh's eyes are wide and startled but the minister looks worried. He stands up and takes a step towards me. "Is everything all right, Isla?"

"Yes. No. I'm not sure." My hands have gone clammy. I wipe them on my jeans and turn to Suresh, who is following Reverend Jack towards the door. "What's going on?"

"Suresh popped in to talk to me about something." The minister smiles at me and gestures to the pew. "Why don't you have a seat and we'll—"

"Why?" My eyes flit from Reverend Jack to Suresh and back as I try to work it out. "Were you the ones who left that message on the wall? Did you do it together?"

"No, Isla, no." Suresh shakes his head. "It's not like that."

"Well, *somebody* did." Frustration sizzles up inside me and sends the words rushing out, all blending together in their hurry to leave my mouth. "Somebody has been sending Flora those messages and they pushed her off the harbour wall, and I can't think why either of you would do that but it was *someone*. Somebody on this island is trying to hurt her, and I need to find out who before it's too late and we lose her all over again."

My face feels hot and my eyes are stinging. I'm so tired of all the worry, all the doubt. I just need to know.

Reverend Jack gives my arm a gentle pat. "Let's have a cup of tea. I've got some biscuits too, if you fancy."

My stomach growls before I can answer – I was too nervous to eat breakfast this morning. "OK," I mumble. "Yes, please."

Reverend Jack goes off to make the tea and I sit down on a pew. Suresh takes the one in front and twists round to face me. "What was that about someone pushing Flora? Is she OK?"

"Mostly." I press my knees together to try to stop them jittering up and down with cold and nerves. "She's been acting strange for weeks now, and that hasn't helped."

"It wasn't me," Suresh says. "I swear, Isla. I would never do that."

His voice sounds sincere but I just don't know who to trust any more. Somebody must be lying. Reverend Jack comes back a moment later carrying a tray with three mugs of the world's weakest tea and a packet of biscuits under his arm. He hands Suresh and me a mug each and sits down beside me.

"I'm sorry I haven't come to see your family lately," he says. "I've been meaning to call and check in on you, but… Well, honestly, I find the trial quite hard to get my head round. That's no excuse, though. I certainly would have come if I'd known someone had attacked Flora. Is she all right?"

"She's fine." I study the minister's face as I sip my tea. It's a kind face, with deep smile lines around his pale blue eyes. "So, it really wasn't you?"

"That's actually what I came to ask too," Suresh says. "I thought Reverend Jack might have written the message on the wall, but I was wrong."

The minister shakes his head. "No, I had nothing to do with it. I wouldn't vandalize a holy building, for one thing. But I also wouldn't want to hurt Flora."

"I'm sorry. I didn't really think you would." I look at Suresh. "But why did you think that?"

Suresh opens his mouth to answer, but Reverend Jack puts a hand out to stop him. "I'm not sure it'll do much good to tell you the story, Isla. It was a long time ago now."

"Please." I lean towards him and send some tea slopping over the side of my mug. "I have to find out why this is happening. This is Eilean Dearg. We're supposed to be safe here. I need to know who's doing this."

The minister looks into his teacup, one leathery finger tracing the handle. He's quiet for such a long time, I start to wonder if he's praying. When he speaks, it's in a low, sorry voice.

"I thought it might…" He breaks off and runs a hand through his thin hair. Reverend Jack speaks quickly and smoothly when he does his sermons, but now he can't seem to find the words. "It could be because, well…"

"Because Flora was the one who started the fire," Suresh finishes.

A slow winter moves through my body, freezing every part of me. I must have heard him wrong. There's been some horrible mistake. Flora couldn't have done that. There's no way.

But the minister nods sadly. "Someone told me they saw Flora at the church that night." He glances at the door, checking we're still alone. "And I didn't know until now but Suresh knew she'd gone there too."

"She sent me a message a few hours before the fire broke out," Suresh says. "She asked me to meet her at the church, said she was going to cycle down there herself. I thought she might be confused – you remember how those drugs made her. Besides, she was so weak, I didn't think she'd get much further than your garden. But she kept insisting, so eventually I gave in."

In a slow, halting voice, he tells me about how he snuck out at eleven o'clock to go and meet Flora. How the smell of burning drifted up to meet him as he pedalled up the hill leading to the village. And how, when he reached the top, he looked down and saw something that almost made him fall off his bike with fear – the church, engulfed in a bright, crackling blaze.

"It was like I went into shock. The smoke was already so thick and even from up on the hill I could feel the heat of the flames." He shudders, reliving the memory. "The MacGregors were already outside, and Annie and Georgie Campbell, all watching it burn. It was surreal."

I stand up and pace between the pews. My legs are like jelly and I feel sick. I try to picture Flora at her weakest, setting a fire and watching it burn, but it seems as ridiculous as imagining her tightrope walking or doing backflips. Nothing about the image rings true.

"That can't be right," I say, shaking my head. "Flora was so ill, and she wouldn't do something like that. Neither of you actually saw her in the church, did you?"

"No, but someone else saw her leaving it. And I found something in the ashes a few days later." Reverend Jack reaches into his pocket. "I actually brought it with me today. When Suresh asked to meet me, I had a feeling it might be about this."

The minister holds something up that makes my stomach flip – a delicate gold necklace with a pendant shaped like a leaf and engraved with a cursive letter F. I take it from him with trembling fingers. Flora's lost necklace. All those hours Mum spent looking for it and it's been with Reverend Jack the whole time.

"Why didn't you say something?" I ask, my voice tight.

"For if ye forgive men their trespasses, your heavenly

Father will also forgive you." Reverend Jack smiles sadly. "Matthew, 6:14. Forgiveness is important."

"But you didn't tell anyone. Not the police or the fire brigade. No one."

"We decided that no good could come from it. Flora was sick, she wasn't herself. I wouldn't want any charges pressed against her." The minister takes a sip of tea. "I also didn't want to add to your parents' stress. They were going through enough as it was without adding that to the mix."

There's a light thump as I sit back down on the pew. Suresh swirls the remains of his tea in one hand, his eyes fixed on the whirlpool in the cup.

"Is this why you've been acting so weird around her?" I ask him.

He nods. "I've really tried not to be but it's too hard, knowing this huge thing about her that she has no memory of. And I felt guilty too. None of this would have happened if I'd phoned your parents and told them she was planning on going out alone, but I didn't want her to hate me for it."

"You were fifteen, Suresh," Reverend Jack says. "You were trying to be a good friend. Give yourself some grace."

"Who was the person who saw her there?" I ask, turning back to the minister.

Reverend Jack hesitates, then shakes his head. "That doesn't matter, Isla. Like I said, it was a long time ago now. I don't want to create any bad feeling on the island."

"But that might be who's hurting Flora!"

"I don't understand why they would do that. I'll speak

to them and find out what's going on, though," Reverend Jack says. "And I'll make it clear that if anything else happens, I'll go to Second Chances myself."

After all these weeks searching for the person behind the messages, it's frustrating to come so close to the truth and have it snatched away from me. I turn the necklace in my hands, letting the thin chain slip between my fingers. When I press my thumb into the pendant, it leaves a reversed F imprinted on my skin.

"Flora wouldn't do that," I say again, though less firmly this time. "That's not who she was. You know it's not."

"No, it wasn't. But people do strange things when they're hurt or afraid," Reverend Jack says. "Things that are out of character. Things that can harm others, whether they mean to or not."

I've seen stories online about inspirational cancer patients. Talk of bravery and fighting and positive attitudes, as if the illness was the bad guy in a computer game that could be beaten with enough practice, and not a question of genes and medicine and luck. Flora wasn't like that. She was scared. She'd shout sometimes, cry and break things. She knew she'd been dealt a horrible hand and she couldn't accept it. Why should she? It was all so, so unfair.

"I suppose she was different in the last few months," I say, turning the necklace in my hand. "She was angry, when she had the energy to be angry."

"She wasn't herself," Suresh says, nodding. "That fire could so easily have been a tragedy – the Flora I was friends with wouldn't put people's lives at risk like that. But she was going through something so awful, it's not

226

surprising it changed her."

"Maybe it gave her a sense of power, when she felt so powerless." The minister puts his hand on my shoulder and gives it a light squeeze. "Anyway, it's done now. What matters is that no one was badly hurt."

Despite the positivity in his words, his voice is sad. The church has been here for over a century; it's seen so many of the island's weddings, christenings and funerals. Even if the building hadn't been completely destroyed, it felt like all that history had gone up in flames. It must have been a hundred times more painful for Reverend Jack and yet he kept quiet all this time.

"I'm telling you this because I don't want you to think I might have hurt Flora, or that Suresh did, either. We both care about her. About all of you." Reverend Jack's eyes meet mine. "I'll do my best to find out who's behind this and make it stop. You concentrate on being there for Flora."

"OK." I look away as another wave of tears wells up. "Thank you."

Suresh offers me the sleeve of his hoodie. I take off my glasses and wipe my eyes on it, laughing lightly, then finish my cold cup of tea and leave before the few people who still attend Reverend Jack's service come trickling in. Before I get back on to my bike, I take another look at the necklace. I could tell Flora that I found it down the side of my bed or in the back of a cupboard. But it's not just a souvenir of my sister any more. It's a piece of evidence from a crime scene. A crime that Flora committed.

So, I go to the harbour wall and fling it straight into the sea.

Thirty-two

I always thought secrets spread far and fast on Eilean Dearg. I thought they grew like weeds, cropping up in unexpected corners, tangling round ankles and dragging people into drama even if they tried to avoid it. But the secret about Flora and the fire has barely moved at all. It took three whole years to get to me, and from the sounds of things I'm still only one of a handful of people who know about it.

When I get home from the church, I realize I don't want it to go any further. Mum is playing Bananagrams with Ùna while Sìth sits in her lap, and Flora is doodling incredibly detailed boats and aeroplanes on the corner of the newspaper. It feels like the past week has been nothing but panic and stress. This is a perfect little slice of normal. I don't want to ruin it.

But more than that, I don't want Mum and Ùna to have to wonder if the Flora we remember was capable of burning down a building, like I am now. I don't want Murdo and Adhiti to know and think less of her. I don't even want to tell Flora. She's already floating further and further away from herself. Something like this could push her out to sea altogether.

But I can't make it disappear. The scene that Suresh described whirls around my head all day. I imagine Flora going to the church, flicking a lighter open… I see her cycling home on weak legs, stopping to push when it got too hard. I picture her watching the church burn from the top of the hill and doing nothing to help or warn anyone. I try to remember how she acted when Dad told us about the fire, if there was a hint of guilt that I might have missed, but the memory of those days is hazy. There was so much going on at home, the fire was just a blurry detail in the background.

A week trickles by, and then another, and I can't get the images out of my mind. I stop going to football. I stop going to visit Dad on Saturdays and pretend I don't hear the hurt in his voice when he calls to ask me why. At school I'm quiet and grumpy, and it makes the atmosphere in the classroom tense. As we're gathering up our stuff to leave one Friday afternoon in November, Murdo clears his throat.

"I was thinking we could have a bonfire on the beach tonight," he says. "All of us. Flora too, if she wants to come."

His eyes are bright and hopeful. Murdo can't stand bad atmospheres, so this has been torture for him. I feel a stab of guilt. He and Adhiti have worked really hard to cheer me up – they're always sending me videos and memes to try to make me laugh – but I've been too distracted to pay much attention. So, this time, I nod.

"Good idea." I smile. It hurts the muscles in my cheeks, like I've forgotten how to do it properly. "I'll ask Flora."

"Great. We should all be there. All six of us." Adhiti shoulders her bag and points at Georgie. "You too,

Campbell. No excuses this time."

Georgie looks up from her computer. "But I've got to go to Eilean Gorm for a piano lesson tomorrow morning!"

"So? If we meet at seven, you can be home before nine."

Adhiti starts poking her lightly in the ribs, and Murdo and Finley chant "come on, come on, come on" over and over until a reluctant smile tugs at Georgie's lips. She eventually shakes her head and laughs. "Fine, fine! I'll see you there."

As usual, Flora is in her bedroom when I get home. I do my "Seven Nation Army" knock but this time I wait for her to answer before I go in. We never used to do that. We were always barging into each other's rooms to find pens or books that the other one had nicked or to show each other something funny we'd found online, before everything changed.

"Yeah?" Flora shouts. I open the door and see her sitting cross-legged on her bed with her laptop in front of her. She glances up at me. "Oh, hey. Did you need something?"

"Uh, no." I lean against the doorframe. "We were thinking we might have a bonfire on the north-west beach tonight. Murdo, Adhiti and the others. They were wondering if you wanted to come."

"That sounds fun." She keeps typing. I linger in the doorway, waiting for an answer. When Flora looks up again, she seems surprised I'm there. She closes the laptop and pats the bed. "Come in and sit for a second. I've hardly seen you this week. What am I missing at school?"

"Not much." I perch on the edge of her bed. "Finley's finally stopped going on about his documentary now that you're not there."

"Poor Finley. I'm sure he'll get his shot at stardom." Flora leans back against her pillows and stretches her legs out. "And how's everything going with Holly?"

My heart gives a twinge at the sound of her name. "It's not."

It feels like a lifetime since I spoke to Holly. I miss waking up and finding photos of Oakley or my horoscope on my phone. I miss her weird would-you-rather questions. I miss *her*, but it's probably best we're not talking any more. My head is still full of fire. There's not much room for anything else.

"Why don't you do something about it then?" Flora asks, tapping me on the knee. "Just talk to her, Isla."

I shake my head. "It's not that simple. There's so much going on at home and I can't tell her about any of it. It's too weird."

Flora sighs. "Well, Project Homecoming won't be a secret forever. You'll be able to tell her the truth one day."

There's a whirring sound as Stephen arrives in Flora's bedroom. Last week Ùna found a packet of stick-on earrings that she used to use when she was little in a drawer and decided they could zhuzh Stephen up a bit. His top is now covered in swirls of colourful gems with a sparkly S in the middle. Maybe it's my imagination but I could swear he's been even grumpier since then.

"Hey, Stephen," I say, waving to him. "What you up to?"

"I'm painting the Sistine Chapel," he says crankily.

"Honestly, what does it look like?"

Flora laughs. As he bustles around her room, Mum shouts up the stairs that dinner's ready. I get up, but instead of coming with me, Flora reaches for her laptop. The screen is open on a photo of a woman I don't recognize. She's around forty with light brown skin, long black hair and a heart-shaped smile. Flora clicks another tab and the image disappears.

"I'm going to give the bonfire a miss," she says. "Thanks for the invite, though."

"But we're all going to be there – even Georgie's coming," I say. "They all want to see you."

"No, thanks. I've got stuff to do. Next time."

"What stuff?" I ask, throwing my hands up. "You're not even going to school any more, how can you be that busy? And who's that woman you're looking at?"

"It's none of your business, Isla. Leave me alone, OK?"

Stephen bumps into my foot, snapping at me to let him do his job and making a huffy circle around me. I step over him and head for the door, my eyes stinging at Flora's sharp tone. When she calls after me, her voice is softer.

"Hey, Lala?"

I turn round. She's looking at me with a strange expression, one I don't know how to read. She gets up and gives me a hug. "Sorry," she says. "And thanks. I know you've tried your best to find out what's going on with these messages, and I know it's because you really want the trial to work. I do appreciate it. I want you to know that whatever happens, it won't be because you didn't try hard enough."

"What do you mean, 'whatever happens'?" I ask with an uncomfortable kick of nerves in my stomach. "What's going to happen?"

"Nothing." She waves me off and turns away, back to the computer and her secrets. "Have fun tonight. Say hi to everybody for me. Tell them I'm sorry."

Thirty-three

The sun sets early here in winter and when I reach the beach that evening the sky is already deep black and filled with stars. Murdo is kneeling to poke at the small but crackling bonfire with a stick, and Adhiti is half dancing to music playing from her speakers as she toasts a marshmallow over the embers. Finley is filming and talking into his phone, as usual, and Georgie is sitting on a rock with her arms wrapped round her legs, looking out to sea.

"Hey." I sling my bag from my shoulder and take out a container. "I made those oat and raisin cookies that you guys like."

"Nice! Thanks, Isla." Murdo sits back in the sand. "Flora didn't come with you?"

"Nah. Says she's too busy."

"Seriously?" Adhiti tuts. "Sounds like she's constantly coding these days. She needs a break."

Finley pockets his phone and reaches for my box of cookies. "Working on what? What's she even doing now she's finished with school?"

"I don't know." I look at Adhiti. "Do you?"

She shakes her head and blows on her marshmallow.

"No idea. I doubt I'd understand it, even if she did tell me. She knows much more about programming than I do now."

Finley sighs. "I was hoping she might finally give me an interview tonight. Seeing as you *still* haven't done yours," he adds, narrowing his eyes at me.

"Well, I did ask her to come but she said no," I snap. "I'm not her boss. Sorry."

My voice comes out so defensive, everyone turns to stare at me. Adhiti looks nervous and Murdo's face is filled with dread. They've tried so hard to cheer me up the past couple of weeks, I don't want to ruin the vibe here too. I take a deep breath and let it out slowly.

"Sorry, it's just…" I trail off. "Can we talk about something else? I feel like all I ever talk about is the trial."

Georgie takes another marshmallow from the packet, pops it on a chopstick and hands it to me. "Good idea."

A song by Taylor Swift starts to play from Adhiti's speakers. She grabs both of my hands and pulls me to my feet. "Let's dance. Taylor will help take your mind off things."

"You know I'm a rubbish dancer," I start to protest but Adhiti won't listen.

"Then let's do a bad dance contest." She starts sidestepping and pushing her fists back and forth in front of her. "I call this move 'Rolling Pastry'. Your turn."

Laughing, I awkwardly shuffle and spin my hands in circles, miming washing dishes. Murdo leaps from side to side, bends his right arm and pulls it back and forth like he's opening and closing the fridge door. Even Georgie gets up and joins in, twisting her hand above her head like she's changing a light bulb. The moves get more and more ridiculous, and soon we're all laughing more than dancing. Finley films the entire thing on his phone, so no doubt it'll end up on Sekkon for the entire world to see. I don't mind. It feels good not to think for a change.

When the song ends, we sit on the sand, open the box of biscuits and toast more marshmallows over the bonfire. I'm struck with a sudden blast of fondness for them all. One day we'll grow up and leave Eilean Dearg, as almost everyone does. Only some of us will come back to this island for good but we'll forever be connected by this place. We've grown up running over the same rough hills and white sands. We have the same sea air in our lungs. That means something.

But as the evening goes on, a dark thought glides over my happiness. What if I never find out who's been sending Flora the messages? Am I going to wonder who it was every time I see one of these people for the rest of my life? I don't want the doubt niggling at me forever, a splinter that I can never fully remove.

I try to push the questions away, but soon they're all I can focus on. While the others are talking about what Christmas presents they're going to ask for, I stare at the fire and think about my orange journal. Adhiti's name was the first I struck off from the list. Everyone else I considered carefully but I barely even thought about if or why she might have sent the messages. I didn't think I had to.

Maybe I was wrong. Maybe she lied when she said she didn't know what Flora was working on. Maybe Adhiti hasn't been helping my sister, but hurting her. Or maybe

Suresh has been covering for her all this time.

I don't know. But it seems like I have more questions for my best friend than I thought.

"Let's play a game," I say, shifting on to my knees. "How about Truth or Dare?"

Finley grins at me over the fire. "OK. Can I start? I want a dare."

"I've got one!" Adhiti points at the sea. "Go and paddle in the water for thirty seconds."

That wouldn't be much of a dare somewhere like Australia or Bali, but in Scotland in November, that's like plunging into a swimming pool of ice cubes. Groaning, Finley pulls off his shoes and socks and runs towards the water. He screeches as the first wave rolls over his feet then splashes around screaming while the rest of us count down from thirty. The second we shout zero, he races back to the fire.

"If I get frostbite and lose my toes, I'm blaming you, Adhiti." Shivering, he leans back and lifts his bare feet up to the flames. "Murdo next. Truth or dare?"

Murdo picks a dare too. Finley tells him to eat some seaweed, but it barely touches his tongue before he gags and spits it out again. Georgie is next and goes for truth. Murdo asks if Georgie would rather be the most amazing violinist in history, but only be able to eat tripe for the rest of her life, or eat whatever she liked and never play music again. Georgie goes for violin and tripe, but she looks a bit sick as she admits it. I'm next.

"Dare," I say.

Georgie dares me to let everyone go through the internet history on my phone for one minute. The idea makes me cringe but luckily there's nothing too embarrassing except a few searches about a weird rash I had on my finger last week. Finley laughs at me for googling *are watermelons berries*, but shuts up when I inform him that they actually are.

After that, it's my turn to ask Adhiti. She asks for a truth, just like I knew she would. My heart is pounding and I feel sick, but I force out the words before I can change my mind. "Were you the one sending those messages to Flora?"

Adhiti's face falls. "What? What are you talking about? Why would I do that?"

"I don't know. You were the one fiddling with her programming. She's been having technical issues ever since," I say, my voice shaking. "Maybe you weren't helping her at all. Maybe you were tampering with her on purpose."

"*Tampering?* She wanted me to help her find out how to do that! It was all her idea, not mine." Adhiti holds up her hands. Her eyes are glossy in the light of the fire. "I would never hurt Flora. She's my friend too."

"Come on, Isla," Finley says, rolling his eyes. "This is getting ridiculous. It obviously wasn't Adhiti."

"You've blown this all out of proportion. That thing with the envelope could have been a misunderstanding," Georgie says. She's not shouting, but her voice is sharper than her usual soft tone. "And the virus... That was probably an accident. I bet none of this is as bad as you think it is."

"Georgie's right," Murdo says, and his voice is so loud and angry and un-Murdo-like that it makes me jump.

"How many times do we have to tell you it wasn't us?"

"Fine, fine," I say. "Sorry I brought it up."

My eyes feel hot behind my glasses. They're making me feel like the bad guy but I'm not the one who's been causing trouble here. I just want to know who's trying to hurt Flora. Murdo and Georgie see I'm upset and jump in to find another truth for Adhiti. While they're debating, something starts to niggle at the back of my head. It's like the feeling you get when you go away on a trip and know you've left something behind. I've missed something. Something obvious.

"Isla!"

Finley is clutching his phone in both hands and staring at the screen. He rushes over to me, drops to his knees on the sand and passes me the phone. The image on the screen makes my heart leap: Flora, sitting in her bedroom, with the words *Project Homecoming* written underneath.

"What is this?" I mumble, but deep down I already know.

Hands shaking, I tap to play the video. Flora is wearing a blue-and-white striped top with her hair in a neat plait and smiling calmly at the camera.

"My name is Flora MacAulay," she says. "I live on an island called Eilean Dearg off the west coast of Scotland. A few of you might recognize me. I used to post here on Sekkon a lot until I got sick a few years ago."

The video cuts to a few clips of her old videos – dancing in her bedroom, posing with Sìth curled around her neck like a scarf, giving a teary update to her followers after she got her diagnosis.

"Unfortunately, I didn't get better. I died. But then

I was recreated by a company called Second Chances." The video flicks back to her bedroom and the present. Flora gives a wry grin. "I know a lot of you will think this is a joke or a hoax. I would too. But I promise, this is a true story."

Using diagrams and footage from the Second Chances training modules, she describes how the company brings returnees back to life, how she woke up in California and was informed she had died three years earlier. The video then shows her own homecoming – stepping off the boat, walking into school on our first day, the graffiti left on the church.

"Second Chances have produced multiple returnees like me. They need to be based on people with years of online data to help rebuild their interests, memories and personalities," Flora says, as a montage of strangers around the world plays on the screen. "As far as I know, they're always Sekkon users – Second Chances and Sekkon are owned by the same parent company."

Adhiti turns to Finley. "Did you know that?"

He shakes his head. That's when I notice the username at the top of the screen: finleyggraham.

"*You* posted this?" I gasp.

"No! I swear," Finley splutters. "I mean, yeah, some of that is my footage, but I didn't film that interview of Flora and I didn't upload anything. I swear, Isla, I didn't."

There are so many things I want to say but they stick in my throat. I can't trust him. I can't trust anyone. Not even Flora. The video cuts back to her in her bedroom, the bedroom where I asked her what she was working on a few hours ago. The bedroom where she lied to me and said it was nothing.

"I understand why my family chose to bring me back," Flora says. "But this isn't the life I've been built to remember. I'm not allowed to leave my island. I'm not allowed to contact my old friends. I'm also not supposed to use my abilities as a machine, even though that's what I am. I am a machine."

Twisting in her chair, she lifts her hair to expose the port on the back of her neck. She moves from side to side to show it from all angles, trying to prove it's real and not just clever special effects. I've always hated hearing Flora say she's just a machine but seeing it on screen makes it hard to deny that this is the reality. Flora is chips and bolts and wires. And now it's online for the entire world to see.

When she turns back to the camera, her eyes are steely.

"This is a half life, an in-between life," she says. "We returnees may not be human but we are people. And we deserve better."

As the video ends, dozens of comments scroll up on to the screen.

This is so weird, I remember this girl…

Pretty sick if it's a joke

Wow! I mean obviously fake but the way you've done that is amazing, they should hire you to do special effects on films

Finley is still babbling that he has no idea how the video got on to his account. Adhiti tells him to be quiet and Murdo asks me if I'm OK. But all I can see are the numbers of views on the bottom corner of the screen. Hundreds and then thousands, spiralling up, up, up and out of control, and taking the trial with them.

PROJECT HOMECOMING:
A GUIDE FOR FAMILIES

Module 18: The Future

Project Homecoming is currently being trialled in
several remote locations around the world.
This allows Second Chances to assess how returnees
integrate into their families and local communities under
the best possible conditions, without interference from
the general public or press. As such, and to ensure
the trial's confidentiality, communication between
returnees is currently not allowed.

We understand this can feel lonely for returnees but
it will not always be the case. At Second Chances,
we strive to create a world where a large returnee
population will eventually live freely and openly, with
all the same rights and responsibilities as their human
friends and neighbours.

While we encourage current returnees to look forward
to that day, it may not become reality for a very long
time. It's far more important that they focus on building
a happy life with their family and community in the here
and now, rather than fixating on a far-off future or the
possibility of meeting other returnees.

These restrictions may seem unfair, but please trust
that Second Chances is working only in the very best
interests of our participants. We always do.

Thirty-four

I've never cycled across the island so fast. The video is already out there, expanding like a cartoon snowball as it tumbles down a hill, but I race home as if I could somehow catch it and stop it ruining the trial. I don't want to believe Finley. I want to think that he was the one who did this. But as soon as I run into the kitchen, I know.

This was all Flora.

Mum is pacing around the kitchen with her phone pressed to her ear and Ùna is scrolling frantically on the computer, but Flora stands in front of the sink, perfectly calm. When she turns to look at me, anger bubbles up inside me like lava.

"What have you done?" I shout. "You've ruined everything!"

Tears spring to my eyes again. After all we've done to try to make this trial a success, all my hard work with the investigation… Flora has thrown it all away. Mum widens her eyes at me and holds up a finger to her lips. A female voice is talking on the other end of the line.

"Yes, of course," Mum says into the phone. "Thank you."

She ends the call then puts both hands on the table,

tips her head forward and takes a few deep breaths. Beside me, Flora taps her foot against the floor.

"That was Marisa," Mum says. "She needs to talk to their PR department and then she'll set up a video call to discuss what we do next."

"Is she angry?" Ùna asks. She sits on her chair with her knees pulled up to her chest, chewing on a fingernail.

"More worried than anything else." Mum sits down and runs her hands over her face. "I can't believe this is happening."

I slam my hand on the wall and turn to Flora. "Why did you do it? And why did you post it from Finley's account? He has thousands of followers!"

"Exactly. I wanted it to spread quickly," Flora says. "Besides, I felt bad about hacking into his computer to take the footage. I figured he deserved some of the credit, he's been going on about that documentary long enough."

Ùna jumps up from her chair. "There's another one!"

She turns the computer round so it's facing Flora and me. On the screen is a skinny man with longish brown hair and a white cap on backwards. He's talking rapidly in a language I don't understand, but the title of the video is 'Second Chances brought me back from the dead'.

"That's the guy I saw you looking at on your computer!" I tell Flora. "Did you know he was going to do this?"

"His name is Pham Duc Duy," she says, nodding. "He lives in Vietnam."

On the screen, the man switches to perfect American English. His story is similar to Flora's. He died in his sleep of an undiagnosed illness, was returned to his village in Ha Giang four years later, but grew frustrated when his friends and family started moving on and he couldn't.

"I've found nine of us so far," Flora says as Pham Duc Duy begins retelling the story in Arabic. "There are three in North America, that I know of. The others are in Nigeria, Peru and Romania, plus me and Duc."

She opens her phone and shows us a series of photos – a girl around our age in a cheerleading uniform, an older man walking through a busy market with a little boy in his arms, the middle-aged woman I saw on her computer earlier, laughing with another woman at a pottery class. I knew Project Homecoming was an international trial but something about this makes me go cold. It feels so … vast. As if Second Chances are planting seeds around the world, hoping they'll grow into a forest.

"So, you've been talking to them?" Mum asks. Her voice has gone dry. "The other returnees?"

"Some of them, yeah." Flora opens her phone again and finds a photo of a twenty-something woman in a restaurant, a glass in her hand and a wide smile on her face. "Ijemma – she lives in Nigeria – she'd hacked her own systems, like I did, so I sent her a message directly. And then she managed to track down Jackson. He's in the far north of Canada."

A ringing sound comes from Mum's laptop. She hurriedly presses a key and Marisa pops on to the screen. "Good morning, Flora," she says weakly. "This is quite a situation you've gotten us into here. And on my day off, as well."

"I'm sorry, Marisa. I didn't want to cause trouble for you personally," Flora says, sitting down in the seat beside Mum. Something about her voice doesn't sound like her any more – it's too stiff, too formal.

"But it was what I needed to do."

"Can you fix it?" Mum asks, gripping the edge of the table. "Cover it up, somehow? Surely most people won't believe it?"

"I've spoken to our PR team. They've already had it taken down from Sekkon but the video's been reposted to other platforms, and it'll take much longer to get those removed." She presses her lips together. "Either way, as far as our legal team are concerned, the confidentiality clause in the contract has been broken."

My heart plummets. "So, that's the end of it? The trial is over?"

"Possibly not. There are a couple of options." Marisa holds up one finger. "The first is that we remove Flora from Project Homecoming and she returns to the Second Chances base. Frankly, that's what my bosses want. I had to pull every string I could get my hands on to stop them from ordering the engineers to shut Flora down immediately."

Ùna lets out a gasp. "No! You can't do that!"

Mum's warning about what might happen if Flora was recalled flashes red in my mind. When I look at her, her face is chalky. "What's the second option?"

"We start from scratch," Marisa says. "But it would need to be in new place, with new identities. Somewhere remote, probably a small town in Australia or New Zealand. We'll set you up with a job, Sarah, and find a school for the girls. But it would mean an entirely new life. Leaving everything else behind."

"We'll do that then," Ùna says quickly. "Definitely."

I nod. "We can leave as soon as you say so. We'll do whatever it takes."

But a sickly feeling churns in my stomach as soon as I say the words. Leaving Murdo, Adhiti, Dad, Kirsty, Gran, Holly. Leaving Eilean Dearg. Waking up every morning in a country I've never even visited, having to pretend my name is Emma or Hayley or whatever they decide I should be called. If that's our only real option then it's what we'll have to do, for Flora. But I don't want that. I don't want any of it.

Marisa is quiet for a moment. The worried look hasn't left her eyes. She pauses before she speaks again, like she's carefully measuring out the words. "When I say start from scratch, I mean Flora too." Her gaze shifts to Flora. "We'd need to entirely reboot your system. It would restore you to your original settings, so you wouldn't remember anything from the past few months. And we'd also have to make some security adjustments so we can avoid any more breaches like this one."

"What sort of adjustments?" Mum asks.

"If we go ahead with this move, we can edit Flora's memories so she feels more settled in your new environment. And we're going to need to tighten security around your operating system too."

Flora stays quiet. Usually I can tell what she's thinking just from her eyes and the way her mouth moves, but right now there's no expression on her face at all.

"We'll need to move fast, but I'll give you some time to talk about it," Marisa says. "How about I check in again in a couple of hours and we can put together a plan?"

"OK. Sure." Mum smiles and lets out an uneasy sigh of relief. "I'm so sorry about this, Marisa, and thank you so much. I can't tell you how much I appreciate it."

There's a beep and Marisa disappears from the video call.

Ùna leans forward on the table, her arms crossed. "Can we can ask them to send us to New Zealand? Australia would be a bit hot for me, and there are so many snakes and spiders—"

I put my hand out to cut her off. "Wait. What was all that about editing Flora's memories? What did Marisa mean?"

"She means they'd remove or change some stuff. Can't miss my friends if I don't remember them, can I? Can't want to go swimming if I always hated it." Flora's voice is calm, but she crosses her arms tight against her chest. "I'm not going to let them do that."

"I don't think you have a choice. You made sure of that when you went online and told the entire world about the trial." For the first time, Mum's voice rises in anger. "Now you have to deal with the consequences."

"No. I won't let them make me something less than I am." Flora gestures to the screen where Marisa was talking a moment ago. "But I also don't want to be sent back to Second Chances and end up like Toby."

"Toby?" I look at Mum and Ùna, but they seem as confused as I feel. "What about Toby?"

Flora takes out her phone and opens it to a photo of the red-haired man who visited us with Marisa back in July. He's lounging in a park on a sunny day – he's tanned and his hair is longer than it was when we saw him, almost to his shoulders. His eyes are crinkled and he's laughing at something off-camera. His face is exactly the same, but his body language and expression are totally different to the person who was sitting in our kitchen a few months ago.

"This is Toby, or rather, the man Toby was based on. His name was Tobias Sandström." Flora flicks to another photo – Toby in a forest, wrapped up in a scarf and hat. "He was from a tiny village in the north of Sweden, only around thirty people. He died in a motorbike accident there when he was twenty-nine."

I suck my breath in. "Wow. That's so sad."

"Second Chances brought him back in a trial five years ago. I managed to access the company's records, and it sounds like it started a lot like ours. Lots of people were against it at first but Second Chances talked them round with cash and promises, like they did here." Flora swipes at her screen and the photo disappears. "But they changed their minds. The trial failed. The people in the town decided to send him back."

Ùna pushes up her glasses, frowning. "So ... Second Chances gave him a job instead?"

"It's not a job, Ùna," Flora says. "They don't pay him. They stripped away all his memories, all his likes and dislikes, all the programming that made him a person, and now they use his body for tasks like driving or carrying luggage. Toby's just a machine now. He can fly planes and repair cars, do any task they programme him to, but he's not much more than a glorified calculator."

Just like Mum told me they could do with Flora. I picture her in a Second Chances uniform, her smile as fixed and bland as Toby's. The thought makes me feel nauseous.

"But ... that's wrong," Ùna says, shaking her head. "They can't do that!"

"They can, Ùna. He's their property. And is it really

249

that unethical, if they've removed his consciousness?" Flora shrugs. "It's not like he has feelings any more. He's not a person."

The sentence hangs heavy in the air. If Toby isn't a person, then maybe Flora isn't, either. But that doesn't make it OK for Second Chances to use them like that. If they created them, they have to treat them well.

"I can't have a future here. I don't age. You two are going to grow up and move away one day, and I'll be left behind." Flora turns to Mum and takes her hand. "You don't need to worry about them shutting me down remotely. I've fixed all the glitches in my system and I've made myself completely autonomous. As long as I have a power source, I can survive independently now."

"What are you saying?" Mum asks, but from the way the tears brim in her eyes, she knows what Flora means.

"I'm saying –" Flora squeezes Mum's hand, then releases it – "that you need to let me go."

Thirty-five

I need to get out of this house. I need fresh air, space to think. I leave Flora sitting with a shell-shocked Mum and Ùna and hurry out into the quiet evening. Sìth follows me, bumping against my ankles and meowing for attention. I stop and pet her while I try to fight back my tears. All this time, I've been so worried about Flora being taken away from us. I never imagined that she might want to leave.

My phone buzzes. I take it out and see Holly's name flash on to the screen. As soon as I open the message, two more pop up one after the other.

Um ... isn't this your sister? she asks, with a link to Flora's video.

Is this a joke?

Isla? What's going on?

I press the video call button. This is too long for a written message, too complicated for a one-sided voice note. The ringtone only sounds twice before Holly answers.

"It's true," I blurt out, before she can even say hello. "They brought Flora back. I'm really, really sorry I couldn't tell you. I wanted to so much but they made us sign all these contracts promising we wouldn't talk about it, and they said they might have to take Flora away again if everyone found out, and—"

"Whoa! Isla, slow down!" Holly says. The walls behind her shift as she sits down on her bed. "Start from the beginning. What's going on?"

So, I finally, *finally* get to tell her the truth. Holly listens in silence as I ramble through the past few months, the words spilling out so fast I trip over my tongue.

"And now Flora wants to leave." My throat tightens but I swallow and carry on. "We said we'd start over, like Marisa offered. They'd reboot Flora and we'd go to Australia or New Zealand or wherever they want to send us. My mum would go to the moon if that was the only option. But Flora doesn't want that. She says she wants to leave us again."

There's a long silence. I can hear Oakley snuffling around Holly's room, one of her brothers playing a game in the distance. Even if we haven't talked since I forgot her birthday, it would hurt to move so far away from her. Like having a piece of my heart flung to the other side of the world.

"What about what *you* want?" Holly asks, pushing a lock of hair behind her ear. "Would you actually want to move that far away?"

"No," I say automatically. "I don't want to leave. I don't want to leave the islands, or my dad and Kirsty, my friends, the football team. Any of it. But it's better than losing her a second time."

Holly falls quiet. I wouldn't know what to say, either. Sìth nudges her head against my ankles, almost like she senses my sadness. I crouch down and rub between her ears. She gives a faint mewl and tilts her head into my palm. Mum and Dad got Sìth from Seamus after one of his farm cats had an unexpected litter of kittens. She's lived her whole life on Eilean Dearg, just like me. If she could have her say, she'd want to stay too.

"I don't think you'd be losing her again," Holly says eventually. "She's not dying. She might have to go away but you can stay in touch. It wouldn't be the same as it was before."

"It's not the same as having her here," I say. "It's not like she can come and visit. It won't be safe. Second Chances will be after her. And if they find her then—"

I break off. I don't want to think about what might happen then. What was it like for Toby's family, losing him in that motorbike crash, then losing the returnee version of him? What if the new Toby bumped into one of his parents or a cousin while he was off travelling the world with Marisa? He wouldn't even recognize them with his memories wiped away. It's hard when Gran forgets my name or who I am, but those memories are still with her somewhere, like nuggets of gold hidden in the earth. If Flora goes back to Second Chances, they'll delete all of that. Her whole self, gone with one click.

The knot of thoughts is growing bigger and bigger, too big for me to untangle right now. Instead, I tell Holly, "I'm really sorry I ran out of your house like that. And I'm sorry I forgot your birthday too."

Holly's face breaks into a smile. "Oh, don't be silly! It's a lot more understandable now I know you've been living in a sci-fi film for the past few months."

She laughs lightly. I join in, though it comes out all

bubbly from crying.

"It was so hard having to act like nothing was going on." I let out a breath and realize that, despite all the chaos Flora has caused, some of that weight has lifted now. "None of you would have believed me if I'd told you."

"I would! I'm not so sure about Eilidh or Tiwa, though. They'd probably think you'd lost it." Holly leans back into the pillows at the head of her bed. "Honestly, I'm relieved. When you left, I thought you… That you didn't like me or something."

"No, of course not," I say, glad the light from my phone flushes out my red cheeks. "Definitely not."

"OK. Good." Holly giggles. Her face turns a little pink too. "And thank you again for the paper cutting. It's amazing! Did you make it?"

"Well, I designed it," I say, "but Flora did the actual cutting. She can basically learn to do anything instantly."

I tell her all about Flora's abilities and about how she managed to keep them hidden from Second Chances all these weeks. Talking about it makes me feel a strange mix of pride and awe. It's incredible that Flora has managed to outsmart the world's best engineers but sort of scary too. There's no telling how powerful she could become.

"That's unbelievable." Holly pauses for a moment. "But … is she really your sister, if she can do all that? I didn't know the old Flora but I'm guessing she wasn't some genius hacker."

"Definitely not."

"And would she really be Flora if they rebooted her?" Holly hunches her shoulders. "That doesn't sound very human."

I think back to what Marisa said, about how they would

have to alter parts of Flora's programming for the trial to work a second time round. Life doesn't work like that. You can't change a person to fit your idea of who they are or who they should be. I don't want that for Flora. I don't want her to be a watered-down version of the person I remember.

"No. You're right. She wouldn't." I look back towards the house. The windows glow gold and smoke drifts from the chimney. You couldn't tell that there's such a huge crisis happening inside. "I'd better go. We need to work out what to do."

"Of course, go." Holly nods quickly. "Keep me updated, though, OK?"

As soon as I walk back into the kitchen, Ùna runs towards me holding her phone. On the screen is a boy a few years older than Flora, sitting in his car and talking rapidly into the screen.

"There's been two more!" Ùna says. "The lady in Nigeria that Flora knows and now this guy in Romania."

Mum sits at the table with her head in her hands. Flora is beside her, one hand on Mum's shoulder. Something about the sight feels off. Then it clicks. Flora's chest isn't moving. She's shut off the mechanism that imitates breathing.

"You all planned this together, didn't you?" I ask her.

"Yes, we did." She turns to Mum, who is staring at Flora with glossy eyes. "We want to join Jackson in the northern territories. A new law on digital personhood has been proposed in Canada. If it passes, there's a good chance they'll help protect us."

"Protect you from what?" Mum asks weakly. "I know

that attack at the harbour scared you, love – it scared me too. But this new move will be a chance to get away from everything. It'll be a fresh start."

"It's not about that." Flora pauses for a moment, weighing up her words. "I feel like I'm stuck playing a role that isn't mine. I don't want to have to pretend to be human any more. That's not what I am, or what I'll ever be. I want to be free. I want to be around people who are like me."

"But we're your family," Ùna says. "We *are* people like you."

Her lower lip is wobbling. Flora links her arms round Ùna's waist and pulls her in for a hug. "You are my family, and that's not going to change. But I'm not the same as you. Second Chances talk about a world where returnees are fully integrated with humans, but that's not going to happen any time soon." She touches the back of her neck. "Why do you think they put the port here, somewhere so visible? It's to make it easy to tell us apart from humans if they need to. We'll never be completely equal."

I think about the future for Flora. She won't get sick or die. Maybe there'll come a time when everyone is recreated as a returnee when they die, but maybe there won't – maybe we'll leave one by one and eventually she'll be all on her own. When I look at it like that, I can understand why she wants to be with others like her.

"You can't do this," Mum says. "You can't go to Canada on your own. You're only fifteen."

"I'm not, though." Flora smiles. "Technically, I'm not even a year old. But now I'm able to access my full capabilities, I have much more knowledge than Flora

ever had – more than you ever will, even. I'll be fine.
I promise."

For a second I'm confused, wondering why she's talking
about Flora as if she was a different person. But then it
finally clicks: something that I've known deep down for a
long time, even if I didn't want to admit it.

"You were never really her, were you?" I ask quietly.
"You're not really Flora."

Tears roll down my cheeks as I say the words. Flora
shakes her head.

"No. I'm not." She reaches for Mum's hand. "I'm sorry.
I know how much you loved her, but Dad – Innes – he
was right. There's no bringing Flora back."

Ùna is crying too now. She takes off her glasses and
rubs her eyes with the backs of her hands. "You seem
so much like her, though," she says, choking on a sob.
"You look just like her."

"Maybe we can do something about that." Flora
stands up and goes to the drawers by the fridge.
"What's something Flora would never do?"

She takes the kitchen scissors from the top drawer.
Before any of us can stop her, she chops off her ponytail.
It falls to the ground, lying curled on the floorboards
like a comma. Mum and Ùna let out horrified gasps.
Sìth sniffs at the long blond locks. Flora runs her fingers
through what's left of her hair and fans it around her
neck. The cut is uneven and too short at the back.

"That's a bit less Flora, right? She was obsessed with
having longer hair," she says with an unsteady grin.
"She googled *how to make your hair grow faster* about
fifty times."

Sadness seeps through my body. I wish this was some normal Friday night, that we were all lounging on the sofa watching a series, or that Flora was scrolling through her phone and talking about some boy from the swim team while I baked in the kitchen. Suddenly I miss her so much it makes my breath catch in my throat, and that's what makes the new Flora's words really sink in. She's not my sister. She never was.

Ùna wipes her eyes on her sleeve. "How are you going to get to Canada?'

"There's a flight from Glasgow tomorrow evening," Flora says. "If I leave on the first ferry, then get the boat to the mainland, the train should get me there in time. It'll be tight, though."

"Tomorrow?" My voice cracks on the word. "That's so soon."

"I can't risk Second Chances coming after me." Flora nods towards her phone. "I trust Marisa is really trying to help us but we don't know about the rest of the company. I need to leave as soon as possible."

This is all way too fast but I nod and start putting together a plan. "I'll set my alarm for half past six. We'll need to leave early if we want to get the first ferry."

Flora's eyebrows rise. "We?"

"You can't go on your own," I say. "I'm coming with you."

"We all are," Ùna says, wiping her sleeve across her nose. "Right, Mum?"

Looking at Mum makes my heart ache. Her eyes are so, so sad – a sadness I can't begin to understand. But I also know that she'll do whatever is best for Flora.

Even if it means saying goodbye.

"I'll call Marisa back and tell her we're accepting her offer of a new beginning. That should buy you some time," she says. "We'll leave tomorrow morning. We'll get there faster if we take the car."

Flora gets up and throws her arms round Mum. Ùna wraps hers round them both and I do the same – just like we did at the harbour that Wednesday in July, the day Flora came home. Beneath my hand, Mum's back heaves with silent sobs. When we finally move apart again, she's forcing a smile.

"OK." She takes a deep breath and looks at Flora, her eyes shiny. "Time to let you go."

Thirty-six

It's still dark when we leave the next morning. Our bags are packed with snacks, a few essentials and a change of clothes in case we have to stay in Glasgow overnight, and Mum has left out enough food for Sìth to last her until we get back. Flora takes her tracker out of her arm and we leave our phones behind – we don't want Second Chances to be able to use them to follow us.

"Ready to go?" Mum asks.

There's a glint of hope in her eyes, as if she's silently praying Flora might change her mind and decide to stay. Instead, Flora hugs her tight and nods.

"I'm ready."

After four or five attempts to get the engine started, Mum drives down to the village and parks by the harbour. Flora gets out of the car and looks around the sleepy village. The early morning sky is still filled with stars, diamond bright and infinite. It's one of my favourite things about the island – the lack of light pollution makes for the most unbelievable skies. Sometimes we can even see the Northern Lights.

"I know I've been programmed to love this place but it

really is beautiful," Flora says. "There aren't many places where you can see the stars like this."

"You must be able to see tons from the north of Canada," I say, climbing out of the car after her. "It'll look the same as here."

"Maybe, but it won't feel the same." Flora tilts her head backwards and spins in a circle, taking it all in. "This place will always be home."

The boat appears, a glowing dot on the dark water. As we turn to go, I get a strange sense that someone is watching me. I look around and catch a movement in one of the upstairs windows of Georgie's house. That niggling feeling hits me again, the sense I had at the bonfire that there was something I'd missed. Something just out of my grasp, like a vanishing word on the tip of my tongue.

Then it comes to me. What Georgie said last night, after I'd asked Adhiti if she was the one sending Flora those messages.

The virus … was probably an accident.

Before I've even finished the thought, my legs are running across the road and then my fists are banging on the door to the Campbells' house. Because I never told anyone about the virus. Not even Murdo and Adhiti. No one outside our family knew about that except Marisa.

"Come out!" I hammer on the wood and shout Georgie's name. "Come out now!"

Una and Mum hurry across the road after me, asking what I'm doing, but I ignore them and keep thumping. A few seconds later, the door swings open so fast I stumble forward. Annie stands on the doorstep in pyjama trousers and an oversized jumper. Georgie crouches on the stairs behind her and holds back Lola, who is barking loud enough to wake the whole island.

"What's going on?" Annie asks, looking from me to Mum. "Is something wrong, Sarah?"

"Georgie's the one who sent those messages," I shout. "She's the one who gave Flora that virus!"

Georgie's face is ghostly pale. Úna lets out a soft "oh" of shock, but Flora doesn't react at all.

"What are you talking about, Isla?" Mum asks me.

"I never told anyone about the virus," I say. "The only way Georgie could have known about it was if she put it there."

My voice is getting louder and louder, drawing people out of the buildings around us. Murdo appears at his bedroom window. The door to the post office opens and Suresh peers out, bleary-eyed from another early start.

Georgie stands up and shakily walks to her front door. "I really needed her to leave," she says, her voice trembling like a tiny bird.

"Why?" Úna asks. "What did Flora ever do to you?"

Georgie looks at her mum with a tearful expression. "She might have told someone."

The door to Murdo's house opens. He steps outside, still in his pyjamas, followed by his frowning parents. Suresh jogs over from the post office too, leaving the door open behind him.

"Told someone what?" Mum asks Georgie. "What could Flora have told someone?"

Something passes between Georgie and Annie, something I can't read. Lola pads through the hallway, presses her snout into Georgie's hand and whimpers.

262

As Georgie kneels down to pet her, Annie turns to face us all.

"I was the one who started the fire," she says. "The fire at the church."

Her voice is barely more than a whisper but it seems to send a shockwave over the entire island. Even the waves hold their breath before they come rolling towards the shore again.

"*You* set the fire?" Andy shakes his head. "But you told me—"

Annie holds up her hands. "It was a mistake, Andy, I swear. I never meant for it to spread so far."

"You could have burned down our whole house!" Katie flings a hand towards the church. "Reverend Jack could have died in there!"

"I know, I know. I'm so, so sorry." Annie gestures towards her cottage. "You remember what a state this place used to be – the roof was about to cave in, it was leaking all over, Georgie had to go to sleep wearing her big coat. I couldn't afford to get it fixed and the insurance wouldn't cover the repairs, but I knew I could get a payout for fire damage. I never thought—"

Mum cuts her off. "What does any of this have to do with Flora?"

Annie looks down at her slippers. "When I went to the church that night, I found Flora there. She was very upset. She didn't understand why she was so sick... I suppose she was looking for answers," she says. "We talked for a while and then I drove her home. She was scared she'd get in trouble, so I helped her back into bed without waking any of you up."

"And then she set the fire and told Reverend Jack it was Flora." My voice is shaking with rage now. "He thought Flora was the one who did it all this time."

Annie finally turns to look at Flora. "I'm so sorry. I was having doubts about the trial earlier this year, about what you might remember, and I told Georgie what I'd done in a panic. When the message on the church wall appeared, I guessed she might have written it – her dad was a big sci-fi reader, we've got that Asimov book upstairs – but she promised me that would be the end of it. I told Reverend Jack the same when he came to see me the other week. I had no idea about a virus or anything else, honestly."

Georgie hides her face in Lola's fur, her shoulders shaking with sobs.

"What if my mum goes to prison? What's going to happen to me then?" She rubs her face and looks at Flora. "I'm sorry. I didn't mean to hurt you but I thought maybe if I scared you enough you might leave. What if you remembered seeing Mum there and went to the police?"

"But Flora doesn't have those memories," I say. "She wasn't programmed with them."

That's the worst part of it: Georgie was worried about something that wasn't possible. Maybe if she hadn't sent the threats, Flora wouldn't have felt so isolated. She might not have started messing around with her programming, working out what she could and couldn't do, and she might not have found the other returnees. She might not have decided to leave. Georgie caused all of this, and it was all over a fear that would never have come true.

"I didn't know." Georgie puts her hands on her eyes and scrubs the tears away. "I'm so sorry, Isla. I just didn't want them to take my mum away."

"But you tried to push Flora into the water!" I shout. "You could have destroyed her!"

"What?" Georgie sniffs and wipes her nose. "I didn't push Flora. What are you talking about?"

"Someone tried to push her into the water at the harbour," I say. Georgie starts protesting that she doesn't know what I mean, but I shake my head. "I don't believe you. Why should I believe anything you say? You told me you felt awkward around Flora because it made you sad that Second Chances couldn't bring your dad back. You've been lying to me the whole time!"

"That part is true! I lied about other things, but not that." Georgie looks at her mum, who stares back with a horrified expression. "And I didn't push Flora, I swear! I wanted the trial to end but not like that. I would never do that."

The boat is pulling into the harbour now. I'm so mad that I could yell for hours but Flora takes my arm and pulls me away from the Campbells' house. Murdo shouts after me, but I'm too angry to answer. Suresh runs after us and catches Flora's arm as we reach the car.

"I'm so sorry, Flora," he says. "I really thought it was you who set the fire. This whole time, I've been wondering who you really were, if you were capable of doing something like that, and…"

His voice trails out. For the first time in months, I'm seeing the Suresh we used to know. The one who would fling himself off our sofa laughing at his and Flora's in-jokes, and left our house sobbing the day she told him about her diagnosis. Her best friend.

"It's OK." Flora takes his hand and squeezes it. "I can tell how much she loved you. She would have understood."

There's a pause as Suresh works out why she's saying "she" and not "I". "You're not her, are you? I didn't really believe you were but I hoped…" He swallows. "I wanted you to be. I wanted her to have more time."

"Me too. She deserved a lot more time. But what little she did have was so happy, and she was so loved." Flora puts her hands on his face. "And she would have wanted you to go out and have a thousand adventures for her."

Tears spring into Suresh's eyes. He puts his hands on top of Flora's and tries to smile. "OK," he says, his voice choked. "I'll have a thousand and one, just for good measure."

Flora smiles and pulls him into a long, tight hug. Ùna and I rush into the car after Mum, giving them a moment together, then Suresh lets her go and she climbs into the passenger seat. I take one look back at the village. Andy and Katie are on the Campbells' doorstep, still asking questions. Reverend Jack is walking over, no doubt woken up by my shouting and Lola's barking. As the boat pulls away from the shore, I have a feeling that the island we're leaving won't be the same one we come home to.

Thirty-seven

It starts to rain on our way to Eilean Gorm. The crossing is rough but I'm too mad to sit still. I pace around the ferry like a tiger in a cage, replaying all the times Georgie lied to me. She made out like she understood what our family was going through, and the whole time she was plotting her next attack. Mum makes me sit and take deep breaths to calm down but I'm still so angry I can hardly speak.

When we arrive on Eilean Gorm, things get even worse.

A minute after the wheels roll off the ferry ramp, Mum's car finally does it. After a thousand near misses and hundreds of false starts, the engine cuts out. Mum slams the steering wheel with the palm of her hand. Ùna says a word that she is definitely not allowed to say but no one seems to care.

"Great," I mutter. "What are we going to do now?"

"We're going to have to ask Dad to take us there," Ùna says.

I look at Flora. A few weeks ago, the thought of being stuck in a car for hours with Dad would have horrified her. Instead, she nods. "Let's go."

Mum sighs but we have no other option. We leave the

car by the side of the road and hurry through the town towards Kirsty's house. The rain is coming down heavy now and we all start to run when we reach the corner of the road. Ùna bangs on the pink door and presses herself against it to try to shelter from the raindrops. A moment later, Kirsty opens up with panic on her face.

"Ùna! What's wrong? Is everything all right?"

Dad appears in the door behind her. He's wearing jogging bottoms and an old HebCelt Festival T-shirt that he's had from before any of us were born. His face goes pale when he sees Flora, then falls when he looks at Mum.

"Sarah – what are you doing here?" he asks. It's so strange seeing them in the same place again – like watching two moons on different orbits finally cross paths. "Is this about that video?"

Flora readjusts her backpack and steps forward. "I'm leaving, Innes. There's a flight from Glasgow to Toronto at five o'clock but Mum's car has broken down. Can you drive us there?"

Dad blinks at her. "To Glasgow?"

"It's what she wants to do," Mum says weakly. "I just need her to be safe."

Dad gives her a look that says he understands. The trial has turned out exactly like he warned us, but one of the good things about Dad is that he never gloats when he's right. He could shout at Mum for ending their marriage over this, for putting us through another heartbreak but he doesn't and he won't. Instead he nods towards the car.

"OK." He grabs his keys from the side table in the hallway and tosses them to me. "Just let me get dressed and grab my wallet."

As he hurries off upstairs, Kirsty steps into the doorway. Her hair is tied up in a messy bird's nest and there are smudges of yesterday's mascara around her eyes.

"I tried calling you last night, Sarah, but I couldn't get through." She turns to Flora. Her eyes are filled with wonder, the way they were when Flora turned up to Dad's birthday. "Can I give you a hug? I never got to say goodbye to our Flora. Can I say goodbye to you?"

Flora smiles. "Of course."

Kirsty pulls her into one of her big, warm hugs and whispers something into Flora's ear. My eyes are stinging so I hurry down to the car and open the doors. The three of us get in the back, Mum into the passenger seat, and then Dad comes running out and climbs in beside her. For a second it feels like old times again, like they're going to put Alanis Morrisette or No Doubt on and belt out the words as we drive around the island. But only for a second.

"We should make the next ferry if we hurry." Dad looks at Mum. "So, the old Fiat finally gave up the ghost, eh?"

Mum smiles. It's a tiny smile, barely a twitch of her lips, but it's there. "It finally did. Talk about timing."

Dad turns the key in the ignition and drives us towards the port. Maybe it's in my head but I could swear a few people do double takes as we pass. News travels as fast here as it does on Eilean Dearg and it won't have taken long for the word to spread that the returnee from the island over is Innes MacAulay's daughter.

"Wait!" Flora shouts suddenly. "Stop!"

Dad slams his foot on the brake. I spin round, frantically searching the quiet street for some sign of an emergency.

Then I recognize the pastel-yellow building at the end of the road. Holly's house. The curtains are still drawn but there's smoke coming from the chimney.

"What's wrong? What are we doing here?"

Flora points to the house. "Go and tell Holly you like her."

My cheeks instantly go so red I can practically feel the heat radiating off them. Ùna lets out a gasp of delight and clasps her hands together. There's a small smile twitching at Flora's lips, but her eyes are serious.

"Now?" I splutter. "Are you joking? You have to catch your flight!"

"And you have to do this. You can't avoid every change because you're scared it'll turn out badly, Isla." Flora gives my shoulder a push. "Go on. Tell her."

Mum and Dad twist round to look at me from the front seats. Their eyebrows are raised in surprise, but then they turn to each other and smile.

Dad cocks his head towards Holly's house. "Go on then, Isles. Make it quick."

My heart in my throat, I run across the road and ring the doorbell of the yellow house. The seconds drag like centuries but eventually footsteps squeak on the stairs. The door swings open and Holly stares back at me. "Isla! What are you—"

"I like you," I blurt out. "I really like you. A lot."

Holly just stares, until Oakley comes bounding through the door and jumps up to greet me. She barks happily and leaves muddy paw prints on my jacket. Holly pulls the dog down and lets out a bewildered laugh.

"You're telling me that *now*? With everything that's

going on?" She runs her hand through her hair and laughs. "It's not even nine o'clock yet!"

"I know, but…" I swallow. "I really needed to say it. And that I'm really sorry for being so weird lately."

"Isla, your sister has come back from the dead. It's fair enough." Holly's eyes are sparkling. She reaches out and holds my hand. It sends electricity sparking over my skin. "But I like you too."

Despite everything that's happened over the past few days and weeks, despite the fact that Flora is leaving once again, a huge smile breaks over my face. Holly reaches up on tiptoe and pulls me into a hug. In a flash, I picture us going to get ice cream or to the cinema, holding hands… And someday, when my parents and sisters aren't sitting in a car a few metres away, our first kiss.

For once, those pictures aren't mixed up with bad thoughts of all the ways it could go wrong. I'm just excited about the good parts that are still to come.

A knock on the car window brings me back to the present. I turn round and see Ùna tapping her wrist.

"I have to go," I tell Holly. "Flora is going to – well, it's a long story, and I don't have my phone with me, but I'll text you as soon as I get home tonight."

Holly leans around me and peers at the car parked further down the road. Her mouth falls open when she sees Flora looking back at her.

"OK! Go!" She shakes her head. "How is this even your life, Isla?"

"I don't know," I laugh. But right now, I'm glad it is.

Thirty-eight

Ùna and Flora demand a rundown of everything I said to Holly, and Mum and Dad talk about the best route to take to Glasgow once we reach the mainland, but the car soon falls quiet. I can feel nerves crackling like static off Mum and Ùna, though Flora is completely still. Right now I'm mostly distracted by the fact I finally told Holly I like her. I wish I could send her a message – something to sign off our conversation, like an *xoxo* or a doodle at the end of a letter.

But as we reach the port, my anxiety starts to bubble up again. The area is chock full of cars, so many we actually have to queue to get into the car park.

"Get down," Mum tells Flora. "We don't want anyone recognizing you."

Flora slides down and tucks herself into the spot behind the front seats. Ùna reaches into the boot, finds a blanket and throws it over her. Dad joins the queue of vehicles going on to the ferry and stops at the ticket office. A woman dressed in the ferry company's dark blue uniform nods as he lowers the window.

"Sorry about all this," she says, gesturing to the traffic.

"Have you heard about that robot girl on Eilean Dearg? Seems like every journalist in Scotland is going over there to find out about it. Four people?"

"Yes, please. Two adults, two kids." Dad hands over a few notes and keeps his eyes down. "They're saying it's a hoax, the robot thing."

"Och aye, it must be." The woman takes the money and passes our tickets through the window. "Good story, though, isn't it? On Eilean Dearg, of all places!"

She grins at him before Dad drives up the boarding ramp and on to the car deck of the ferry. You're not supposed to stay down here during the crossing but none of us wants to leave Flora alone, and obviously she can't go up to the deck. In the end, Mum, Dad and Ùna go upstairs to get breakfast from the ferry café while I stay in the car with Flora. I crouch down beside her and pull the blanket over my head so no one will see us if they walk past.

"This is so weird," I whisper. "It's like we're fleeing the country."

"I *am* fleeing the country." Flora grins, her eyes bright. "Are you all right? You were so mad at Georgie earlier."

"I still am! She's been lying to us for months." I remember Flora flat on the sand at the harbour and grit my teeth. "I'm never, ever going to forgive her for this."

"She was scared, Lala. Can you blame her? She lost her dad, and her mum might have gone to prison if anyone found out she burned the church down. She still might, now that the truth is out." Flora pokes me in the knee. "Come on. You can forgive her."

"I can't! She ruined everything. Things probably wouldn't

have turned out like this if it wasn't for her. And besides, she sent you a virus *and* tried to push you into the sea. That's beyond forgivable."

"Um, I have confession to make about that." Flora picks at a loose thread on the hem of her hoodie. "No one pushed me off the wall. I jumped. I turned off my pain sensors so it didn't hurt."

I stare at her. "Why? Were you trying to damage yourself?"

"Not exactly," Flora says. "I'd already started planning to go and meet the other returnees. I thought that if you and Mum believed that people on the island were really that hostile towards me, that it was dangerous for me to be there, it might be easier for you to let me leave."

"Wow." I swallow. "Any other lies you want to let me know about?"

"Just one. Georgie did put the virus on the USB but it wasn't nearly as bad as I made it look. My firewalls caught it, like Marisa said they should. I let it run on purpose. I knew it would look worse that way." She holds up her hands. "That's all, I promise. I'm sorry. I felt really bad about lying."

I pull the blanket from my head and take off my glasses to wipe my eyes. It's bad enough Georgie was lying to me, but Flora… That feels much worse.

"Why did you even make that video?" I snap. "You could have picked up and left in the middle of the night if you were so desperate to leave."

"I couldn't do that to Mum," Flora says. "I needed to put myself in a situation where I *had* to go. It would have hurt her too much if I'd disappeared without saying goodbye. You and Ùna too."

274

"So, you were trying to make Second Chances the bad guy." I find an elastic band under the driver's seat and twist it between my fingers. "Acting like they pushed you into this, when actually you planned the whole thing yourself."

"I don't know if they're bad guys, but they're not as transparent as they claim to be," Flora says. "They really are trying to do something good. I just don't know if they'll ever manage it. There's no machine that can get rid of grief and pain. They're part of life."

"They don't have to be for you." I let go of the band and ping it against the chair. "You don't have to care about us at all if you don't want to. You could turn those parts of you off, like you turned off your pain sensors."

"Would you do that, if you could?" Flora asks.

I don't even need to think about my answer. There have been so many bad parts of the past few years but they're outweighed by the good. Flora dying ripped our world apart, but it can't get rid of all the happy times we had together. I would never trade those in for a life without her, even if it meant less sadness now.

"No, I wouldn't." I pull the blanket back over me and lean against Flora's shoulder. "I guess it's a good thing you cared enough about us to want to make it easier."

"Of course I do. I'm not Flora. I'm not human. But I'm not some totally unfeeling machine, either. At least, I don't think I am."

We're quiet for a moment, both listening to the waves outside. I think about Flora – the real Flora – and wonder what she would have thought of Project Homecoming. Back when she was texting her friends or filming her Sekkon videos, she had no idea all the data she was generating would be used to recreate her after she died. I think she would have loved it, but there's no way to know for sure. She never got to have her say.

"Maybe you should choose a new name," I tell the new Flora now, wiping my nose. "It feels a bit weird calling you Flora, if that's not who you are."

"You're right." She presses her lips together and screws her mouth to one side. It's such a Flora-like mannerism that it makes my throat swell. "It should be something related to your sister, though, and I want to keep MacAulay as my surname. You're still my family, no matter what."

I give her a small smile. "Something related to Flora... Fauna, maybe?"

She laughs. "Bit on the nose, don't you think?"

We try out loads of names but nothing seems to fit. Twenty minutes later, as the ferry draws closer to the mainland, Mum, Dad and Ùna come back downstairs and join us. I ask them for suggestions.

"How about some type of flower?" Mum says, passing me a polystyrene cup of hot chocolate and a croissant from upstairs. "A wee nod to our Flora."

Flora smiles. "That's a good idea. Plus it's kind of ironic, picking something natural to name a machine."

We go through names of flowers: Lily, Daisy, Poppy, Rose... I like them all but nothing feels quite right. They all seem too delicate for her, this sort-of-but-not-quite-a girl, my sort-of-but-not-quite sister. Then, right as the ferry docks and the doors open to let the cars out, Dad has an idea.

"How about Heather?" he says. "It was actually a really unpopular plant in the past. Gardeners associated it with poor rural areas, so for a long time they wouldn't use it at all. It was only later that people began to appreciate it. It's a useful flower too – it feeds sheep and deer, it makes heather honey, and it can be used to dye wool and flavour beer."

He catches my eye in the rear-view mirror. I smile back. He's trying to say that though people might not understand returnees now, just like he doesn't, maybe they will one day.

Flora tries the name on for size. "Heather," she says slowly. "Heather MacAulay. I like that."

"Heather," Mum repeats. "It suits you.'

Ùna sticks out a hand. "Nice to meet you, Heather. Welcome to the family."

Ùna and I both fall asleep on the long drive down south and by the time we arrive at Glasgow airport it's already dark outside. It's been over a year since I've been to a city, and it makes me feel claustrophobic after so long on the island. The tall buildings crowd the sky, a mouth with too many teeth.

Usually I like the anonymity of being in such a big place but today the size feels threatening. Pulling into the airport car park, I watch people haul suitcases out of car boots, pat their pockets for lost items, wave to loved ones, and wonder how many of them have read about Flora's – no, Heather's – story. Without a phone, it's hard to know how far it's spread and how many people believe it. Dad switched on the radio a few hours ago and caught the end of three scientists discussing the trial, but they were all convinced it was a hoax – there was no way

Second Chances could have managed to outpace their competitors so quickly, they said.

Heather stares through the window at the departures entrance. "Maybe I should go alone. I'll blend into the crowd better if I'm by myself."

"Of course you're not going in alone." Mum twists round from the front seat. Her eyes are watery but she gives a brave smile. "I want to make sure you get on the plane safely."

"Actually, how *are* you going to get on the flight?" Dad asks Heather. "You don't have a passport, do you?"

"No, but I can hack into the Wi-Fi network here and get myself through security," she says. "Getting on to the plane is going to be more difficult. Hopefully I can follow a member of staff, hide with the luggage and sneak into the hold. I've got three spare battery packs with me, so that should be enough to last until I get to Canada."

We all stare at her. It sounds like the plot of some over-the-top action movie. The past few months have been stranger than fiction but this is a whole new level of dramatic.

"Flor— Heather," Mum says, correcting herself. "That's far, far too dangerous."

"It's a terrible idea!" Una says. "What if you get caught?"

"I have to try." Heather takes a scarf from her backpack and wraps it round her neck to hide her charging port. "If I stay here much longer, Second Chances will track me down themselves."

Dad buys a ticket and parks near the entrance. To my surprise, he gets out and follows the four of us into the airport. Inside, the terminal is busy, so busy that Heather's

278

idea about slipping into the crowd without anyone seeing might actually work. But then we turn a corner and her plan unravels.

Standing right by the security gates, bags slung over their shoulders, are Marisa and Toby.

Thirty-nine

"Hello, Flora."

This isn't the polished, smiling Marisa who appears on Mum's computer screen every Wednesday. There are shadows under her eyes, her usually neat hair is slightly mussed up on one side, and her teal blazer is wrinkled from what must have been a last-minute flight across the Atlantic. Toby is wearing a black anorak, jeans and a scarf instead of the uniform he had on last time we saw him, but his face is as calm as I remember. He even smiles as they walk through the crowd of travellers to meet us.

"It's Heather now." She takes a step forward, one hand gripping the strap of her backpack. "How did you know where we were? I covered my tracks. I was so careful."

"Our security team were able to listen in to your conversation through your mom's phone last night. You told her what flight you were planning to take."

"What?" Mum gasps. "You're not allowed to do that!"

"We are, actually, Sarah. There's a clause in the contract that says we're allowed to use your phones as mics in the case of emergencies. You signed that contract, so…" Marisa runs a hand over her hair and sighs. "Believe me, we don't like to abuse our power like that. But after what Flora did – the way the company sees it, they had no choice."

She casts a nervous glance round the airport. People criss-cross all around us, hurrying to security or dawdling towards the door with tired eyes and heavy luggage. Unless they've seen Heather's video, there's no way any of them could tell there are two returnees in their midst. Their ports are hidden behind scarves and Heather's turned on the mechanism that makes her chest rise and fall like she's breathing again so she looks like anyone else.

"Are you here to bring me back to Second Chances?" Heather crosses her arms. The look of defiance in her eye is exactly like my sister's. "You're recalling your product, is that it?"

"I wouldn't put it like that, but yes. You've left me no other option, Flora."

There's something in Marisa's expression that doesn't match her words. This is difficult for her, and not just because it's causing her trouble at work. She put a lot of effort into bringing our family back together. It must hurt for her to see it break apart like this.

"I have a question first," Heather says. "Did you know Toby before his trial failed?"

At the sound of his name, Toby moves slightly towards Heather. Dad draws in his breath in surprise. He hadn't clicked Toby was a returnee, either. Marisa frowns and shifts closer to Toby.

"Yes. I was Toby's Family Liaison Officer too. He was my first assigned case." She takes another look round the terminal. "Flora, I'm sorry, but we really don't have time for—"

"What was it like for you when they stripped all his personality away?" Heather asks. "It must have felt strange. Someone you'd spent hours with, travelled thousands of miles beside, being reduced to a basic machine."

Marisa's jaw tightens. "It was very difficult, yes, but given the circumstances, it was the right thing to do."

"What will happen to me when I get back to the centre?" Heather asks. "Who will I be assigned to?"

"That's not how it works," Marisa starts to argue, then pauses. It's like she's fighting with a voice in her head. "Yes, there's a possibility you'll be reworked into what we call an IPA, an intelligent personal assistant. But we might also… We might repurpose your hardware to use for another returnee."

"Wow. Like a robotic organ donor." Heather gives a short laugh. "There's no mention of that in the family user manual, is there?"

"Please don't do that." Mum rushes forward and clutches Marisa's arm. "Please, Marisa."

"What if this was Hana?" I ask, remembering her story about her cousin who died so young. "A returnee based on Hana, I mean, with her memories and her personality. You wouldn't want that to happen to her, would you?"

Marisa flinches. She's obviously struggling, but I'm sure she's on our side. She was the one who stopped Second Chances from shutting Heather down after she released the video last night. She wouldn't have done that if she didn't care.

"This trial isn't working, Marisa," Heather says gently.

"Maybe one day you'll discover a way for returnees to fit into this world but we can't right now. Please, let us go." She reaches for Toby's hand. He stares at her fingers, unsure how to react. "Both of us."

"Both of you?" Marisa says, blinking.

Heather nods. "Toby too. The real Toby," she adds meaningfully.

Marisa is silent for a long moment, though her eyes still dart nervously around the airport. Toby's do the same, as if he's scanning for possible dangers. After what feels like forever, Marisa mutters something under her breath and quickly reaches into her bag. She takes out a Health Hub and clicks on the screen. A familiar dashboard appears, but this one has the name Tobias Sandström at the top right.

"OK," Marisa says, passing the tablet to Heather. "Do what you have to."

Heather's fingers fly over the tablet. A minute or two later, Toby blinks. The calm smile disappears, replaced with a confused frown. He says something in Swedish, then seeing our blank faces, switches to English.

"Where are we?" His American accent has gone, replaced with a faint Nordic lilt. Even his voice was changed when they brought him back to Second Chances. "Why am I in an airport?"

Heather replies in perfect Swedish (both Mum's and Dad's eyebrows shoot upwards at that) then falls silent, her face completely blank. At first I think she's glitching again, but then I realize – she's talking to Toby over the network. There's nothing miraculous about this – it's as basic as setting two computers to play chess against each other – but to me it feels like telepathy.

"Come with me," Heather finally says in English, talking out loud so we can understand. "I'm going to join other people like us. We can be free there."

Marisa swallows. "If that's really what Toby wants…" she says, her voice rising slightly as if she hopes he might say no. But he nods, even if he does still look confused.

"It is," he says. "I think so."

Fear and sadness flash in Marisa's eyes but she reaches into her bag again and takes out a black folder. "Passports and documents for both of you, in case you need them," she tells Heather. "Take the company plane to the airport in Yellowknife – I'll call ahead and make the arrangements – then hitch a ride north, or travel by foot if you can. That'll buy you some time, but not much. They already know you're going to Canada, so if you want to stay there you'll need to get good at covering your tracks. And whatever you do, remember to charge."

"What are you going to tell your bosses?" Ùna asks as Heather tucks the documents into her bag. "Won't they be mad at you?"

Marisa lets out a bitter laugh. "Oh, they're going to be furious. I don't even want to think about the trouble this is going to cause. But I'll tell them the truth: that Project Homecoming has failed."

"It didn't fail," Heather says, shaking her head. "You helped create us. That's huge! We just didn't turn out exactly how you thought we would."

"Kids never do," Dad says with a light chuckle. When I turn to look at him, he's holding Mum's hand tight.

Marisa smiles sadly. "I honestly was trying to help, you know," she says. "It wasn't for the money or the prestige.

Most of us at the company felt the same. We were really trying to do something good."

"I know." Mum puts her other hand on top of Dad's. "So was I."

Marisa holds her hand out for us to shake, but Ùna and I throw our arms round her in a hug. Marisa whispers something to Toby, squeezes his hand, then turns back towards the departure gates. As she disappears into the crowd, Toby steps away from the rest of us, lingering instead by the queue of people waiting to check in to a flight to Leipzig.

Heather turns back to Mum, Dad, Ùna and me. "Well, that's me off," she says, smiling and swinging her arms exactly like Flora would. "Going to see the world."

A thought flashes into my head. If the real Flora had lived, she would probably be setting off on her own around now too. She might have left to go to university already, or maybe she'd be saving for a gap year. I picture her travelling around Cambodia or Peru, maybe with Suresh or her friends from the swim team. I know that Heather is her own person now, but even so... I'm sure there are sparks of my sister somewhere in all that code. Maybe Heather will have some of the adventures that Flora never did. It might be easier to accept her leaving if I think of it that way.

Dad puts his hand on Heather's shoulder. He looked slightly to the side when he talked to her before, like he was trying to avoid looking directly at a solar eclipse, but now he makes proper eye contact with her for the first time. I watch the way his jaw tightens and his expression softens.

"*Sealbh math dhuit*, Heather," he says, wishing her luck. He turns and squeezes Mum's shoulder. "I'll give you all a minute. I'll be over there by the shop."

He wanders to the gift shop near the exit, pretending to be interested in the shelves of shortbread and stuffed Highland cows. The four of us are alone again. I picture the long journey back up north without Heather, that empty chair at the kitchen table, the silence behind her bedroom door again. Hot tears spring to my eyes.

Beside me, Ùna is already crying. "I don't want to say goodbye," she tells Heather, wrapping her arms round her.

"So, don't." Heather pushes Ùna's hair away from her face. "This isn't the end."

Ùna sticks her fingers under her glasses to wipe her eyes. "Will you at least keep in touch?'

"Of course, Ùnes! I'll let you know where I am as soon as it's safe."

Heather gently lets her go and moves to hug me. Even with her bad haircut and a glint in her eye that isn't quite Flora, she looks exactly like my sister. So, I pretend I'm talking to the real Flora. I whisper how unfair this all is, how much I'm going to miss her, how much I wish she was still here to grow up with us. I give her the goodbye I never got to say three and a half years ago, when she slipped away without warning. By the end I'm crying properly, but Heather doesn't rush me.

"She's still with you, Lala," she says, tapping my heart. "And I am too, OK? Always."

"I know," I say, nodding. "I'm going to miss you too. Both of my big sisters."

That leaves Mum. She's smiling but there's so much hurt in her eyes that it's painful to look at her. Before she can say anything, Dad comes back from the shop with something in his hand.

"Here. I got you all something."

In his palm are four brooches shaped like a sprig of heather. Cheap souvenirs for tourists, really, but pretty ones. He hands one to Ùna, one to Mum, another to me.

Ùna takes the fourth and pins it to the collar of Heather's jacket. "You'll keep it forever, won't you?"

Heather smiles. "Forever and ever. I promise."

She gives Ùna and me one last hug each, then Dad walks us towards the door and leaves Mum to say goodbye. I keep my eyes fixed on the heather brooch in my hands, turning it so the gems glow bright purple when they catch the light. When Mum comes back to us a few minutes later she's wiping her eyes but she's OK. We're all going to be OK.

Dad puts an arm round Mum's shoulders and pulls her close. Standing together, the four of us watch as Heather waves from the gates. Toby comes to join her and they disappear into the crowd. A flash of blond and she's gone for good.

I look at Ùna as Mum and Dad slowly make their way towards the exit. There's so much to say. Too much. Instead, I nudge my glasses up my nose with my knuckle. She sniffs and does the same, and we both smile. Me and her, in this together.

But it's always been the three of us, and it always will be. Flora is still with us. I'll feel it every time I freewheel down the road on the bike, the sun on my face and the wind in my hair. No matter what happens in life, where I go or who I meet, Flora is always going to be a part of me. It's never going to be OK that she was taken from us so soon. I'm never going to get over that. But I can shape a life around it. And it's going to be a good one.

Epilogue

Six weeks later

The tyres of my bike slow as I reach the north-west beach. Ùna skids to a dramatic halt beside me and sends a curve of sand flying towards the sky. Behind us, Mum and Dad are pushing their ancient bikes up the path, both of them red-faced and panting.

"Remember how quick Heather could cycle up here?" Ùna asks me. "They'd never have been able to keep up with her."

"Neither could we. She was always miles ahead of us." I drop my bike in the sand. "Flora might have been able to, though."

"Yeah. She was a lot faster than us."

It's a Saturday morning at the end of December and we've come here to finally scatter Flora's ashes. The sky is powder pink with the embers of the sunrise, and the waves glide smoothly over the sand to greet us. There's never going to be a perfect time for something you should never have to do, but a day like today comes pretty close.

Ùna and I walk to the edge of the water and look out across the Atlantic. Beyond that blurry horizon is the east coast of Canada. I know she might have moved on by now but I still picture Heather somewhere over there, walking through barren, snowy landscapes with the other returnees. They don't need to drink and they probably don't feel cold any more, but I like the thought of them all sitting around a fire in a log cabin, sipping on hot chocolate. Sometimes, I wish I could dive into the freezing-cold water and swim across to join them.

So much has changed since Heather left. For one thing, the Campbells have moved away. Suresh, Reverend Jack and the MacGregors all decided they wouldn't tell anyone else about Annie starting the fire – they'd been through a lot, and no one wanted to see Georgie lose another parent – but Annie decided it was time to go anyway.

"The house is on the market and we'll stay with my sister in Edinburgh until we find a place," Annie told us when they came to our house to say goodbye. "A fresh start will do us both some good."

Georgie brought us a card and a huge bouquet of tulips to say sorry for what she'd done. Inside, she wrote about how guilty she felt and how upset her mum had been when she found out about it. It didn't even start to make up for everything, and I still haven't forgiven her, but I've talked it over a lot with Mum and Holly and I'm on my way. Like Reverend Jack said, forgiveness is important. If he can forgive Annie for burning down his church, I'll get there with Georgie eventually.

Not long after that, two more returnees shared their stories online – one in Morocco, the other in Australia. There's no doubt now that Project Homecoming was real, and the news has been filled with reports wondering how

Second Chances managed to create such sophisticated machines. Every day Mum and Dad get interview requests and offers to go on TV shows to talk about our experience. We've said no to all of them, except one filmmaker – Finley Graham. We're all scheduled in for an interview next week.

But for now, Project Homecoming has been put on pause. Marisa got in touch with us a few weeks ago to tell us that the company was halting it for the time being. Fortunately, there was a loophole in the contract that meant that no one had to return their money to Second Chances if the returnee was the one to go public about the trial, so everyone will get their full payment. The lawyers are still investigating, but it looks like the company will even have to rebuild the church like they promised.

"So, no one will lose out financially. I know that's probably not much comfort after everything you've been through, though," Marisa told us, smiling sadly. "I'm afraid that's all I know. I'd tell you more if I could but they fired me as soon as they found out I let Toby go."

Mum and Dad couldn't stop apologizing but Marisa shrugged it off. She was headhunted by a ton of businesses after the story came out and recently accepted a role as head of AI at some big healthcare company. When I told her that Adhiti was the one who helped Heather hack into her systems, Marisa invited her to California for an internship any time. Adhiti's thinking about going next summer, since her mum recently got the all-clear after her last cancer treatment, and Suresh is getting ready to start university in Glasgow next year.

So, everything is changing around here. And for me,

maybe the biggest change is that I haven't panicked about any of it. If Project Homecoming taught me anything, it's that life is full of curveballs. I'm trying to learn to smash them and run, instead of cowering and hoping I don't get hit.

I think Heather would be proud of me. I wish I could tell her about it myself but it's been ages and I still haven't heard a word from her. I've even started posting on Sekkon more often, hoping I might get a like or a comment from a user called heylala or tangerinessuck, some clue just for me ... but there's been nothing. She must have her reasons, but I miss her – not in the way I miss Flora, but a lot all the same.

As I walk along the wet sand, watching the waves swallow up my footprints, Mum and Dad finally reach the beach. They leave their bikes in the long grass and walk down to the shore to meet us, their hands linked together.

Ùna is crouching to collect tiny white shells. Mum runs her fingers over her dark hair. "Are you ready to say goodbye, love?"

"I think so." Ùna looks up at her and squints in the sunlight. "Are you?"

Mum gives a wobbly smile. "Honestly, no. I'll never be ready. But it's time to let her go too."

Dad puts his arm round Mum and pulls her towards him. She wraps her arms round his waist and presses her face into his chest. He's come to visit every week since Heather left, and he spent Christmas with us too. It's nice coming home and seeing him washing up or playing Dobble with Ùna, just like before. He still hasn't bought the house on Eilean Gorm that he was talking about, so maybe there's still a chance he'll come back home for good. Either way, our family is going to be OK.

"We need music," I say. "Flora would not stand for a goodbye ceremony without a decent soundtrack."

Dad laughs. "You're right. Put Pandora21 on, Ùna."

Ùna takes out her phone and puts on our playlist of Flora's favourite songs as Dad takes the urn with her ashes out of his bag. My heart throbs with sadness, the way it always does when I see it, but it feels right that she's back home on Eilean Dearg with us, instead of alone in Kirsty's kitchen.

The December air is cold but we stand on the beach and talk for a long time – what we miss about Flora and what we loved about her, the things she was and the things she might have become. Behind the music, the waves lap softly at the sand. Seagulls caw overhead and the wind whispers through the long grass bordering the sand. I don't know where Flora is now, but I can feel her here, in this place she loved.

We're all crying by the end. One by one, we each pick up a handful of the ashes and scatter them. Some are carried away on the wind, off to explore the world around us. Others fall at our feet, mixing with the grains of sand. Part of us and part of the island, forever.

When we get home later that morning, there are three letters waiting for us on the front step. One is addressed to Mum, one to Ùna and one to me.

Ùna snatches them up and shrieks with excitement.

"Look at the stamps!" she says, jabbing at the right-hand corner of the first envelope. "Canada!"

I grab the one with my name on it and run upstairs to Flora's room. It's changed a lot since Heather left. Mum finally took the posters and photos down, and she gave away most of the clothes and some of Flora's things to a charity shop on Eilean Gorm. She's still a long way off turning this into a guest room or anything else but she sees now that we don't need stuff to hold on to our memories of Flora.

My hands trembling, I open the envelope and pull out a sheet of paper. Behind it is a Polaroid photo of Heather, grinning and making a peace sign at the camera. The landscape behind her is snow, nothing but pure white as far as the camera captures, but she's dressed in a short-sleeved purple T-shirt, as if it was still that summer day in July when we all went to the beach together.

Dear Lala,

I'm sorry it's taken me so long to get in touch. We had to keep moving and until now I couldn't take the risk, even via "snail mail", as they used to call it. Do you think I'm the first ever robot to post a letter? Feels a bit like teaching a vacuum cleaner to use a pan and brush. (How is Stephen, by the way? I hope he's as grumpy as ever.)

Things are good here. I'm happy — or whatever mechanism inside me simulates the emotion called happiness is working well, at least. There are seven of us now, our own little returnee family. Second Chances are still looking for us, but we've found a place where we can be relatively safe. It hurt to leave you all, so much — more than makes sense for a machine. But this was the right thing for me. Even if we're still on the run here, I feel free.

I love that you've been posting a lot on Sekkon lately – it feels like a way for me to still check in with you, even if we can't talk often. I'm happy that you're playing football again, that you're still baking enough to feed the entire island and that Holly finally got to meet Sith! More pictures of that beautiful cat, please. I miss her, even if the feeling isn't mutual.

I hate that you lost another person in your life because of me. But don't worry, I'll see you again one day. I promise.

Lots of love from your other big sister,

Heather xx

I look through my window, towards the Atlantic. Outside, a starling murmuration has filled the crisp winter sky. It ripples and glides above our house, a great, pulsating cloud of fluttering wings and slick tails. Hundreds of tiny birds, together mapping out something strange and fleeting and beautiful, and then disappearing into the air.

Acknowledgements

A huge thank you to everyone at Little Tiger, especially to my editors, Mattie Whitehead and Ella Whiddett, for all their brilliant ideas and enthusiasm for this book, and to Pip Johnson for giving it such a gorgeous cover.

Thank you to my agent, Hellie Ogden, for all her help and support.

Thank you to Dan Shapiro, Linda Freund, Andrew Critchley and Grace Kavanagh for their feedback on early drafts, and to Liam Redmond and Robert Pringle for checking my dodgy Gaelic.

Thank you as always to my family and friends for their support. Special thanks to Naïa for making sure I had time to start writing this book while we were in lockdown with two babies, and to Ezra and Noah for helping out by being excellent nappers.

Finally, thank you so much to the readers, bloggers, librarians and booksellers who have supported my books over the past few years, and to anyone who takes the time to read this one! I really hope you enjoy it.

About the Author

Sophie Cameron is a YA and MG author
from the Scottish Highlands. She studied French and
Comparative Literature at the University of Edinburgh
and has a Postgraduate Certificate in Creative Writing
from Newcastle University. Her debut novel *Out of the
Blue* was nominated for the Carnegie Medal 2019.
She lives in Spain with her family.

Read on for an extract from

When Gala moves to Scotland from Spain, she feels
lost and lonely. Just as she's making friends and settling
into her new life, the actions of an anonymous classmate
threaten to take it all away. Will be she be able to find out
who's behind it and show everyone who she really is?

"A wonderful story about what happens when we take
control of our own narrative, and find ways to communicate
across the gaps in language. Clever, brilliantly written,
and thought-provoking, it will stay with you."
Sinéad O'Hart, author of *The Time Tider*

One

The head teacher had *slugs* on his face. Lime–green, right in the middle of his chin.

Not the animal – the word.

The word *slugs* stuck to his chin in lime-green letters.

"Welcome 〜〜〜〜〜, Gala," Mr Watson said. "〜〜〜〜〜 〜〜〜〜〜 school."

At least, that was how it sounded to me. I tried to read the missing words as they fell from the head teacher's mouth – they were bright and bold, egg-yolk yellow – but I was too distracted by the *slugs* on his face. Why had he been talking about slugs so early in the morning? Maybe he was a gardener and was worried about his vegetables. Maybe he stepped on one on his way into school and felt bad about it. Maybe he'd eaten them for breakfast. Maybe that was normal in Scotland.

Mr Watson must have noticed me staring because he brushed his hand over his chin, and the word *slugs* fell on to the desk. "I think you 〜〜〜〜〜 〜〜〜〜〜," he told me. "〜〜〜〜〜 〜〜〜〜〜 change, but 〜〜〜〜〜."

The sentence dropped

piece

by

piece

from Mr Watson's mouth and disappeared into the pile of words in front of him. It wasn't even nine o'clock yet, and his desk already looked like he'd spat out half a dictionary! I saw a few words I knew – a small grey *cold* caught behind the space bar on the keyboard, *music* in cursive purple letters by his coffee cup – but I still had no clue what he was saying.

Beside me, Papa smiled and nodded. "Gala is very 〜〜〜 〜〜〜," he said, putting his hand on my shoulder. His voice slipped into that funny up-and-down thing it always did when he spoke English, as if his vocal cords were riding a carousel. "I am sure 〜〜〜 〜〜〜 happy here."

The word *happy* caught on the collar of Papa's jacket. It was a light blue lie. I wasn't happy to be here. I didn't want to be in Scotland at all. It had only been five days since we'd moved here from Cadaqués, a little town by the sea in the north-east of Spain, but I already missed it so much it hurt. I wanted to be back at my old school, racing my friend Pau down the corridor and getting into trouble for talking too much in class. I wanted to go home.

As words spilled from the head teacher's mouth, there was a knock on the door. Mr Watson said a large orange, "Yes?", and two girls stepped into the office. They were both around my age, almost twelve. One was White and very tall with freckles and light brown hair, and the other was Black and short with smiley brown eyes and braces on her teeth. The tall one said something, and Mr Watson nodded.

"Thank you, ～～～. Gala, this is ～～～ and ～～～," he said, turning back to me. "They ～～～."

The girls smiled awkwardly at me as Mr Watson talked. There was a word he kept saying, something I'd never heard before. I realized from the way he was pointing to the girls that it was a name. When Papa nudged me to reply, I quickly scanned the desk and found it dangling from the tip of a pencil in Mr Watson's pen pot: *Eilidh.*

"Hello –" I tried to sound out the word – "Eyelid?"

The girls blinked at me, then the tall one's eyes went wide, and she said a lot of bright pink words very, very quickly.

Seeing I was lost, Papa finally switched to Catalan, the language we spoke at home. It turned out *Eilidh* was their name – both of them, Eilidh Chisholm and Eilidh Obiaka – and it was pronounced 'A-lee'.

Mr Watson and Papa both chuckled at my mistake, and the girls giggled too. It wasn't a mean sort of laughter, but I felt my cheeks go red. Why bother spelling it E-I-L-I-D-H if they weren't going to pronounce half the letters? That made no sense whatsoever.

Outside Mr Watson's office, a bell rang. He and Papa stood up and moved towards the door, so I did the same. From the way the Eilidhs lingered by the doorway, I guessed they were here to show me to my first class. The one with braces, Eilidh O, gave me another smile and stepped aside to let me into the corridor.

It was noisy now, dozens of kids laughing or swinging their bags or shoving last-minute breakfasts into their mouths as they went to their classes. This place was bigger than my last school, and with everyone rushing around it felt enormous – there must have been twice as many kids here. But that wasn't the reason my mouth fell open.

It was because of the words.

Hundreds and thousands of words falling out of mouths

and flying through the air,

bouncing off

walls

and

fluttering

to

the

floor.

ANGRY RED WORDS and happy yellow ones. *Timid whispers in pastel tones* and **excited shouts in bold, thick fonts**. There were tired words that **blurred with a yawn around the edges**, and *sleek cursive words that could only have come from rumours and secrets*. There were so many that they already came up past my ankles – a glittering stream of speech curving past the reception desk and along the corridor as kids splashed through it without a second thought.

My old school was filled with words too. Back there, I never paid them much attention. Sometimes my friends and I would flick them across the desk to each other when we were bored in class, but I'd never thought about how many there were around us. Not even when the school cleaners came to sweep them all away at the end of the day. When I was speaking Catalan or Spanish, I hardly noticed when the words left my mouth – I just brushed them off my clothes or picked them away if they landed in my food. Here they were all I could see, all I could hear. And I could barely understand anything.

"Are you OK, bug?" Papa asked me in Catalan. "I know it's a lot but you'll get used to it."

Seeing words in our own language and Papa's familiar ochre shades felt like a lifebelt, but it was quickly pulled away when Mr Watson said a loud white, "Oh!" He went to reception, spoke to the woman standing behind the desk and came back holding a sheet of paper.

"Your ～～～, Gala," he said, handing it to me. "Eilidh and Eilidh will ～～～."

On the paper was a timetable with Class 1C at the top and my subjects printed below. When I looked up,

Mr Watson was pointing towards the corridor behind reception, but I couldn't catch what he was saying. There were too many words whirling round us, and I couldn't pick out the ones I needed. Papa explained in Catalan that the Eilidhs were in most of my classes, and they would show me to registration. I didn't even know what 'registration' meant. It sounded like it might be something to do with computers or filing cabinets.

"OK, Gala?" Papa touched my hair and smiled. "Have fun. I'll see you at home."

Papa shook Mr Watson's hand, said a bright blue goodbye to the Eilidhs, then waved to me again before walking towards the main doors. Ever since we arrived in Scotland last week, all the English words that I'd learned at my old school and from Papa and TV shows had been jumbled up in my head, a puzzle that I couldn't put together. But, as I followed the two Eilidhs towards the next classroom, a few pieces finally connected.

This is NOT my home.